Steven walked softly to the window and pulled the curtains aside. He stood for a long moment, staring forlornly into the darkness. I went to his side, but all I saw was a large backyard with a glacier of snow and ice in the angle where the garage abutted a tool-shed.

I started to hug him, but he withdrew in a rigid silence. Instead, I tried to reassure him. "She'll be back, you'll see."

He stared at me like I was an utter idiot. Slowly he shook his head, shivered and pointed to the back-yard. "That's where the vampire ate Elena."

★

"Jorgensen endows her heroine with a combination of savvy and foolishness that makes her just right."

—*Kirkus Reviews*

Previously published Worldwide Mystery titles by
CHRISTINE T. JORGENSEN

A LOVE TO DIE FOR
YOU BET YOUR LIFE
CURL UP AND DIE

Forthcoming from Worldwide Mystery by
CHRISTINE T. JORGENSEN

DEAD ON HER FEET

DEATH
OF A DUSTBUNNY

CHRISTINE T.
JORGENSEN

WORLDWIDE®

TORONTO • NEW YORK • LONDON
AMSTERDAM • PARIS • SYDNEY • HAMBURG
STOCKHOLM • ATHENS • TOKYO • MILAN
MADRID • WARSAW • BUDAPEST • AUCKLAND

*This is dedicated to Paulot and Hannah,
cherished newcomers*

DEATH OF A DUSTBUNNY

A Worldwide Mystery/May 1999

Published by arrangement with Walker Publishing Company, Inc.

ISBN 0-373-26308-2

Visit us at www.worldwidemystery.com

Printed in U.S.A.

Acknowledgments

It always amazes me how many people it takes to write one book. I wish to thank all the people who have so patiently contributed to this book, through their special knowledge, their tireless reading and rereading, their moral support, and their humor. It takes a lot of humor to survive a book.

Endless thanks go to my patient critiquers, Lee Karr, Kay Bergstrom, Dianne Mott Davidson, Dolores Johnson, Leslie O'Kane, and Peggy Swager; and Liz Hill, Alice Kober, Mary Stobie, JoHanna Gallers, Lucy McGuire, and the saints of Capital Hill, all Rocky Mountain Fiction Writers.

Any errors found are mine and not the fault of the incredible assistance I received from Special Agent Nathan Galbreath, U.S. Air Force, Forensic Science Consultant, and to the Immigration and Naturalization Service.

And very special thanks to my agent, Jane Chelius, my editor, Michael Seidman, and to Tom and Enid Schantz of the Rue Morgue Book Store.

Finally, I must thank my most beloved critic, Jim Jorgensen, whose love and humor mean so much.

ONE

THE NIGHT-LIGHT in little Steven Holman's room glowed, casting soft shadows across the floor.

Steven whimpered and turned over in his bed. His toy tank was poking his ribs. He shoved it away and was almost back to sleep when he remembered the salt. Elena forgot to sprinkle the salt.

The vampire could come get him because she forgot. Salt was his protection. Elena said so.

Through the bathroom that linked their rooms, Steven could see into Elena's room and her bed, her pillow propped against the headboard, dented where she had been leaning against it. Where was she?

"Elena?" he called. No answer.

Where was she? She was his nanny. She was supposed to stay with him.

He listened. There was kitchen noise from downstairs. Maybe Elena went downstairs. Why?

"Elena!" he whispered.

Maybe Elena would have magic ears this time and hear him. She said she did, sometimes. He listened hard till his ears rang, but she didn't come.

The back door opened. He could always tell when someone opened it, because it was right under his room and the spring squeaked. Maybe Elena was going to the backyard.

Steven felt cold in his stomach. The backyard was dangerous. The vampire lived back there. Elena mustn't go there!

He threw back the covers and ran through the bathroom into Elena's room, then to her window, ducking under the curtain.

Light from the kitchen window lit the frozen lawn and the path from the back door to the tangled, winter-bare vines of the grape arbor.

At the very back of the yard, where it was darkest, the roof of the garden shed stood black against the light from the alley. The shed was bigger and darker at night; its windows looked like blank, mean eyes.

The shed was dirty and smelled like dust and had old tools crusted with dirt, left by the people who had lived here before. Daddy said to leave them alone. So did Elena.

The back porch door opened wide, then banged softly shut.

He saw Elena on the garden walk, dragging a large, awkward bag of trash, nearly as big as she was. Her slacks and shoes blended into the dark, while the light from the kitchen window reflected stark white off her blouse.

Halfway down the walk, Elena picked up the bag and trudged toward the shadowy grape arbor. Then she was under the bare vines and he could see only the light occasionally bouncing off her blouse. He heard the sharp clink of a glass bottle in the trash.

"Careful, Elena. Don't trip on the bricks," Steven whispered. "Hurry, before the vampire comes after you."

She made it to the trash barrels, put down the bag, turned, and started back, picking her way past the tools and the wheelbarrow.

Steven's words choked him. "Elena, watch out!" he whispered. He lifted his hand and waved, bumping the curtain open so the light sprang out. Elena looked up. She saw him.

"It's me, Elena. Hurry!" he whispered. "Don't let the vampire get you."

Elena started to raise her hand to wave back, then stopped and turned. A dark figure emerged from the grapevines, partially hidden in the shadows.

"No! Don't talk to it! It's the vampire." Steven whispered.

Elena backed away. The light from the kitchen fell on her face. She was mad. And saying something to the vampire. But she mustn't!

"Run, before it's too late," Steven whispered.

The dark shape reached out from the shadows and struck Elena. She stumbled, fell. It leaned over her, pulling and pushing.

"Get up, Elena. Run!"

But she didn't get up. The vampire grabbed Elena's hands and dragged her to the shed.

Steven's heart drummed against his ribs. He had to hurry. He had to do the salt, or the vampire would get him, too. Steven threw himself away from the window, stumbled, his feet tangled in the curtain. He jerked free, then ran to Elena's dresser, dragged open the bottom drawer, grabbed the salt box, and ran to his room.

His night-light made long, scary shadows on his Legos and toy cannon. His bedroom door was shut tight so Heather wouldn't see him when she and Daddy came upstairs. He didn't like Heather. And that made Daddy mad, 'cause she was his girlfriend.

He shook a thin stream of salt around his bed. It disappeared into the carpet, but it would work. He'd be safe now.

Steven crawled into bed, pulled the salt box tight against his stomach, and pulled the covers over his head. Then he squeezed his eyes shut tight until he saw the magic lights.

He wished his mother were here. She was soft and smelled good. His eyes began to sting. After he rubbed them they were wet. Daddy would be mad if he cried.

Big boys don't cry. Never.

But it was so hard.

TWO

Elena Ruiz was late. And I was worried.

We were well into the middle of March, but winter was clinging to the underside of Denver. The snow piles, all nice and white two months ago, had melted down to grimy heaps, and mini-glaciers lay on the north side of every building, slicking the sidewalks where they were shaded by buildings or evergreen bushes. The squirrels in Cheesman Park near my apartment, searching the frostbitten earth for buried food, were lean and humorless, and so were the die-hard joggers wearing Spandex leggings, nylon jackets, and ear warmers. We all had the mid-March glums.

Friday afternoons are usually dead quiet at the *Denver Daily Orion*, the weekly newspaper where, as Stella the Stargazer, I write an astrological column for the lovelorn. This one was no different, except I had a very nasty feeling in the pit of my stomach. And it wasn't indigestion from the shrimp and anchovy pizza.

The rattle of the wind on the windows grated on my nerves. Any distraction would lighten my mood and keep me from worrying about Elena, but the other two occupants of the newsroom, Jason Paul, the *Daily Orion*'s only reporter and my current love complication, and Andy Whitman, gofer, were out on TGIF assignments, which translated to beer and nutzels at the local sports bar. I was the only minion there.

Zelda, real name Sally Ann Miller, was in the front office, thoroughly into her Zelda persona, complete with gum-chewing authority. She was cursing over a crossword puzzle. Zelda isn't a minion, she is the paper's receptionist and virtual director. She runs the place. I nicknamed her Zelda the first time I saw her, because with her dramatic blond hair, wise mouth, and whiskey voice she was my idea of a Zelda from the days of Mike Hammer.

Mr. Gerster, editor, owner, and publisher, was buried in his office at the far end of the building. I've never been quite sure what he does behind his closed door, but I'm sure he works very hard at it.

The *Denver Daily Orion* specializes in human interest stories, church reports, local street closings, and my astrological column for the lovelorn...news that's local and happy. Oddly enough, that includes death notices. I guess it depends on your point of view.

I checked the time again, then riffed through my correspondence, selecting an onionskin paper envelope with little butterflies in the corners, addressed in feathery blue handwriting.

From my totally biased, unscientific survey, I've concluded that stationery reflects the writer. To test this theory, every so often I guess the contents of the letter before I open it, to see how close I come to the actual message. Based on the paper and the handwriting, I decided this particular writer was romantic, trusting, and earnest. The problem would be infidelity or finances.

I slit the envelope and shook out a beautiful pastel blue onionskin letter with background butterflies.

Dear Stella,

Sometimes I have trouble making up my mind, so I'm writing to you. I've been in a relationship with this man for five years, and I just found out he has been writing to two other women besides me. When I first met him, he was honest and told me he was in jail for killing three men and a chicken during a robbery, so I never dreamed he would lie to me.

He says I should show some compassion and forgive him. I don't know what to do. I think compassion is overrated.

Penelope, a Gemini

I penciled a note on the bottom of the letter: "a romantic Gemini...trouble with decisions. Support her. In this case, compassion vastly overrated." I put it in my growing stack of read, noted, but as yet unanswered correspondence.

It was two-thirty, a solid half hour later than Elena said she would be here. Some of my friends, like Meredith Spenser for one, could be a whole day late and I wouldn't be too concerned, but Elena was different. I gnawed on the pencil eraser.

I first met Elena three months ago at the Denver Literacy Project, where I had just started as a volunteer teacher, thinking I might earn a few badly needed stars for my heavenly crown. She was my assignment.

Petite, dark-eyed, and pretty, though not in the conventional sense, she was in her early twenties and worked as a nanny and light housekeeper for a widower, Grant Holman, and his five-year-old son, Steven, a very high-maintenance child. The long hours would have been intolerable for most people, but Elena was a Taurus, devoted and determined to the point of stubbornness.

The front door of the newspaper office opened, then slammed. Elena? I glanced at the wall clock. Two-forty-five p.m. Then Meredith's voice carried through the quiet. Seconds later she sailed into the room.

She pulled off her hat, shook out her thick chestnut hair, and tossed her gloves onto an empty desktop, shrugging out of her coat as she talked. "Well, at least try to say, 'Hi, Meredith. So glad you came on a dull Friday when no one else bothered.'"

"Meredith, I'm thrilled—"

"You're looking worried. Did your landlord refuse to renew your lease after all?"

That was one more worry, but Elena was a more immediate problem. "I haven't heard yet. Did you come for a particular purpose? Elena is due—"

Meredith paused midstride, then frowned. "That's odd, she's never late." She threw herself into Jason's desk chair. "So, I won't take long. I came for your advice. I'm at crisis point. I'm depressed. I've come to the conclusion that I need to live a more contemplative life."

"Well, that's enough to depress you."

"I think I need to put more value on the esthetic side of...things. Concentrate on *being* instead of *having*. So, would you do my horoscope?"

"I can't concentrate now, Meredith. Last night Elena called, almost whispering. She said it was *muy importante* to see me today. She was upset and worried about something, and as soon as I said okay, she hung up."

"So?"

"At her last lesson she asked for a reading, wanting to know if this thing she was working on would be successful. So I did a real general one, she doesn't know what time she was born, and—"

"And—?"

"It was terrible, but I didn't want to scare her, so I just said she'd have to be careful and try real hard."

Meredith grimaced. "You're still not responsible, Stella."

"What if I am?"

THE NEWSROOM WAS silent and empty after Meredith left. It's easy for me to overreact when I'm feeling down, so I watched the dust motes circling in the feeble sunshine and tried to be calm and patient. Of course that made it worse.

I straightened the pile of correspondence and tried again to concentrate. I slit open the envelope from the top of the stack.

Dear Stella,

I'm a Scorpio in desperate need of a sexy guy. I'll settle for anything decent that walks on two legs, but they're in short supply. Any suggestions for places to meet men? Any good dating services based on the signs of the zodiac? You're talking to a desperate woman.

Starved in Aurora

My heart wasn't in it. I had gotten as far as "Dear Starved" when the Chinook rattled the windowpane at the back of the newsroom and the sun burst through the grimy glass, distracting me.

I reached for the telephone to call Zelda, almost afraid to tell her Steven would be coming today. Last Friday I'd found him crouched before her rounded knees, his teeth bared and holding out his bony little hands like claws, chanting, "I'm a vampire. I'm going to suck your blood. You're old. Wriiinkled. Graaaaaay. You're going to diiiiiiie."

I shouldn't have laughed. Zelda was barely speaking to me a week later.

I put the telephone receiver to my ear and punched in her numbers. She lifted it on the fourth ring.

"Any messages, Zelda?"

"Have you been here for the last hour?"

"At my desk."

"Did your phone ring?"

"No."

"There's your answer."

"This is important, Zelda. If Elena calls, interrupt me and put her right through."

"Jesus, Mary, and Joseph! She's a saint, but I'm not, so don't tell me she's bringing Steven again."

"Zelda—"

"Do you know how much work that means for me? That

kid could slip the skin off a snake and leave him smiling. I'm gonna have to clear my desk. And lock it."

"Zelda, it's Friday. There's nothing *on* your desk."

By 3:10 in the afternoon, inactivity and the rattling of the windowpanes had my nerves in a royal twist.

I dug out the telephone number for the Dustbunnies, the company that employed Elena and leased her nanny services to Grant Holman for Steven. I'd never laid eyes on either Holman or Louise Braden, who owned and managed Dustbunnies, but I figured she was the best place to start.

A recording gave a cellular phone number. I tried it, and on the third ring I got an answer from a living person.

Louise puffed into the receiver as though she'd been running, "Dustbunnies, Louise Braden."

I asked about Elena, but she didn't respond right away. Thinking she might have misunderstood me, I started to repeat myself. "I'm trying to reach Elena—"

"Who are you?"

Elena had sworn me to secrecy about the fact that she couldn't read. Unless, or until, I absolutely had to, I wasn't going to break that promise. "I'm...her friend, Stella. I write a column called Stella the Stargazer for the *Denver Daily Orion.*"

"Oh, yeah. You're the one Steven likes."

Steven seldom spoke or made friends, but for some reason he had liked me. He had dark hair that hung over a broad, intelligent forehead and guileless blue eyes that were so sad you could see tears in them. Elena said he never smiled, but the last time I'd seen him, he had smiled at me. It lasted only seconds, but it transformed his face. And stole my heart.

"Elena was supposed to meet me at two o'clock."

Louise was quiet so long I began to think she wasn't there. Finally she spoke, her voice sort of thick, as though she'd just swallowed a huge hunk of fudge. "I don't think she's going to make it."

The windowpanes shook, nearly drowning out Louise's voice. "Grant Holman called me early this morning and said she left a note that she was gone until Monday."

"A note? But—" I bit my tongue. A sick, nasty feeling rolled around in my stomach. The windowpanes kept up a steady funereal drum roll. I closed my eyes. Elena's whispery voice echoed in my mind, *I must see you. It's…muy importante.* "She called last night, specifically about meeting me."

"What for?"

"She didn't say. What was in the note?"

There was a slight pause before she answered. "Actually, I didn't see it. Holman said she'd said she would be back Monday."

"Did he call the police?"

Her voice was a little choked. "I suggested it, but apparently because the note said she'd be back on Monday, the police said they'd wait. Holman's actually being quite good about all this. He and his partner, Barry Quinley, were supposed to go to San Diego on business this noon."

"So where's Steven?"

"Grant managed to get a seat on the plane for him and took him. What else could he do? Imagine how much business they're going to get done."

I pictured Steven's thin face, large, sad eyes, and incredibly stubborn chin and imagined how he'd cope.

Louise continued, her voice a little edgy. "I can't hold this job for her, and I don't have the time to go looking for her. I'll bet anything Elena got another job for more money. I'll have to start advertising this weekend for a replacement. What a mess. It is *so* inconsiderate of her."

"But I can't believe Elena would leave him, unless something terrible had happened. Who's listed as next of kin on her application?"

Louise audibly caught her breath, then I heard papers rattle. "No one. She doesn't have any."

Of course. Elena would leave as much blank as possible, so she wouldn't list her sister, Maria. She could sign her name and grasp a few simple words, enough with her personal charm to hide her illiteracy, but that was about it. I wondered what else Louise had neglected to check on. "Louise, Elena had a work permit, didn't she?"

Her reply was immediate and defensive. "Of course she has papers."

"You actually saw them?"

"Do you think for a minute I could risk employing someone who was illegal? I could be closed down for that, you know. You've heard the phrase 'independent business owner'? Well, between the INS and the IRS I'm barely able to go to the pot by myself. Independent, my foot."

That wasn't quite true. A number of people employ illegals and then plead ignorance when they're caught. If Louise couldn't afford the minor fine, then her business was running on a very thin margin.

"I don't know what I'll do for someone to take care of Steven starting Monday. It's not everyone he tolerates." Her voice grew throaty. "Elena told me you get along well with him. You'd be willing to fill in until I can get someone, wouldn't you?"

"Not on your life."

I cradled the telephone receiver, trying to absorb it all.

Holman was out of town, Louise in her heart believed Elena had gone to a better job, and the police wouldn't do anything until twenty-four hours after she said she'd return. Three and a half days from now, at the earliest.

Elena couldn't have written the note.

But because of that damned note, nobody would do a thing.

THREE

ELENA AND HER SISTER, Maria, were very close, and Maria was the most likely person to have written the note.

I'd used Maria and her family as the subject of Elena's last reading lesson, trying to help her with addresses and familiar things. I plowed through my desk and Elena's file looking for that lesson with Maria's address on the back of a picture of a gentle garden scene that Elena had drawn for Steven to keep him busy coloring while I tutored her. I would never have thrown it away by mistake.

I went through everything again. Nothing.

I decided to try another approach. I picked up the telephone and rang Detective Lee Stokowski, whom I had first met when he investigated the murder of a friend of mine. He was chronically short on humor and anything but a soft shoulder to cry on, but he was intelligent, persevering, and fair, and he didn't laugh at me and generally didn't dismiss my concerns, entirely. And he was currently seeing Zelda, who had almost turned herself inside out to catch his attention. He answered on the second ring.

After I finished telling him my worries, for a minute he was silent, then he spoke, sounding barely patient. "There's a note that says she'll be back, there are no signs of violence, no reason to suspect foul play, nothing. Stella, every day people walk out of their lives for a whole bushel full of reasons, usually just because they're sick to death of things the way they are. Stop looking for disaster."

"But she can't write, Lee. She's illiterate. And she called me last night, very worried, saying she had to meet me. And she was whispering as though she didn't want to be overheard."

He was quiet for a moment. "It's all too vague, Stella. But if someone has filed a report, then you've done all you can do for now. I know it's tough on the kid—"

"Damn well bet it's tough on the kid."

"Stella, let's get real here. Most missing people aren't really missing. Someone knows where they are. Another huge percentage are people who just need a break, they'll be back. Most of the rest are determined to disappear. And they have the right to do so. Chances are, she up and left on her own. Maybe she didn't have the nerve to say goodbye to this kid because she knew it would be hard on him. Maybe this was the only way she knew to get out."

Elena had told me what Holman paid her...and the monthly commission she paid Louise. It all amounted to a tidy sum, one Louise would want to keep. I thought about the fact that Elena had seldom mentioned Grant Holman; she didn't seem to like him, but leave? I couldn't buy it.

Stokowski cleared his throat, his prelude to a tough question. "Is there reason to think she's an illegal alien and has been picked up? Have you checked with the Immigration and Naturalization Service? She may have left to evade them."

That was the big question. Because of that too-quick response from Louise, I was about 40 percent sure she'd lied to me about Elena's papers.

It was always possible she'd been picked up and had no papers. I made up a story and a very similar name so I wouldn't identify Elena but could still get the information, then punched in the numbers for the INS.

A harried voice answered.

"Could you see if there were any women at all picked up in the metro area since last night at, say, six p.m."

"I don't have time—"

"It's *real* important—there's a small child involved."

"Well, this once. Hold, please."

A rush of cold air and a fresh, masculine smell laced with

beer and fried onions blew into the newsroom. I looked up, my hand over the mouthpiece of the receiver.

Jason Paul grinned, loped across the room, and folded his long frame into his desk chair, swiveling around to watch me. A year ago he had been a green cub reporter barely able to grab a pen and write with the pointy end. Somehow between then and now he'd not only discovered how to wield a pen with skill, he'd managed to fill out in some very masculine way. His shoulders fit his worn leather jacket and narrowed down to powerful hips and thighs. Not that I cared, but he was pretty gorgeous even with the beer and onion fragrance.

I was about to ask him why he was there when the woman at the INS came back on the telephone. "Sorry, miss. No women detainees, last night or this morning." She emphasized the word *women*.

I thanked her profusely and hung up. The good news was that neither the INS nor Denver homicide had had contact with Elena, which ruled out two large, disastrous possibilities.

Jason, with a sly look on his face, was flipping a pencil back and forth in his fingers, exercises for the feeble. I figured he wanted something, and it was probably significant that Andy, the gofer, wasn't with him.

"Okay, Jason. Why are you here in the middle of the infamous Friday-afternoon sports bar mania? And what have you done with Andy?"

Injury spread across his face. "He had to go home early. He's meeting his girl for a big weekend, so I thought I'd come see how you and Elena were doing."

This had all the earmarks of working up to a favor. "So if Andy had to go home, what was it he couldn't do for you?"

"Oh, Stella. You are suspicion incarnate." He rose and peered around the room. "Where's Elena? I thought she'd be here."

"She didn't show." I felt my chest tighten with anxiety. "Jason, I think something's happened to her."

He frowned. "What do you mean, happened to her?"

"Louise Braden, owner of the Dustbunnies, said she left a note saying she'd be back on Monday. This just isn't like her. It's not right."

"Maybe she needed a break from that kid. Who wouldn't?"

"Elena couldn't read *or* write. She couldn't possibly leave a note saying she had to go and would return."

"She was a quick learner?"

"Not that quick."

He draped his lanky frame over the corner of my desk and grinned at me with his melt-your-heart brown eyes, soft and warm, and a little shadowed. He grabbed my hands, holding them as though that would somehow impart confidence to me. It did, of course. "She probably got someone to write it for her. Hey, look, maybe she got fed up and had to take a break. Or maybe she got bad news. She'll show up. Give her credit."

"I do give her credit. Short of learning that her mother was dying, she'd never leave Steven like that. It's too traumatic for him, and she knows that."

"Maybe her mother *is* dying." He shrugged.

"She would have mentioned it when she called last night."

Jason sighed. He looked tired underneath his efforts to cheer me up. "Have you called her sister?"

"I don't have a telephone number for her. Her name is Maria Ruiz, her husband is Alberto Reyes." I pulled the telephone directory off the shelf. "I'll find the address in a minute. You want to go with me to see her?"

Jason rose uncomfortably from the desk.

"Stella!" Zelda called from the reception room. "I need a four-letter word."

Dozens leaped to mind.

Zelda strolled in, crossword in hand. She paused, considering the possibility I might tolerate her sitting on the corner of my desk. I pushed a stack of letters to fill it and discourage her.

Zelda grinned, grabbed the back of the gofer's chair, dragged it over, and settled herself, smoothing her exceptionally short skirt in the direction of her rounded knees. "What's a four-letter word for March?"

"Walk? Trot? Step? Zelda, I don't have time for—"

"No. It ends in an *s*."

"Oh, give me your crossword puzzle. Where? Oh, here. Beware the blank of March," I mused.

I looked at Zelda, and a little shiver crawled over my shoulders. "Ides, Zelda. Beware the ides of March."

"Yeah, smarty, whoever heard of ides of March?"

"The ides are the thirteenth day of the month in the Roman calendar, with the exception of March, May, July, and October, when the ides are the fifteenth day." I thought of Elena's horoscope.

"Cool! This is the fifteenth. The ides of March." She peered at me. "Is something wrong? You don't look so good."

"The ides of March have a bad-luck connotation. And Elena didn't show."

"Well, Stella, the truth is hard to hear, but not everybody thinks Steven is a bundle of joy. Maybe Saint Elena got sick of being told she was old and gray and wrinkled and took off."

"Zelda, Steven is five years old, a child, a rather sad child."

"Well, you can have a soft heart if you want, but I'm going to be realistic. That kid needs help. Look what he left on my desk last week."

She thrust before me the picture Elena had sketched for him to color. I turned it over. Maria's address was on the back.

Zelda flipped it back over to the garden scene. "Look what he did to it," she said, tapping it with her fingernail.

I bit my lip to keep from grinning. In addition to coloring the simple little garden scene, Steven had added a large tombstone and a thick black stick figure with globs of red falling from large, sharp teeth.

"Real creative," Jason said, not quite hiding a smile.

"Yeah, right." Zelda's bloodred fingernail jabbed at the bottom of the picture. "And look at that!"

Printed across the bottom was the caption "blud sukers" in small, uneven letters.

As I stared at them, the room around us seemed to grow dim. My fingers holding the picture began to tingle. Then my cheeks grew cold, and the beating of my heart grew steadily louder in my ears, my breathing harsh. The room seemed to darken.

A fine cold mist of perspiration covered my upper lip, and a strong metallic taste like blood filled my mouth. My legs felt suddenly rubbery, and I leaned against the desk, a little dizzy and lightheaded.

The room grew dimmer. A wispy figure, human, but neither male nor female, took shape before my eyes, my skin rose in prickles, and I shivered. A terrible heaviness weighed on my chest, and it was hard to breathe. The form began to remold into a silhouette.

I tried to focus on the facial features of the shape, but the essential details were elusive. The shifting shadows revealed only an outline, and I think I had more of a sense of terrible urgency than any identifiable feature.

The windowpanes rattled in a sudden burst, and Jason's arm, warm and protective, wrapped my shoulders, recalling me. Immediately the room brightened, the roaring ceased, and I regained normalcy, whatever that was.

I was cold, my head ached, but most of all I was frightened by the last thing I'd seen: a head and shoulders framed against a backdrop of flames, screaming in terror.

FOUR

I'VE HAD THESE SPELLS off and on since I was a child. As a young girl I would just "know" that someone had done something. Usually it was a very specific thing, like the time I knew that Tillie Olafson ate cat food because she was too poor to afford regular food, or when I "knew" that Harry Ballgreen, nicknamed Greenteeth, was visiting LydiaAnne Smelton in the afternoon, although at the time I didn't understand quite why. Even now, when I do know what they were up to, I still don't understand why she would have wanted to.

In my teens I tried to block out these little spells. I ignored them, pretending to myself they hadn't happened. For a while it seemed as though they had gone, then in my late twenties they returned more vividly than before and more sinister, but less clear. I no longer "knew" exactly who and what they were about. It was as though the increased menace had driven away specifics. The more I tried to discern detail, the less I could see. Meredith, the only one with whom I discussed them, believed my mind couldn't stand the evil content and turned it into a metaphor.

Whatever it was, it was frightening.

I seemed to receive a kind of telecommunication, intense images or emotion-laden ideas, from another person's mind. Even then it doesn't fully explain what occurs, or why sometimes it's present and other times future.

Recently, the touch of something belonging to the person involved has initiated the spell. Steven's picture had precipitated it this time, but since it had originally been Elena's drawing, I didn't know which of them was in danger.

Zelda was peering into my eyes. "Stella? Are you all right? You were like, gone, for a minute."

"I'm fine. If Elena calls—"

"Yeah, yeah. Find out where she is. And call you ASAP." Zelda left with her crossword puzzle.

I had to assume that Steven was safe with his dad, but Elena... "I have to find Elena." I folded the picture and put it with some of my correspondence into my purse. No finger tingling this time. "I'm going to Maria's. Coming, Jason? We can go for burritos afterward."

He stiffened, his gaze shifting uncomfortably to the floor. "Well, something has come up, Stella. I've got to go out of town this weekend...."

I'd noticed his awkward hesitation a little earlier. I gave him a steady, unflinching gaze and saw discomfort in his brown eyes. He wasn't being quite forthright. Talk about deflation, disappointment, anger, irritation. My mood, already anxious and low, plummeted.

I let him dangle for a long moment. "Let me guess, a sick friend?"

He looked up, face alight, astonished. "Yeah. How'd you know? It's that extra sense you seem to have, isn't it?"

I didn't tell Jason, of course, but the "sick friend" was an excuse I'd heard several times in a previous relationship marked by a disastrous lack of fidelity and trust. In spite of my protests that the relationship was over and forgotten, shreds of it clung to me like a virus to a host cell.

Jason must have read some of that in my eyes, because he sighed and shook his head. He stood over me for a minute, then leaned down and put his hands on the sides of my face, lowered his lips to mine, and kissed me softly. "I'll be gone for the weekend, maybe longer, I don't know. I'll leave you the number where I can be reached. I want to hear about Elena. Now, will you take me to the airport?"

"Maybe—"

"I need to be there by six."

"Are you packed?"

"Everything's in the car."

"So, we can go by Elena's sister's place before we head out for the airport."

I SHIVERED IN the front seat of Jason's car as we headed west over the Eighth Avenue viaduct. Jason was driving fast but carefully, threading in and out among rush-hour traffic.

"Stella, what happened to you back there in the newsroom?"

"Nothing, I was just thinking about Steven's picture."

"It was more than thinking. You looked as though you saw something."

I didn't answer. Jason didn't know about my spells, and I didn't feel like trying to explain them. Besides, what would I say? Yeah, Jason, actually I was seeing a vision. I get them every so often, and then disaster usually strikes.

I scrunched down in the car seat and cracked the passenger window open. Cold, exhaust-laden air hit my face and pierced my pea jacket and thick cherry red sweater, conservative leftovers from my former existence as a nose-to-the-grindstone accountant.

Elena's sister, Maria Ruiz, lived in the near northwest side of the Platte Valley near Thirty-eighth and Mariposa. It was an area that had housed waves of immigrants to Denver beginning late in the last century. The Germans, Poles, Irish, Italians, and now Mexican/Central American people filled the little homes. Over time, the neighborhood hadn't changed much with its different inhabitants; some of the little houses were brightly kept up, but many had porches sagging lower and lower with age.

Jason turned into a narrow side street. The leafless trees and shrubs offered no graceful cover, and each blowing piece of paper that littered the street emphasized the dead winter drab. The last rays of late-afternoon sun caught and outlined the flaws and dilapidations of the homes.

"Stella, I don't like this, and I'm going to miss my plane."

"It won't take a minute. There's always another plane. There is no other Elena."

If I had been less worried about Elena, I would have grilled Jason and found out why he was leaving. As it was, I was a bit resentful of his preoccupation with his visit to his "sick friend" when Elena could be in trouble. However, I figured if I started asking him about it, we'd end up arguing.

Jason parked across the street, and we stepped out of the car into the raw March wind. I led the way toward a tiny, dingy house. Jason came grumbling behind me.

I picked my way up the narrow, broken sidewalk toward Maria's house, so small it seemed barely able to hold three people. Paint was peeling around the foundation, and the one large front window was covered by a pink cloth that looked a lot like a wornout sheet, roughly tied to one side to let in light.

The brief afternoon sunshine had dried the exposed ground, but under the sagging branches of a very tired old juniper were patches of hard black ice. My right foot slipped, then my left. I was skating up the walk. Loafers are miserable on ice.

At the edge of the porch a lone red plastic flower jammed into the ground bobbed in the wind next to a child's mitten, half-buried in frozen mud. The porch boards creaked under my weight, then groaned when Jason added his.

I knocked. At each strike of my knuckles, the screen door banged against the doorjamb, like an echo.

Jason checked his watch again, sighing unhappily. "We have to leave by five, or I'll never make my flight."

I nodded. We could leave by five-thirty and still make it if he drove fast. I heard footsteps and a child's voice behind the door. The doorknob rattled, but it didn't open. The cloth at the window fluttered. A smudged face pressed against the glass, solemn brown eyes unblinking, examining me suspiciously. I smiled encouragingly and waved. The face disappeared from the window, then the doorknob rattled and the door swung slowly inward. A warm old-house smell rolled out.

A second young girl, smaller and round-faced, with a tangled mop of dark hair and similar solemn eyes, looked up at me.

"Is your mama home?"

No answer. She twisted back and forth, her staring dark eyes never leaving mine, then abruptly she turned and darted away. I opened the screen and stepped inside. When I realized Jason was still outside, I grabbed him and pulled him in, too.

The living room was small, dim, and stuffy. A large old floor-model television, too large and too old to be easily stolen, occupied the whole of the far corner, topped by a flock of family pictures. A lumpy, overstuffed couch leaned against the wall under a crucifix decorated with more red plastic flowers. With Jason and me both in there, the room was full.

I edged closer to the television to glimpse the framed photos. A proud young man in a navy uniform and a rigid pose stared solemnly out of a polished frame next to a wedding photo complete with palm trees. My gaze halted on a snapshot of Elena, in a thin, flowered dress, proudly holding the hand of a small, thin, dark-haired boy, maybe three years old. For a second I thought it was Steven, but then I saw the round, dark eyes and knew it wasn't.

"That's Tia Elena." The older girl jostled the younger aside. "And that's Eduardo. *Il muerte.*"

I didn't know much Spanish, but I got the gist of that. Eduardo was dead.

"Who is Eduardo?" I asked. The child glanced to the doorway and darted away. I lifted my head and saw in the doorway to the kitchen a tired young woman, rounder, taller, and older than Elena. From the facial resemblance I knew it was Maria. Elena's dominating feature was her eyes, and they were her sister's, although where Elena's eyes had a tragic quality, the sister's merely looked tired and harried.

I swallowed and tried to smile. The last thing I wanted was to upset Maria so much she wouldn't talk to me. "I'm Elena's friend, and this is my friend Jason. I was supposed to meet Elena today, but she didn't come. I thought you might know where she is."

The sister looked blankly at me. "She's at work."

I shook my head. "She left a note saying she had to leave. No one seems to know where she's gone. I thought she'd call you or come by last night."

Maria was suddenly bewildered. "I didn't see her. She left a *note?* But—"

"Did you write it for her?"

She shook her head. "No."

"Did she call you last night?"

Maria's eyes slowly filled with tears. "No."

"When did you see her last?"

"Last Sunday. You sure she isn't at work? How could she leave a note?" She shook her head, puzzled. "Is the boy, Steven, all right?"

"I think so. He's with his father. Why do you think he might be with Elena?"

"He is always with her. His father is too busy, and his mother is..." Her voice trailed off, and she left the word *dead* unsaid.

"Maria, this is important. Did Elena say anything to you about leaving there? Going anywhere else?"

Maria shook her head rapidly, as if trying to clear it.

"Was she afraid of Grant Holman?"

She shook her head impatiently. "It was a great job. She had everything."

"Did she talk about getting another job?"

Maria frowned, her gaze unfocused, as if she were thinking. "No, never." She bit her lip with worry. She wasn't acting. I could feel her alarm.

Through the front window I saw an ancient rusted red truck pull up in front of the house. Footsteps tramped on the porch, the front door swept open, and the broad shoulders and strong torso of a man in his late thirties filled the door frame.

Maria smiled wanly. "It's *mi esposo,* Alberto," she said.

Her husband was a squarely built man with thick dark hair brushed back from a broad forehead, prominent cheekbones, and well-defined lips that curved up naturally, as though he laughed a lot and easily. His jacket was worn, his hands red and rough, and he was dressed in work clothes and boots.

Both little girls squealed and clutched his legs. Alberto laughed and patted their heads, then he glanced at me, surprised. His smile faded. He eyed Jason slowly, then glanced questioningly at his wife. "Maria?"

She replied in fluid Spanish. His solemn expression turned to a frown.

I spoke up. "Mr. Reyes, I came to see if you or your wife have heard from Elena. I'm very worried about her. I can't believe she'd just up and leave, especially without talking to someone."

He shook his head. "We didn't hear anything." He looked searchingly at his wife.

She shook her head slowly, eyes filling again. "Nothing."

"I talked to Elena's boss, Louise Braden of the Dustbunnies—"

Alberto interrupted. "Did she give you our address?"

"Elena gave it to me last week, as part of our lesson."

"Did you give it to anyone else?"

"No. Would it matter?"

"Yes. We don't give it out."

"Louise didn't have any information about you. Your

name wasn't on Elena's application for work. She didn't even know about you and Maria."

He crossed to Maria. "That's how it should be. It's nobody's business."

"Is Elena here illegally? Is that what you're worried about?"

Alberto said something quickly and softly in Spanish to Maria, then disappeared into the back of the house.

An expression I didn't immediately recognize crossed Maria's face as he moved out of sight. She ran her hand over her hair, shoving it behind her ear, her gaze troubled. "Please," she said. "You must go. I don't know where Elena is. She's supposed to be at work."

Whatever Alberto had said to Maria changed her mood completely. I was willing to bet it had to do with Elena's legal status.

She hesitated, distracted. Her gaze skipped around the room as if she were looking for something. "You must go. He's tired—"

I interrupted. "What about Elena? Aren't you worried?"

Suddenly I understood the expression on her face. Fear. She was now suddenly very afraid.

"What's the matter?" I asked. "Do you know where she is?"

Maria shook her head emphatically. "No, no. Nothing," she said, but her face started to crumple with tears.

"What are you afraid of?"

"Nothing, please—"

"What did she talk about last week?"

"She was worried about the boy. All she would talk about was Steven and how he needed to have his mother. She was crazy about that."

"Anything else?"

"Nothing. You must go now."

The younger child seemed to sense her mother's anxiety.

She teetered over to the television set, lifted down the picture of Elena, and brought it to me.

I took the picture from her absently. I didn't understand what had just happened between Maria and her husband, but I thought if I could get Maria to calm down and talk more, I might be able to figure it out. "Maria, who is this child?"

She reached for the photo in my hand. "Please..."

I squinted more closely at the picture. It was a younger, rounder-faced Elena than I knew, standing before a stucco house with a broken pot of geraniums on the ground behind them and dust at their feet. Sun streaked across Elena's and the boy's faces, and a trick of the light made a glow over the child's head, almost like a halo. Squinting closer I saw that someone had scratched the picture to create the effect.

Then, as I looked at the picture again, my fingers tingled and the room dimmed. I saw Elena's face change. Instead of a smile on her face, I saw fear. Instead of pride in the child, I saw protection for him and her hand raised toward me in supplication. I had the overwhelming sense she was asking for help not for herself, but for the child.

Jason's hand was warm and rough on my arm, shaking me. Then Elena was smiling once more, in the sunshine, holding the hand of a small, thin boy. I searched the picture, but the sense of danger, of protectiveness for the child, of Elena's pleading, were gone. Had I imagined the whole thing?

Jason put his arm around me. "Stella?"

I felt shaken, unsure of anything except that Elena was in trouble and needed help. I turned to Maria. "Who is this boy? Is he yours?"

She shook her head.

The child in the picture looked so like Steven, except for the dark eyes. Could Elena have had a son? Surely she was too young.

There was a thump from the back of the house. Maria flinched at the sound and took the photo from me. She pushed me gently but firmly toward the door. "Please...I'm sorry. You have to go."

Jason pulled me forward, toward the front door.

"Is the boy in the picture Elena's brother?" I asked. Maria didn't answer.

Jason opened the door. A flush of discomfort colored his neck. He'll go for details, but he doesn't have the killer instinct of a really tough snoop, like I do. I shook his hand off my elbow.

Maria pressed on my arm, her hand trembling, but pushing.

"Let me give you my number." I fished for a name card, then for a pen, always a good stalling technique. "Would Elena return to Mexico to visit her mother?"

"No, no. She died, two, three years ago...."

"Maria!" Alberto's voice boomed from the back of the house.

"Please, you must go."

"Stella, for God's sake, come on," Jason said.

But I just couldn't leave so easily. "Who is Eduardo? Is he Elena's son?" I asked, pushing the card with my name and phone number on it into her hand.

Maria, now desperate to get me out the door, burst out angrily, "Yes, he was Elena's boy."

"How did he die?" I asked, but her door slammed shut.

FIVE

"DAMMIT, STELLA, I don't know how you do it," Jason said.

We were speeding east on I-70, past the cloying smell of soybeans and dog food from the dog food factory. Half of the world was going east on I-70, the other half appeared to be going west on I-70. I was feeling queasy.

"Did you ever think you could be making it worse?"

"Elena's in trouble, Jason. And no one is looking for her."

Jason wanted me to pay attention to what he was saying, but my mind kept going over the conversation with Maria. Elena had talked about how Steven needed his mother. Nothing new there; she had confided the same to me, plus the fact that she thought Grant Holman was too harsh with Steven. That she had lost her own child might explain why she was so devoted to Steven, but it also argued that she would never desert him by simply walking away. There were so many things I hadn't had a chance to ask. A jumble of houses slipped by now as we zipped eastward.

"Stella, Maria was begging you to leave, and you stayed on and on."

"Leaving two minutes one way or the other wouldn't change what happens to them, Jason, but it might change what happens to Elena. Alberto was practically afraid of us. How come? And there's more. I think Maria was shocked when I told her Elena was gone, and so was Alberto, but then I'm sure he told her not to talk to us. Why?"

"I don't know, Stella. They just don't trust us."

"Oh, God, Jason! I forgot to tell her that I had checked and the INS didn't have Elena."

"You can call her later. Now tell me, what was going on in there with you?"

"I was trying to find out about Elena."

"You know what I'm talking about. You were, like, out of it for a minute or two, looking at that picture. It happened before, in the office. Your face went all gray and sick when you were looking at Steven's drawing. What was that all about?"

I let my gaze slide over the wintry, forlorn yards of the houses below the raised interstate highway. I didn't want to tell Jason about my spells. I didn't want his concern, his smothering, his questions, or his disbelief. It's hard enough for me to deal with them. I sure didn't understand them well enough to explain them in the middle of a highway, during rush hour, when he was leaving to visit a sick friend I didn't believe existed.

"The stuffiness got to me. I thought I saw something in the picture, then I got a little dizzy from the heat, I guess, that's all."

Jason's jaw set in disbelief. I studied the city, now turning to industrial warehouses with incongruously trim lawns.

"She never mentioned a son, dead or alive."

"Stella, no one in their right mind goes around telling about their tragedies."

"Men don't, maybe, but women do."

"Like hell they do. I've never heard one." He glanced at me. "Call Stokowski, tell him what you're worried about, and leave it alone."

"I did. He was polite, he was pleasant, he wrote down the information, and he's doing nothing. Now, try this on. Suppose Elena is an illegal alien, no green card in spite of what Louise says. Maybe Elena thinks she's been turned in and flees to avoid being picked up. Alberto and Maria would know whether she's illegal. Maybe they'd think they were protecting her. In fact, maybe they're illegal, too, and afraid I'll turn them in."

He thought about it. "Probably explains it."

"One way or another, I've got to find her."

"Why, Stella? Do you know something you aren't telling me?"

I looked at him, his stubborn jaw, his drawn brows. Who was he to talk to me about keeping secrets? "Jason, you have a few things you aren't telling me, too."

Impasse.

We continued in silence.

My relationship with Jason was in a complicated phase, if it really was a relationship and not merely a hormone rush. Aside from a healthy dose of lust, I wondered if we really had much in common. I had a hefty load of old relationship baggage, and he had a truth and history problem. He never visited relatives nor indicated he had any, although I had discovered that he had a sister, and his family had a post office box in New York City. He was always brushing aside questions about his family and his past, so I had a nagging suspicion that he had a nasty secret.

At this point my pet lizards had a more trusting relationship than we did. It was a good thing he would be gone for a while. A little distance might clarify things.

At Denver International Airport, Jason preferred a curbside drop-off. I took over the driver's seat while he pulled his luggage from the trunk. I was waiting for him to remind me to take good care of his precious Miata, to park it inside, etc.

"Stel—"

I braced myself for his car caretaking lecturette.

"If the lease on your apartment isn't renewed, you can stay at my place with me."

I stared at him. This was totally out of the blue. "Jason, what are you talking about?"

"Your apartment lease... You don't have the best record at your apartment building, you know. The break-ins you've had, the explosion, the weird people they think they saw and hold you responsible for...you've had a complaint or two, at least. I know you've applied for renewal, but I thought that, well, if you need a place—"

"Jason, I don't need a place to live. I have one. They'll renew. And I certainly don't need your pity offer."

"It's not a pity offer."

"Then what is it?"

His face underwent a series of changes. For a moment he seemed about to say something that might actually have made my heart beat faster, then he shook his head and smiled ruefully. "Hey, Elena will show up. She'll be coming to the newsroom again, bringing Steven with her, he'll be messing with everything and liberating my pens, and it will all be great. Call and tell me all about it. And protect my desk, will you? Don't let that kid take my stuff."

"He doesn't!"

"Stella," Jason leaned over me, his melt-your-heart brown eyes so close to mine I could practically see myself reflected in his irises. "Darlin', I love you. You're smart, you're brave, you're usually honest, and you always stand up for the underdog. I even agree that the kid is depressed rather than depraved. But promise me."

"You've locked up your desk. He can't harm a thing."

"The kid's magic. Trust me."

As I DROVE away I was sure I heard Jason yell after me. "And please don't scratch the car."

He knew I had a thing about cars. It's not that I didn't like Jason's car. I did. It was cute, had a tight response, leaped at a touch of the gas pedal, and parked like a dream. I knew why Jason loved it. But the Miata was small; I was barely able to squeeze into the front seat with him and his ego, and there certainly wasn't any room for anyone else...however tiny.

My record with cars is not a good one, and I didn't want to add a mangled car to our already tangled companionship.

I drove the Miata quickly and carefully to his underground parking space in his apartment building, locked it, and pocketed the garage door opener.

It was a quick, cold walk in the dusk to the newspaper office where I'd left my car, and it gave me time to think.

Elena Ruiz was a woman of strong convictions, determined to the point of stubbornness. If she were hiding voluntarily, she'd have found a way to call me. Furthermore, I knew Elena didn't write the note, and I believed Maria when she said she didn't write it. Finally, I figured that whoever wrote the note knew it would prevent a police investigation or delay it by at least a few days, when the trail would be good and cold.

I got in my car and headed back to northwest Denver. It was just after seven o'clock. The sun had dropped behind the mountains well over an hour ago, and the city streetlights were glowing. Traffic was brisk with Friday-nighters, some of whom were already weaving in their lanes after happy hour twofers. I took Speer Boulevard, which runs along Cherry Creek until it meets the Platte.

Denver was initially settled along the banks of Cherry Creek in hopes of a major gold find. That didn't pan out, but by then the settlement had grown north along the confluence of Cherry Creek and the South Platte River. Denver remains divided east from west by a broad stretch of industrial land containing the South Platte, the railroad tracks, Elitch Gardens Amusement Park, and the Coors baseball field, as well as some open derelict acreage.

I crossed over on the Speer Boulevard viaduct going west. The mountains were blanketed by clouds, the foothills purpled in the evening gloom. Once I reached the west side I drove north on Zuni to Thirty-eighth, where I turned back east, then south, to the triangle of several blocks of old houses nestled in next to the highway. Maria's neighborhood.

At Maria's house I parked in front. The old red truck was

gone and the house was dark. It was 7:25. The wind had shifted, now out of the northwest in icy, biting gusts, instead of the earlier, warm Chinook wind. The temperature had plunged below freezing. It felt like snow was in the offing.

I hustled to the front porch, the wind catching my hair and chilling my spine. I knocked, the screen banging in a floppy echo. I shifted my weight from one cold foot to the other and shook myself, as much to ward off discouragement as anything else. I knocked, loud and insistent.

It had been barely two hours since Jason and I left here, but there was no glow of light from inside, no twitching of the window curtain. I pounded on the door.

No answer.

MAYBE THEY HAD gone for fast food, perhaps even the Burrito Ito, a place Elena had mentioned as having tamales and Jannina, a waitress she knew.

Back in my car, I drove west on Thirty-eighth a mile toward the mountains without finding it, then turned around and headed east again, toward Globeville. In the midst of the Indian alphabet streets, I found the Burrito Ito, a cubbyhole restaurant on the north side of the street. I pulled into the minuscule parking lot, surveyed the place, and wished my high school Spanish was better. The rich scent of chili and menudo washed over me even before I entered.

Not surprisingly, the inside was as tiny as the outside. A counter at the back held a telephone, tortilla baskets, flatware, and napkins and served as a pass-through to the kitchen. Three booths were crowded along one wall, and two tables were squeezed in the middle space. The sudden hush in conversation and the dark, blank stares made a table suddenly far too exposed. Two of the booths were filled; I aimed for the empty one at the back.

I slid in and fiddled with the shaker of chili peppers, rearranged the salt and pepper, and tried to be subtle, staring back at everyone staring at me.

Three men filled the first booth. The one facing me had thick dark hair, a widow's peak, and one eyebrow raised slightly over dark eyes with squint lines at the corners. He could have been grinning at something his buddies said.

The second booth held a family of five or six and at least three generations, maybe four. One of the children stood on the seat facing me, eyes solemn, wisps of dark hair falling across her forehead, and a finger caught between her lips.

The young waitress swiveled over to their table, balancing oval plates laden with burritos, beans, rice, shredded lettuce, and cheese. She had bangs sprayed into a three-inch crest and long dark hair, caught in a thick braid. Her apron had a large kiss painted on it. I hoped she was Jannina.

Gradually the verbal buzz returned, but on a noticeably lower scale. The young waitress came to my table, swiped at it with a cloth, and set down a basket of chips and a tiny bowl of salsa. Her dark eyes were quick and intelligent, her expression so closed it could have been called suspicious. "Know what you want?"

"Are you Jannina?" She didn't deny it, so I went on. "Elena said your tamales were great." I smiled, trying to win her over. She tossed her head. "Not bad."

"Elena says your green chili is the best. Seen her lately?"

She shook her head. "She's busy," she answered with a lilt. "You want me to come back?"

I ordered and waited until she returned with my burrito, asked for extra hot sauce, then asked when Elena was last in.

Jannina's lips thinned out. "Thought you were her friend."

"I am. Last night she said she would see me this afternoon, but she didn't show up. I tried to call her, but couldn't get an answer where she works."

Jannina held the order pad, totaling the bill. She had a tiny cross crudely tattooed in the web skin between the thumb and first finger on her left hand. She pursed her lips and her eyes shifted around the room, seeming to fall on someone. She shuffled her feet uncomfortably. "Could be she's out."

"Yeah, could be. How would I find her boyfriend?"

She shook her head. "I don't know about any boyfriend. She never talked about one."

"She had one though, didn't she?"

"I don't know."

I couldn't tell if she didn't know or wouldn't tell. "Look, Jannina, I'm worried about Elena. She always came when she said she would. So this isn't like her. You know any way I could find her?"

Jannina put the bill on the tabletop. "You want anything else?"

I looked at my watch. "Could you make this to go? I gotta run."

She took the plate back to the kitchen pass-through. In seconds she was back with a Styrofoam carton. "Box will be an extra fifty cents."

I paid, and when she brought the change I pulled out a ten-dollar bill and put it with my card. "If you see her, tell her Stella is worried about her. She's got my number. Here's my card. If you hear anything, call me."

Jannina's eyes flickered. "I don't snitch."

"You don't have to. Have her call me. It's important. I'm only worried she needs help."

She hesitated, then picked up my card, scanned it, and shoved it into her pocket. The ten she shoved back at me. I wondered if she'd call Elena then, or wait. Or if I was totally wrong. She left.

I pulled on my jacket, picked up my food, and on impulse went toward the kitchen. Jannina was making a call from the pay telephone, leaning into the wall as though she might be able to disappear into it. I reached for her. "Jannina—"

A thickly muscled hand circled my wrist, tight and bruising. There was a cross with two bloodred drops in the webbing between his thumb and first finger. The letters TRUE were tattooed on his knuckles. "Try another phone."

I found myself practically eye level with a man, five foot seven or so, maybe an inch taller, but broad, all muscle, the sort I associate with weight lifting and steroids.

My wrist was turning to mush in his fingers. "Who the hell do you think you are?" I said. I wanted to shout, but his grip had tightened as soon as I started speaking, a very effective volume control.

"Call somewhere else."

"This is a public restaurant, and this is a public phone."

"Not now, it isn't." His grip tightened down. Clearly I had a choice. I could insist on my rights and get my hand pinched off at the wrist, or I could leave. The pain was hideous, and my fingers were already numb. I left.

He watched me to the door but didn't follow me outside.

Jannina's sudden call made me think she knew where Elena was. I decided it would be worthwhile waiting, maybe to talk with her after she left or to follow her home. I moved my car to a spot where I could see people exit from both the front and back doors of the restaurant and waited for my fingers to return to normal. After that I filled time by munching down the burrito, terrific, incredibly spicy, but cooled and slightly congealed. It was a long wait. The muscle man left about eight-thirty and the restaurant closed at nine. Jannina came out at 9:20, dashed across Thirty-eighth, and headed south down Mariposa Street, walking fast.

I thought I remembered that Mariposa dead-ended at the Valley Highway about three to five blocks away. I was afraid I'd lose her if I tried to follow her in the car. I jumped out, locked it, and hustled after her.

When the city doled out streetlights, they missed this street. It was inky dark with fluid shadows, and my footsteps on the sidewalk made soft little scuffing sounds that were muffled in the bare-twigged hedges. I had the creeps before I'd gone a block.

Jannina was a power walker worthy of mention. She whipped around a corner, and I had to jog to catch up. I reached the corner and saw her half a block away, mounting the porch of a small older home with a steep pitched roof and tiny windows under the gable. It was set next to the alley and looked like a converted coach house. No lights shone inside.

She entered quickly, never looking back. A light flicked on in the front, then off, and another went on in the second floor. I saw Jannina briefly, a figure in front of the light as she pulled the window shade down.

I weighed the possibility that Elena was inside. That would have meant that she had waited in the dark for her. It was possible. Anything was possible.

I circled the little house, then crunched down next to the Dumpster in the alley and watched for half an hour. I could trace her progress through the house by the turning on and off of the lights, but there was only Jannina's shadow.

The temperature might reach 45 degrees Fahrenheit in the afternoons, but at night it plunged well below freezing. Even the promise of spring in the form of today's feeble sun and Chinook wind weren't enough to shake the winter out of the city. My hands and feet were cold, and I had a significant and growing case of heartburn from the burrito. I was tired. I finally gave up and returned to my car at ten o'clock.

I made one more trip by Maria's place. Midblock it was dark, with only the reflected glow of downtown on the low-flying clouds for light. Porch lights weren't lit on this block, shades were drawn across the windows.

I parked across the street from Maria's house, looked around at the street, and cursed. The rusty truck I'd seen parked in front of the house was still gone. I should have taken down the license number earlier, but I hadn't. I'd been too busy thinking about Elena and her dead child, Eduardo.

I knocked on the front door. Nothing. Not a sound. No flickering television glow lit the windows. I peeked across the yard to the neighbor's. That house was dark, too. On the other side the neighboring house had a For Rent sign in the window. I hadn't noticed it before. One more time I knocked, loud and persistent. Nothing.

Maria's house was dark as a tomb.

SIX

SATURDAY MORNING I woke at the stroke of six on the far edge of a nightmare where Technicolor witches were pointing at me and chanting, "Elena, Elena."

My eyelids were scratchy, and my jaw muscles ached from clenching my teeth. I was still tired after a night of thrashing in the covers, seeing Maria's tomblike house in my dreams, and trying to convince the bad dream demons that it wasn't my fault that Maria and her family had gone.

I pulled on a Cleota original burgundy thermal lace teddy, with extra-warm cups made especially for those chilly mornings, topped it with my favorite fuchsia sweats, and brewed a pot of strong black coffee, no fancy flavors, no lacing with additives like cream, milk, or sugar, simply a jolt of caffeine from the straight stuff. I wondered where Maria and Elena were this morning and if they were having coffee. I hoped so.

I checked with Fluffy, my pet lizard, actually an American green anole, but he was snuggled in with Lips, his fiancée. He turned away from me when I held out my hand for him. He was a much more content, not to mention lusty, lizard with Lips around, but he sure wasn't much company for me. Lips had not been a good influence on him.

Every time I looked at him he was either nibbling on her neck, his little lizard arms wrapped around her, or doing push-ups and blowing out his throat in a beautiful cherry red balloon, the height of reptile ardor. When I tried to make friends with Lips, she dove under the log.

I sighed. "You've been in lizard rapture long enough, Fluffy. It's time for a break." I put my hand in again, but he dove for the log with Lips. He stuck his head out once and flapped his lips, then pulled back under the log.

The sun was out, bright but cold, and I shivered in my jacket all the way to the corner newspaper box. It was too cold to power-walk to the bakery for cinnamon rolls.

Back in the lobby I ran into Larry, the manager of my apartment building. I waved and smiled. He looked uncomfortable and darted back into his apartment.

"Larry, wait up a moment. Have you got my lease? I didn't find it." He stuck his head back out and shook it, his gaze dropping uncomfortably to the floor. "There isn't any problem, is there?"

He scratched his ear, never a good sign, I've noticed. "Yah, there's a problem. Not with me, of course. Uh, the owners said they wouldn't renew—"

"And why not? I pay regularly and on time."

"Uh, there's been a couple of complaints. And they said that you were too expensive and caused trouble. Uh, they mentioned the little explosion last fall, the strange people, the cops—I'm sorry. You need to be out by the end of the month."

"That's only two weeks away! I can't pack up my lingerie in that time. You tell them I'm going to appeal this!"

"With who? This isn't public housing, you know. It's private. They don't have to be fair."

I rode a wave of indignation all the way back to my apartment. It wasn't that this apartment was so great, or that I couldn't bear to leave it, or even that it was a good deal. It was the idea of having to find a new place, but most important, it was the rejection.

I stewed awhile, munched cold leftover pizza, read the paper, scanned the for-rent columns of the classified ads. Finally I showered, slipped on hot pink lace panties and bra, and pulled on respectable, conservative slacks and sweater. I chose sturdy, rubber-soled ankle boots I could negotiate ice in, since I figured I was most likely going to be slogging around outdoors today. Then I called Mom, before she called me for a change. Her advice was simple.

"Janie, dear, you move back in with your father and me. You can get rid of that Stella name and have your old room back, and I'll call Norman Schlangwanger, your father's golf buddy. He advises us on all civil legal problems."

"He advised you to go ahead and put up the fence even though it was on the neighbor's property and against the zoning regs."

"Yes, and he advised us to take it down again, too. He's very flexible." Somehow, Norm Schlangwanger wasn't my idea of reassuring legal support. I shelved the housing problem; Elena was more important.

I WENT BACK to Maria's house. The mitten still lay on the ground, encrusted in ice, and the ragged sheet still hung across the front window, but even in the midday sunshine the house had a discarded, lifeless look.

If Maria and Alberto had truly moved, then it was my guess they all were illegal and were frightened about being picked up.

I knocked on the screen, the sound seeming to echo in the house, then crunched over the frozen ground around to a side window and peered in. It might have been a bedroom, but there was no bed, no clothing, only a few tangled coat hangers on the floor. I tromped around and peered into the kitchen. Barren. It looked like they'd done a midnight flit.

Where does a family with two small children go in an emergency? To another family. To a shelter...to friends.

I crunched over the frozen ground to the house next to the one next to Maria's. An elderly man peeked out the window at me, then dropped the curtain and hollered at me to go away. I went door to door up and down the street, but of the few who were home, no one could tell if the family had come or gone.

By two in the afternoon I was starved. I stopped at the

Burrito Ito again, and Jannina took my order for another fiery burrito, smothered green, but she refused to make eye contact and shook her head curtly when I asked about Elena. She hadn't heard from her, she didn't know her sister Maria, she "didn't know nothing." I wondered if she was lying as I fired down the best burrito I'd had in several hours.

When she brought the check I held out a twenty-dollar bill. "Last night there were three men in here in the booth toward the front. One of them didn't want me to wait at the pay phone for you. Who were they?"

She looked flatly at me. "My brother and his friends. He doesn't like for people to bother me. I don't know nothing. Leave me alone."

I was sure she knew more than she was telling me, but she looked scared, and I was clearly the one scaring her.

At six-thirty Saturday night, Louise Braden called. "Stella, have you found her? I need to know. I'm so afraid she won't show Monday. I have to say something to Grant Holman."

"I haven't found her."

"Would you consider filling in for a few days if Elena doesn't turn up tomorrow?" She talked fast and positive, the way salespeople do when they're trying to convince you to buy something you can't possibly afford. "Please? Just until I find a suitable replacement?"

"Absolutely not."

"You have to. You're the only one he likes."

Housekeeping businesses like the Dustbunnies are a hard way to make a living. Most don't last two years, and Louise's was going on three now. Louise tried to shame me into taking care of Steven because she wanted Holman's account, and it was working because of my soft spot for Steven. "No."

"It wouldn't be for long; think what it would mean for Steven and Elena...and Holman's house is so great. You'll love it. And it'll only be from Sunday night till Monday, whenever Elena comes back."

"No, Louise, I'm not doing it. This is your problem."

"When I mentioned you to Steven, he smiled."

"He smiled?" I thought of him needing Elena so badly, feeling abandoned. I weakened. "All right, but just till Elena is back."

SEVEN

BY SUNDAY AFTERNOON I was tired, worn, and had checked my messages so many times my voice mail threatened to wear out. The only message was one from Jason in Los Angeles, saying he'd be out of the hotel for a while and he'd get in touch.

I finally called Detective Stokowski to see if there had been any new homicides. He wasn't at the station, but I found him at Zelda's. He'd heard nothing. There wasn't a trace of Elena. The only place I hadn't checked was Grant Holman's house, and the only people I hadn't talked to were Grant, his girlfriend, Heather, his partner, Barry Quinley, and Barry's wife, Millie. And I was still holding out hope that Elena would come back on Monday, as the note said.

By five o'clock Sunday evening a thumbnail moon lay in the eastern sky, and a bank of clouds hovered over the mountains in the west, threatening to roll down over Denver. The weathermen were predicting a skiff of snow at midnight and fifty degrees by Monday noon. I looked at my apartment with the eyes of a woman who might have to move. I had a new, raw appreciation for what Maria had accomplished.

Meredith lounged on my couch, contemplating where on her body the extra fifteen calories would reside if she ate another green pepper ring off the top of the pizza I had ordered. I always order because when she orders we get naked lettuce salads, the big treat being a mini-ear of baby corn.

Meredith was born to wear Spandex, but she could wear a gunnysack and look great. Tonight she almost was wearing one. She had on a beige muumuu thing that fell from her neck in folds, topped by a bulky shawl around her shoulders.

The grunge look for grannies. It was definitely not the usual Meredith outfit.

We were finishing our Sunday-night pizza early, shrimp and roasted red and green peppers. I had ordered conservatively; the burrito was still giving me fits. Meredith had feasted on the green pepper rings. I sacrificed and ate the rest while I considered how best to announce to Meredith that I'd finally broken down and agreed to take care of Steven, and that I was to start that night.

"The name Grant Holman sounds so familiar. Wasn't there a Grant Holman in our class in grade school?" she asked, then answered her own question. "I'm sure there was. A skinny kid with glasses and freckles all over. You used to call him Frog Face, I think. Do you still have your old photo album?"

I pointed to the bottom shelf of the bookcase.

She strolled over, pulled out the thick old green album, and leafed through it. "I found him. Oh, lordy, was he appearance-challenged! The smallest kid in the class, glasses, bat-wing ears. I can't believe he found someone to hook up with and make a kid."

"Money makes up for a lot of deficits, Meredith."

She glanced up. "You're a little jaded tonight." She sat down in the rocker by the window. "You're letting this business of Elena get you down. You're basing all this distress on your 'special sense' and on your belief that Elena wouldn't leave Steven in the lurch, but you don't know that. Maybe something came up with her family. Her mother may be sick or something."

"Her mother died a couple of years ago."

"Well, some other sibling then."

"Then Maria would have known." I dropped onto the couch and leaned back against the cushions. "I've looked everywhere and talked to everyone, except Holman and his partner. Louise called last night and I agreed to fill in. Starting tonight."

"What?"

Meredith's my best friend, so she is frequently torn between loyalty and truth. Generally it takes half an hour of internal struggle before she'll tell me what she really thinks. This time, it took maybe five split seconds. She threw her hair over her shoulder in a chestnut-colored huff and snorted. "You're nuts! Freaking, outrageous, fantastically nuts!"

"You think it's a bad idea?"

"I know you had some experience at the child development center, but that was years ago, and it's not like you're some child psychologist—and that sounds like what he needs."

"Steven's not really so far from the norm. He lost his mother, and he's in a perfectly normal monster stage trying to master a huge, scary world."

"God, you've been reading those psychology articles. Now I know you've lost it. Why don't you do something solid and helpful for her? Such as redo her horoscope. Maybe it would tell us where she is."

"They don't tell locations, and her horoscope won't change. It was too lousy."

"How lousy?"

I rubbed my forehead, shoving my hair back. It's straight, brown, and just above shoulder length, and it slips out of a pony-tail in wisps to fall in my face. It's growing out, my euphemism for neglecting to get it trimmed. "Elena's horoscope warned of danger in her relationships and betrayal and was adverse for home and money matters."

Meredith frowned. "I think a lot of what you see in those horoscopes is your interpretation. I don't know where it comes from, or what you did to get it, but it seems like you're getting even more…sensitive, Stella." Meredith rose from the rocker, clutching the album to her breast, and looked out the window for maybe four whole minutes. Something was coming.

She sighed heavily and turned to me. The light fell on her

face, highlighting her cheekbones and brows, giving her an aesthetic look. "Have you ever thought of going back to being just plain Jane Austin Smith? I know you got bored with the accounting thing, but you had money then and you never got into trouble. Your life was safe. The only weird person in your life was me. It was so much better that way. I was the flake, and you were the steadying anchor. The only thing you went wild over then was underwear that no one saw. And now—" Her lip trembled. "I miss the old you."

Well, I hadn't expected that. "Meredith, this is the old me. And the new me. Maybe I'm getting more sensitive to the intuitive side of me, but I can't help it. It just comes. We're both changing as we grow a little older. I'm happier than I've ever been. I'm not totally broke, perhaps financially anorexic, but I adore my column. What more could I want?"

She sighed again. "You're so...out there."

"*I'm* out there! Look at you. You're wearing sackcloth and sashes with no makeup. You look great, as always, but this isn't you. You're depressed and feeling sorry for yourself, right? Isn't that what all this is about?"

She drew herself up. "I'm practicing celibacy until I find my true inner self and understand her."

Meredith practicing celibacy was actually good news, and if she could do it without all the drama, it would be truly great. Meredith tends to live between two equations: Meredith equals extremes, and Meredith minus romance equals depression. It cycles about twice a year, and the only effective way to interrupt a depression cycle is to distract her with a new project of some kind, but I didn't have any brilliant ideas at the moment.

"Right—look, Meredith, I'm having trouble concentrating on anything other than Elena right now. I figure if I can find her address book—"

"If she can't read," interrupted Meredith, "why does she have an address book?"

"She has things written down that she can copy, like her sister's address, for references, and then she can always point to them for others to see. And of course, everyone always assumes she can read. It's all part of her pretense. She makes a little icon next to the different entries, so she can remember what's what." Meredith's brows were crumpled into worry lines, and the distance in her eyes told me she wasn't listening. "Meredith, what else are you worried about?"

A little tear trickled out of the corner of her eye. "I spend all my time searching for love, and you spend all your time running away from it. I'm afraid neither of us will find it."

"Oh, for God's sake! Of course we will." I wished I felt as sure about it as I sounded.

"We'll just die trying..."

Fortunately the door buzzer rang and saved me from any further tragedy talk. The voice that came over was deep and masculine. "Miss Stargazer?"

"Yes."

"It's Grant Holman. I'm down here in the lobby. May I come up and see you?"

I didn't even have to think. I pressed the buzzer to admit him.

Meredith stiffened, pulling her shawl nervously across her shoulders, then spoke in an unusual shrill voice. "You're really going to go through with this?"

I looked at her. "Meredith, I'm going to start watching Steven tonight. Holman's come by to finalize things."

"Steven's going to stay here?"

I shook my head. "I'm going there."

"What? You don't know, he could be an impulse killer."

"Like an impulse shopper? Meredith!"

"Well, Jason's going to—" She was cut short by a firm knock on the door. "I'm going to the kitchen," she whispered, and drew her finger across her throat.

I opened the door. For a blinding second I stood there,

stunned. Grant Holman, aka Frog Face, was drop-dead gorgeous.

He topped me by maybe four inches, which put him close to six feet tall. He had thick dark hair, piercing blue eyes, a cleft in his chin, and a strong jaw. All of that was perched over very broad shoulders, of the sort guys get when they work out a lot. He could have been a former jock in one of the rough sports.

He wore a camel-colored cashmere sports jacket over a navy turtleneck sweater, snug jeans, and the kind of casual leather shoes that shriek "Needless Markups."

Grant Holman was like a sleek, powerful shark, exactly the kind of man that Meredith hoped would take a bite out of her. I find them attractive myself. He was halfway across the room, and I was still following his butt before I even noticed the brunette with him and Steven dragging his toes at the end of the group. You never really notice the pilotfish swimming with the shark.

While I did double takes, Grant introduced himself and Louise Braden. Louise was slim, in her late thirties, with short, efficient hair and a trim, athletic body; she was fully as tall as I am. She wore beige slacks and sweater with a blue scarf that set off the blue of her eyes. She murmured something about how nice to meet after talking on the phone, then smiled nervously as though she were afraid I'd suddenly change my mind, and settled in on the couch next to Holman.

Steven, scowling, wandered to the middle of the room. His face was pale, and there were puffy crescents beneath his eyes. He glanced uncertainly at his father, as if needing a prompt.

"Steven, come here," Grant said.

Steven turned his head from side to side, slowly enough that it could have been interpreted as glancing around the room if you were obtuse. Holman wasn't. He flushed uncomfortably. "Steven, I said come here. Sit with us."

On cue, Louise smiled woodenly and patted the couch next to her. "Right here, dear."

I thought she nearly choked on the word "dear." And when I looked up I found Steven's blue eyes locked on me. A knowing half-grin played around the corners of his mouth. He remained in the center of the room, as if he hadn't heard a word.

I pulled the rocker from in front of the window to a spot comfortably close to both the kitchen and the front door.

"Well, what can I do for you?" I asked, as if I didn't know. I felt Meredith's glare on the back of my neck. Her interest in Holman came right through the kitchen door. I ignored the clatter of silverware dropping to the kitchen floor.

Holman glanced toward the kitchen, and his right eyebrow inched up his forehead in a mute question, but I ignored that, too. When he saw I wasn't going to respond, he drew in a breath. "I need someone until either Elena returns or I find a replacement for her. Steven has had a difficult time, and Elena's leaving has been hard on him."

In the middle of the room, Steven twirled on his heels, his arms out like a helicopter until he ran out of momentum and staggered, obviously trying to get attention. I ignored that, too.

"Steven, don't do that while your daddy is talking," Louise murmured, effective as a feather in a cyclone.

Steven twirled again. His lips pinched closed, keeping his reply inside. Holman was clearly uncomfortable, his eyes followed Steven. "Steven is a very..." Holman searched for the right word. Steven twirled carefully, listening to how his father would describe him.

"Creative?"

Holman flashed a thank-you smile. Great teeth. "Yeah, maybe creative is the word."

"Doesn't he go to school?"

"Uh, not yet. Next fall."

"Kindergarten?"

"No. Elena was teaching him the alphabet and stuff at home."

Actually I was the one teaching the alphabet and reading, but I saw no reason to tell him that. It was interesting that Holman seemed unaware of Elena's inability to read. Steven's twirling ended in a dizzy crash to the floor.

"Steven! Stop that!" Holman ordered. "Steven!"

Steven giggled and got to his feet. Louise leaned forward. "Steven, what have I told you?" she asked softly, her straight dark brows drawn, her gaze intense.

For a moment Steven and Louise glared at each other, then Steven seemed to deflate. He began to drift around the room, inspecting things. He was particularly fascinated with my little brass lizard on the end table.

Holman watched Steven, distracted for a moment, then began to speak again. "As I was saying, I need someone who has the time and patience. And I'll pay well. It's only until we find Elena or a replacement. I never realized how important Elena was."

The words were right, but no emotion came from Holman. His face was closed, blank, and I couldn't tell whether he genuinely felt something or was reciting the words he thought would work. Steven twirled again, closer to me, listening. Louise, of course, sent a silent plea. I realized she was desperate for me to take care of him.

That put me in the power seat, and it felt good. "Steven needs consistency and someone who has the skills—"

Steven stopped twirling abruptly and threw himself into my lap. "Heather is a vampire."

"Who's—?"

Louise cut in, "Heather is a friend of Grant's. Steven doesn't like her very well."

Steven didn't like Louise very well, either, but who was counting? "Mr. Holman, you—"

"Call me Grant."

"How did you know Elena was gone?"

"I saw the note when I went in."

"And that was what time?"

"Uh, the morning, maybe eight o'clock. Steven actually discovered it. He came and got me." Grant was smooth, scarcely missing a beat, but his eyelids did a little triple blink that made me think he was hedging the truth.

"Do you remember what it said, exactly?"

He did that little triple blink again, rat-tat-tat. "It was to the effect that she had to go away for the weekend."

"But you aren't sure?"

"Well, it's a little hard to remember exactly."

"It was a long, complicated note?"

"Well, not that, but with all the upset, Steven, you know, I just don't remember every word."

"How was her writing? Firm? Shaky?"

"Hard to say." He frowned. "It was just regular, I guess. Slanted a bit, real loopy looking."

"Slanted, as if she wrote fast?"

"Yeah."

I remembered Elena's labored printing, the uneven characters, the difficulty she had with spelling. He'd have noticed it, too, if it had been there, so someone other than Elena wrote the note, unless he was lying about it. "And she said she'd be back when?"

He was oddly uncertain about what it said. "I think it said after the weekend."

"So why don't you wait? As important as she is to you and Steven, you could at least wait until tomorrow."

His expression hardened. "I'm in the midst of very delicate negotiations right now, and I can't risk not having child care for Steven. Tomorrow morning I have to be there at seven, without fail. At this point, if I have to cancel or even be late to meetings it could ruin things, and I can't take that chance, not after all this."

"What is it you do?"

"I'm an entrepreneur. My partner, Barry Quinley, and I are about to close a very big deal involving a genetic engineering laboratory, a brand-new artificial blood product, and a great deal of money. I don't believe in leaving things to chance, especially where Steven is concerned. I need someone starting tonight."

Louise was nodding, pleading through her eyes with all her might.

At that moment the kitchen door burst open, and Meredith came out, shawl now tied suggestively about her hips, her chin high, holding a tray.

"Coffee? Tea?" Meredith set the tray down on my little desk and stared even harder at Grant Holman than I had. "Don't I know you? Your name sounds so familiar."

Ah, Meredith, not even an original line.

"Didn't you go to Park Hill Elementary and Gove Junior High?"

Louise bridled. Holman may not have recognized the look of a circling predatory female, but Louise did. Interestingly, she fired right up. "Grant and I are both Colorado natives, aren't we?" she said. It really wasn't a question.

Holman looked startled. "Yeah. But my family left when I was in eighth grade."

Meredith settled herself in the easy chair, where the light caught the sheen of her hair and highlighted her cheeks. Her voice was pure velvet. "I thought I recognized your name. You've really changed."

By all indications it looked to me as though Meredith's depression cycle was interrupted. She had a new project. Grant Holman. I wondered how he would take her interest.

Grant grinned. "Well, I believe I remember you quite well, Meredith." He looked speculatively at me. "But I don't remember..." A little lightbulb went off in his head. "You aren't—?"

"Jane."

"The smart girl with the smart mouth. What was it you used to call me?"

"I forget."

"I remember. Frog Face."

Steven suddenly leaned on my knee. He looked at me solemnly. "Vampires are bad. They eat people."

My throat constricted, but I forced myself to smile reassuringly. "Yeah? Well, they won't eat you. You've got your daddy to take care of you."

The room was suddenly quiet. Steven put his hand on mine, gripping me lightly, his fingers thin and vulnerable-looking, his eyes very round. "The vampire ate Elena."

EIGHT

GRANT HOLMAN'S HOUSE was up the hill from Sloan's Lake in an area of northwest Denver built in stages beginning in the 1890s with ornate brick mansions. Then before World War I small one-story brick squares were added, and finally during the fifties small ranches, mostly blond brick. In the seventies the old elms fell to the beetle, to be replaced by locust, silver maple, and green ash, all still young and leaving the area rather bald except for some ancient spruce and pine trees.

Holman's house seemed isolated because of the looming blue spruce trees planted around the edge of the property, which cut it off from the rest of the neighborhood and gave it an almost spooky aura.

I parked my car at the curb, wishing I hadn't agreed to do this. I hadn't been cheap or easy, and of course, it had nothing to do with his good looks. Holman had agreed to an exceptional wage, and so long as Steven was with me, I had the freedom to come and go. I didn't want Holman to think he could order me around.

Grant Holman's bluff statements about his need to plan for Steven didn't carry much weight with me, especially when I'd seen poor Steven trying his best to get his dad's attention. Holman had talked about his intentions that night, but he never actually reached out to the kid or praised him or patted his shoulder. He patted Louise's shoulder though, and I thought Steven might just put a knife into her if he had the opportunity.

I'd had a vague hope that when I announced that my chameleons had to come along Holman would say never mind, but he hadn't. He'd only asked how big they were and whether they'd be caged. So now I looked up at Grant Holman's sparkling, imposing house and felt totally overwhelmed.

I wished I'd been able to talk with Jason, but the hotel had said he was out. So I'd packed my lizards, my letters, my lingerie, and a few clothes and dragged myself there. Maybe keeping up with Steven would banish the emptiness Jason had left.

The lack of interest from the missing persons department and the chance to go through Elena's things were the final selling points. If I could figure out Steven's vampire and find Elena's little green address book, I might find her.

The house was three stories of chimneys, gingerbread gables, cut glass windows, and even a turret, standing at the top of a gentle hill. Steps led from the street up to a sandstone walk and a wide porch. It could have been the model for a Victorian Christmas tree decoration, the proverbial gingerbread house, almost too good to be true. I briefly wondered if I would find Elena caged in the basement, being fattened for the witch's dinner.

A gust of wind sighed in the spruce trees, then a crumpled McDonald's bag bounced up the street, blew onto my windshield, and brought me out of that nonsense.

Fluffy and Lips were in their travel cage, which was wrapped in a thermal pack for warmth, but Fluffy rattled the bars to tell me he was chilly. I had to get them inside or they'd catch cold. Nothing worse than a lizard with a snotty nose. Unless it's two lizards with snotty noses.

I gathered the lizards and my bag, locked the car, and trudged up the steps to the walk and up to the broad front porch. Since Meredith knew where I was, I reassured myself I didn't need to drop shiny pebbles in order to find my way home again. All the same I felt I was entering a strange, new world; it was worthwhile, though, if I could find Elena.

Jason had said the kid was magic. Maybe Jason was right, or maybe it was the fear I saw in Steven's eyes, but I was here, a bit rattled by his announcement that the vampire had eaten Elena. I wasn't sure what it meant, but I figured in time he would tell me.

Seconds after I rang the bell, the front door swung open. Warm, spicy air rolled out in a rush, and I was face to face with Grant Holman in a tuxedo, the stark, pristine white of his dress shirt setting off his suave tan, ruddy cheeks, and dark brows. He was smooth around all the important edges. In a heartbeat my hand rose to his.

Holman shook my hand warmly. "Thanks for making it. Let me introduce everyone. I'm due at this charity thing, so it'll have to be brief." It was nice he could interrupt his social life for me.

He led me into the vestibule. "This is Barry and Millie Quinley, my partner and his wife." He punctuated their names with intense and unsettling glances at me. I hoped he was assessing my suitability to manage his son. I feared he either thought the Quinleys were especially wonderful people or thought I was especially dull and needed the visual cues to remember their names.

Millie Quinley was tall, blond, breathtaking, and wrapped in a shape-hinting cloud of mink and Private Collection perfume. Her long oval face and hazel eyes were carefully made up. She couldn't have been an ounce over a size ten or a day under thirty-nine. My guess was closer to forty-four.

Millie smiled at me with a mixture of fervor and pity. "Welcome," she breathed. One-hundred-twenty-proof vapors rolled past my nose.

Barry Quinley was barely noticeable in the wake of his wife. He was bulky, stood about five feet ten inches tall, and was clothed all in brown. He looked like a wallet kept in the back pocket, thick, worn, and used. Far from a female fantasy, he had the sort of soft-lipped smile that promised a moist lip print if he kissed.

His palm was damp, and he pressed my hand a degree too warmly, reminding me of the furtive assessments I got when I was still an accountant and arrived to do an audit. His clear, no-color eyes, however, were sharp, intelligent, and constantly scanning, like a wary, abused child checking the safety level. I had the feeling that he'd memorized every detail of my face and entered it into a mental database.

"This is such a shock about Elena," he said. His gaze fell to the left as he spoke, as though too much intimate eye contact was dangerous. He stared at my left shoulder as he continued. "I was always so struck by how loving she was...to Steven. And he's so...er...uh...interested in... things."

It was a puzzling shift in conversation. I wondered if this was characteristic of him, or if he'd found himself at a conversational dead end and was trying to back out. He adjusted his glasses. "I guess you've done this sort of thing before, then?" he asked.

I chose not to answer. "So you both knew Elena fairly well?"

"Not really, I guess," Millie replied.

"Yes," Barry said.

Interesting.

The Quinleys opted to wait in the vestibule while Grant took me to Steven and collected Heather. Grant explained the layout of the house as he led me across a long formal living room done in oyster white with vivid overlaid oriental carpets, to the double, sliding oak pocket doors of the library. "Steven and my friend Heather Jordan are in here."

They were playing checkers. I stopped. I'd never seen a five-year-old play checkers. He was dwarfed by all the polished golden oak in the bookcases, ceiling beams, and fireplace mantel. A fire in the fireplace crackled and cast flickering light eerily over the pair, emphasizing Steven's hollow eyes and thin frame.

His tennis shoes looked as though they'd just come out of the shoe box. His jeans were equally new. A thick belt with silver studs and his initials, SH, imprinted in the back circled his waist. His thin shoulders were clad in a navy cotton knit long-sleeved turtleneck shirt with a little polo pony on the left breast. Nothing but the best.

Heather, in a sequined dark green satin miniskirted dress, with her dark gold hair in voluptuous upswept curls, stared at the checkerboard with a pondering finger stuck between her teeth. She leaned forward and pushed a black checker in a slant to the last row. "King me!"

Steven pouted, disgusted. "You can't move that way unless you're taking a piece."

"Yes, I can."

"No, you can't."

"Can too!"

I had to look twice to make sure these weren't two five-year-olds. Nope. Heather Jordan was a beautiful, childlike girl-woman. My immediate impression was that she could no more mother Steven than hoist an eighteen-wheeler overhead.

However, Steven was talking. I'd been afraid he would retreat to silence, as he had when Elena first knew him. I stepped into the room. "Hi, Steven. What'cha doing?"

Steven flung himself back in his chair, whacking his head against the wooden rim. "She cheats!"

"Hah! At least I got you talking," Heather said triumphantly.

Steven's lips compressed into a thin white line, and his body went rigid with anger. He stalked to the desk in the corner of the room, threw himself into the chair, and bent his head low over several sheets of paper, coloring in angry slashing movements.

Holman's brows drew together, forming a dark line across his face. "I think we'd better be going, Heather. I'll get your coat." He nodded at Steven. "Steven, bedtime." Then he turned back to me. "Well, see you. Steven will show you the upstairs." He started to leave, but the telephone rang and he lifted it to his ear.

I moved to the desk and peered over Steven's shoulder. He'd drawn a picture of a woman in a black cape with blood dripping from her face and a spider eating her cheek. He labeled it "hether."

He laid down the crayon, got up, and gravely took the picture to Heather, laying it in front of her on the checkerboard table.

She glanced at it, then quickly at Grant's back, then softly said to me, "The best thing about this kid is he sleeps from seven to seven."

Well, it was way past seven tonight, and Steven was anything but sleepy. Seven must have been when Elena and Steven were banished from sight.

Once everyone was gone, Steven led me out of the library, pointing first at the dining room, dark with old oak paneling, and then at the kitchen, stark in modern white tile and granite-colored counters. It had an enormous industrial-sized oven—big enough to bake a calf, or Hansel and Gretel.

The staircase was old-fashioned carved oak in two flights with deep, wide steps covered in the centers with thick white carpeting. The banister ran from the base to the top in one long, beautifully carved strip of highly polished oak. A perfect slide.

Steven started upstairs, one arm slung over the banister, clinging to it, placing each foot carefully on only the uncarpeted portion of each step next to the banister. I followed suit. The fourth step up creaked under my weight. Steven glanced back at me as if to say I'd just let the enemy know we were here, then resumed his climb. He didn't say a word.

"Steven, if it snows tomorrow, do you want to make a fort?"

Silence. It took us several minutes to negotiate the stairs because if Steven wobbled and touched the rug, he had to back up and redo the step. His small sidewise glances at my face told me this was a test. I thought I passed.

At the top there was a large, U-shaped gallery hallway,

dark from oak wainscoting and smelling of old wax, warm and lemony. To the right, the front of the house, was the master suite. Straight ahead was Steven's bedroom, and on the left, at the back of the house, was Elena's room, now presumably my room.

White carpeting covered the floor wall-to-wall, and Steven teetered across it as though he were on a log crossing a stream, then proceeded toward the back of the house. At the corner of the hall Steven opened a door, reached for the light, flipped it on, and walked inside.

His face was pinched, his eyes tense. "This is Elena's room. You sleep here."

It was beige and white and almost as personal as a motel room. I swallowed and put Fluffy and Lips on the dresser top.

Steven walked softly to the window and pulled the curtains aside. He stood for a long moment, staring forlornly into the darkness. I went to his side, but all I saw was a large backyard with a glacier of snow and ice in the angle where the garage abutted a toolshed. The lights from the kitchen and another room at the back of the house lay in shafts on the dark grass, making an eerie scene.

I started to hug him, but he withdrew in a rigid silence. Instead, I tried to reassure him. "She'll be back, you'll see."

He stared at me like I was an utter idiot. Slowly he shook his head, shivered, and pointed to the backyard. "That's where the vampire ate Elena."

NINE

HE HAD SEEN SOMETHING, and he was scared to death.

That thought made the air on the chilly windowpane feel suddenly icy cold against my face. I reminded myself that whatever he saw would be filtered through his five-year-old understanding. If I made light of his fears, he would think I didn't believe in him when I actually did. At the same time, I didn't want to make his fears worse by overreacting.

I wasn't sure what I should do or say, but I was convinced that if I could find the key to unlock this kid I'd know what happened to Elena, and I'd take a huge weight off his little psyche. Who knew, maybe he would turn out to be normal.

I searched for words to tell him it would be okay, but I couldn't find any right away. His fear was beginning to affect me. So I patted his shoulder and mumbled something about his father loving him. We stood together, gazing at the dark yard, until he finally turned away from the window.

Until then I had thought I could simply pursue finding Elena with Steven's problems as an aside, but at that moment, I realized the two were intertwined. It made worms crawl in my chest.

I followed him into his room, decorated boisterously with cars and sailboats. In spite of all the cheery decoration, the room felt sterile and comfortless. He had a bazillion books and toys, all neatly arranged on shelves along the walls. The only sign of a living child was the tiny Lego building blocks scattered across the floor in front of his bedroom door, one of the better foot cripplers ever designed.

He had a jungle-gym bunk bed with cubbyholes full of toy guns, rubber knives, GI Joe, and Power Rangers. There was barely room for him in there. I tried to pinpoint why there was no joy in the room and finally decided that it looked like a red, white, and blue arsenal.

"Do you want a story?"

He shook his head.

"You want to go straight to bed?"

He nodded. He didn't strip and drop his clothes like most children. He removed each item of clothing and folded it laboriously, even his socks, then piled them neatly on a chair. His skin gleamed pale, with an almost blue cast, in the harsh overhead light. He pulled on knit Superman pajamas, then washed his face, brushed his teeth, and hung his toothbrush carefully in the holder. He marched to the bedside and said prayers. Absolutely nothing was spontaneous. All this he completed in such a silent, obsessive routine it was oppressive. I felt compelled to talk to fill the void.

"Steven, it's all right to have a little fun. All the children I know toss their clothes on the floor, have to be told to wash, try to skip brushing their teeth, and jump on their beds. Most of all they ask for bedtime stories, hugs, games, and several drinks of water."

He made no response to my attempt to lighten the mood. I could feel defeat gnawing at my stomach, or maybe it was merely anxiety, but I wanted him to respond. Anything, to tell me what he was thinking, or what he'd seen. I'd settle for a grunt. For a second I thought he was going to say something, then he pressed his lips together.

"Steven, I'm exhausted watching you. Do you do this every night?"

He nodded and went to his dresser, opened a drawer, and pulled out a box of salt.

"Snacks before bed?" I asked. No answer.

Very carefully, he sprinkled a thin line of salt across the threshold and windowsill of his room, then around the bed. "Oh, boy." It was a bizarre routine. It certainly didn't have much to do with the prayers he'd just said. "Sweetheart, you're not a french fry, you don't need salt to be good."

He looked at me again like I was nuts. It was hard for even me to smile at my attempts at humor. I tried to impress him with strength. I squared my shoulders and put authority into my voice. "Steven, I'll be here all night. If you need anything, *anything,* you can call out."

He closed the salt box and placed it in his bed. So much for my show of strength.

"Steven, why did you sprinkle salt?"

He looked sullenly at me.

"If I don't know, you aren't going to tell me. Okay, fine." Now I was not only talking to him, I was answering for him. After another day of this, I'd be a babbling idiot.

"Steven, come here." I pulled him onto my lap. A good old-fashioned fairy tale might help. "Have you heard the story of Rapunzel in the tower?" He hadn't, so I regaled him.

He slid from my lap and trotted to his bed. Climbing into bed was no simple matter, either. He rearranged the war toys with tortured concentration, then pulled down one corner of his covers and crawled in, clutching the salt box to his chest. By the time he was in, he was salted and armed to the teeth.

I crossed the room, stooping to tuck him in and give him a kiss, but he turned away, faced the wall, and refused to respond. Now that stung.

It was bad enough to be depressed because Jason was nursing a supposedly sick friend, but to be pained because a little kid rejected me, after all I'd sacrificed, was—was immature on my part. I took a deep breath and stroked his forehead and told him we'd get things set straight somehow. I was sure he heard me, but he didn't respond.

It was so scary to see him turn inward this way. I'd read about childhood depression, and how children can become so despairing after abandonment they withdraw from all human contact and literally wither away. I wanted at least to connect him with some living thing. If I could hook him into a warm, fuzzy feeling, he'd be better for it, and maybe I'd sleep better, too. I remembered his interest in Fluffy. "Hey, Steven, you forgot to say good night to Fluffy and Lips."

His breathing stopped for a second.

"They'll be lonely. They like you. They'll think you don't like them."

He shook his head.

"Fluffy will be sad, maybe have bad dreams."

The idea of bad dreams did it. He turned over.

"Fluffy needs you."

He considered it for a second, then slid carefully out of bed, marched into my room, and leaned over the travel cage on the dresser. Fluffy was stretched out on a twig; Lips had crawled on top of him. Steven's intense little face flattened against the side of the cage. I prayed Fluffy and Lips wouldn't dart away. Lips especially is flighty and shy.

Steven crooked a finger at them, then marched back to his bed, slid in, and turned resolutely away from me.

It was tiny, but it felt like a giant step forward. That's how grim this situation was. "Do you want the light on or off, Steven?"

He pointed to a night-light.

"Can you say good night to me?"

Silence.

I LEFT HIS night-light on and the bathroom door almost shut, returned to my room, and threw myself on the bed. It would be so much easier if I could merely turn him upside down and shake the words out of him like coins out of a pocket, but of course I couldn't.

It disturbed me down to my core that in the midst of his own home, with his powerful father to protect him, he didn't rely on adults, reach out for comfort, or want contact.

I wasn't positive, but I thought I remembered that the salt routine had something to do with keeping evil spirits away. Had Elena shown him that? Did she do it, too?

I flicked on all the lights in my room and bent close to

the threshold of the door. Sure enough, little grains of salt were imbedded in the carpeting. I crawled around the bed and found it there, too. There was even salt on the windowsill where Steven had stared out into the backyard. Good God, what was going on around here?

Clearly Elena, too, had been frightened of something.

She was basically a gentle, talkative, trusting person, yet she hadn't talked to me about it. Would she have talked to Maria? Probably, but I couldn't find Maria. Someone else? Possibly.

Her little green address book held all her friends' names. She had had me put my name in there, too. I needed to find the book.

I stopped, partway across the room. If she had left on her own, she would have taken it. If I found it, it would mean she didn't leave on her own. It would mean...I left it unformulated. I wasn't ready to give up hope. My eyes stung briefly. *Please let her be all right.*

There was a simple sliding bolt lock on the bedroom door that led to the hall. I shoved it into place. The door to the adjoining bathroom I left ajar so I could hear Steven if he called out.

Fluffy and Lips were still perched on a twig, their little eyes beady black, waiting for me to do something. They usually go to sleep by seven at night, so I was pretty sure Fluffy was upset and telling me to get the hell out of there and take them home.

Elena's room was neutral beige, the liveliest accent being a swatch of dried flowers hanging upside down on the wall. It reminded me of the women's rest room in a funeral home. All it needed was the smell of Formalin and carnations. A week of this place and I'd be begging for Prozac.

Except for the crucifix over the bed and the rosary dangling from the right-hand knob on the headboard of her bed, it was completely impersonal. Elena had lived here for at least six months. Where were the photos? Where were the little mementos of life, pictures Steven had drawn, keepsakes from her nieces, all the little things that a person collects over time?

Fluffy rattled the bars of his cage to tell me he was cold, even with Lips for a blanket. I moved his cage to the bedside stand and turned on the light for warmth.

Then I went through the closet.

Heather had said she didn't even take her own clothes, but there were so few in there I found it hard to believe. There were three blouses, a black skirt, and a pair of black slacks, both in petite size three.

There were also several very expensive pastel outfits, sizes eight to ten, which I assumed were castoffs from Heather. Elena was tiny, barely over five feet tall. She would have had to almost remake Heather's clothes in order to wear them.

The top drawer of the dresser held a meager supply of underwear, a pair of stockings, two pairs of black socks, and a gray cardigan.

I searched everywhere, including behind the radiator, on the bed slats, behind the mirrors, and on the dresser drawer bottoms.

An hour later I was hot, tired, and no further ahead. The most personal items I found were her rosary, a bowl of dried rosebuds, a necklace, and an old church bulletin from Our Lady of Guadalupe Catholic Church on Thirty-sixth and Lipan, barely three blocks from Maria's house. The sermon had been "A Mother's Love." I couldn't tell from this collection whether Elena had packed anything or not, but I'd found no little address book and no purse.

I gave up, undressed, pulled on one of my favorite Little Nothings nighties, electric lime green with a fringe, and went to bed. At least I could feel sexy, even if there was no one there to admire it.

Sleep wouldn't come. I missed my own bed, my own clutter, and most of all, I missed Jason. At midnight, I called the hotel where Jason said he would stay. He had checked out.

I plotted his torture in a multitude of tiny, painful ways, then consoled myself with correspondence from my purse. I chose a sensible-looking envelope from Loveland, Colorado.

Dear Stella,

Please give us your opinion. My boyfriend says fidelity is sticking to one belief, and his belief is that polygamy is the natural and honorable state and men need more than one woman to keep their manhood.

I say fidelity means being loyal or constant to one person, and he's being a cheat and a philanderer.

My second question is, what shall I do? I love him.

Troubled in Loveland

I resisted the urge to suggest that she help him combat his fear of losing his precious manhood by sticking it to his leg with a little superglue while he slept. Then he wouldn't lose it anymore.

Instead, I penciled a note at the bottom of her letter: "1. You are right; 2. Dump him; 3. If you can't dump him, buy a lifetime supply of condoms to protect yourself, check in at heartbreak hotel, and prepare yourself for a life of sharing." I read that over and decided that it wasn't any more helpful than my original inspiration. Usually reading other people's problems takes my mind off my own, but that letter came uncomfortably close to home.

Several letters later, at the deepest time of night, the house moaned and groaned in a rising wind until it sounded as though it had a life of its own. At that point I almost believed in vampires myself.

I was drifting off when a piercing scream came from

Steven's room. In sheer fright, I levitated from the bed, stumbled over my shoes, cursed the strange room, and headed for Steven through the adjoining bathroom. He was still shrieking when I reached his bed.

"Steven, it's all right. I'm here. You're okay."

I shook him gently and pushed his sweat-dampened hair off his forehead. His eyes slowly focused on me, then his face crumpled and tears streamed from his eyes. "It's all right, honey. It was only a bad dream."

He hiccupped and started to talk. "Elena was—"

The door to his bedroom burst open. Grant Holman, wrapped in a terry cloth robe, hair sticking out at angles, swept barefoot into the room. "What's going on? What happened?"

I tried to warn him about the Legos. "Watch it—"

He was coming too fast. "Yeow, oh damn!" He cursed, hopped up and down, rubbing his foot, and cursed again under his breath. I winced in sympathy, managed to quell a giggle, and glanced Steven's way. I swear I saw a flicker of a smile on Steven's lips, even though a tear trickled from the outer corner of his eye.

Manfully, Holman walked on his injured foot and reached down to Steven, pushing in to be at his side. "Are you all right, son?"

Steven nodded. Grant patted his shoulder awkwardly, as if he were uncomfortable with Steven and didn't know how to comfort him.

I tried to reassure them both. "Kids his age tend to have nightmares, especially after someone leaves. He'll be all right."

It seemed to rile Holman. "Of course he will. He's a man, and men are tough, right, Steven?"

"Well, he's only five."

"Old enough. No tears now, okay, guy?"

Steven's lips compressed in a thin line. He nodded, turned on his side, and faced the wall.

Grant tucked the covers around him, then turned to me, his face haggard. "Have you been asking him things, Stella?"

"What?" I said, surprised. "Let's step out, we can talk better. Let Steven get back to sleep."

We went into the hall, closing the door to Steven's room. It was so dark I could barely see to find my way. "What do you mean, asking him things?"

"I mean," Holman said, sounding a little calmer in the hallway, possibly because his foot hurt less, "I mean, were you talking about Elena?"

"I only asked if he'd seen her the night she left."

"Don't ever talk to him about that."

"Why? He has to have questions. He may even know something. He's scared. The more you talk about those things, the less scary they are, you know that."

"I just got him over nightmares, and you'll bring them back." His voice rose irritably. "I absolutely forbid it, do you hear?"

His anger was way out of proportion, as though he himself could not bear to hear the topic, almost as though he were guilty or knew something about Elena. I needed to get back to the relative safety of my room. "I hear you, Grant. He's your son, so you have the final say, but I don't agree with you. You're wrong, and you will prolong his fright."

Holman started to wind up further, so I raised my hand to stop him, even though I doubt he could see it. "Please turn on the light so I can find my room; I can't see out here. I said you have the final say. I mean it. But I want you to know, I believe it's a mistake to cover up."

A soft sconce light flickered on. Holman's gaze dropped to my nightie. His eyes widened in surprise, then his lips twitched with suppressed laughter. "I can see you don't believe in cover-ups."

Lime green with fringe doesn't lend itself to dignity, but I tried. I turned on my heel, marched to my bedroom door, and wrenched on the doorknob. It might have been a redeeming and dramatic moment, but the door was locked, of course. I had locked it earlier.

I gathered the fringes of my dignity, passed by Holman, and retreated. Back in my own room, I tried to convince myself that there was something positive in that little humiliation. Holman's near laughter was the first sign of humor, however primitive, that I'd seen in him so far.

It would be so easy to leave in the morning; I could tell Holman I'd made a mistake, Steven wasn't responding to me, I needed to take care of my own business, any number of excuses. But I still felt responsible for Elena. And no one else would look for her, because of that note.

I checked the door to the hall to make sure it was locked and started to shut my door to the adjoining bathroom.

Steven's thin little voice came out of his covers. "Leave it open. Please?"

TEN

MONDAY MORNING came through the window blinds in bars of sunshine. I turned away, trying to hang on to the ragged edge of sleep a little longer.

Thoughts of Elena intruded. I could not count the times I replayed Elena's lessons. She had confided she was troubled in her heart, but hadn't told me exactly what it was, and I assumed it was about Steven, but was it? I hadn't taken the time to get the specifics, I just told her to do what she knew in her heart was right. Another time I had consulted the tarot, but had downplayed the danger in the cards.

Where was she now? Hiding? Hurt? Worse? Wherever she was, I hoped she had spent the night in a warm, safe place, and I prayed she was with Maria.

I thought about Grant Holman's attitude last night. After practically begging me to come here, he had handed out orders like some minor tyrant. At this rate my stay in the Holman household could be very short. Getting Steven to talk was top priority, and finding out about this vampire business was next. And I'd go for specifics.

Slowly I became aware of another presence in the room, at the far side of the bed. I rolled over and pried open my eyes to see Steven, fully dressed in a turtleneck T-shirt, chino slacks, and the too-long belt, like a miniature man instead of a little boy, standing at my bedside, staring at me with round, tired eyes. He looked as though he had slept very little.

"What's the matter?" I asked.

He pointed to the clock.

My eyes were gritty from lack of sleep, and my neck was stiff. I glanced at the clock. Seven-thirty. I usually wake at six, without fail. I sank back on the pillow. "Steven, if you'll play in your room for a few minutes, I'll get up, shower, and get dressed. But I need to do it alone, okay?"

He nodded and started across the room.

"Wait," I said.

He stopped.

"I'm not getting out of this bed until you say yes."

He struggled with the decision. I closed my eyes and pretended to snore.

"Yes," he said, and slammed the door.

Coffee waited in the kitchen along with a note from Grant Holman, stuck under a corner of the kitchen knife block so it wouldn't blow away. One of the knives was missing, and out of curiosity I checked the dishwasher, but it wasn't there. Things like that usually don't bother me, but this time I was uneasy.

"Steven, there's a note here from your dad," I said. "He'll be home at six, and we will all go out for burgers."

Steven shrugged, noisily dragged a chair across the floor to the cupboard, got a bowl and a box of cornflakes, and took them back to the table. It was going to be very hard to get him to talk.

I opened the refrigerator. It was stocked with orange and tomato juice. Maybe I could joke him into talking. I grinned. "Orange juice for your cereal, or milk?"

Steven thought for a minute, then pointed into the fridge. I pulled out the orange juice. He frowned.

"Most kids like milk on their cereal," I said and got ready to pour the orange juice on his cornflakes. He put a hand over his bowl just before I poured and pointed again at the fridge. I smiled and then got out tomato juice and threatened to pour that on his flakes. "Which do you want?"

He stared at me, biting his lips, his hands over his cereal bowl, holding out. I can recognize a power game and we were in one. My brilliant idea wasn't working. "Why don't you come show me the one you want?"

By the end of breakfast I started thinking more objectively about why he wouldn't talk. Last night he had pressed his fist against his mouth, and later he'd abruptly stopped talking when his father came into the room. It occurred to me that he might be afraid of talking in his house. Perhaps he'd talk somewhere else.

I'd hoped to search the house today, but there still might be time this afternoon. "Steven, today we're going places." He looked up, listening. "I need to see my friend Meredith. You met her when you came to my house, remember?"

He nodded.

"Then we'll...go to the newspaper office to see Zelda and get my mail, and afterward we'll go to the park if you like. Sound good?"

He nodded, his lips tight.

I had another idea. "Steven, do you like songs?"

He looked puzzled, then shrugged.

"Okay, try this one.
I know an old lady who swallowed a fly
I don't know why she swallowed the fly,
Perhaps she'll die."

He smiled. I went on, adding the tune.

"I know an old lady who swallowed a spider
It wiggled and jiggled and tickled inside her,
Perhaps she'll die."

He loved it and started humming with me.

"I know an old lady who swallowed a bird,
Have you heard? She swallowed a bird,
Perhaps she'll die."

When I ended on the horse verse he laughed, but he didn't say a word.

The sky overhead was bright blue and cloudless, the air was probably crystal cold. We left Fluffy and Lips slumbering on a twig, bundled ourselves up, and trailed out to my car.

Meredith's flower and candle shop is in Capitol Hill near

Ninth and Corona. We parked a block away and walked up the street, looking in the shop windows. Our breath puffed in little clouds as we walked past the Zooey Soopers grocery haven and the old green-and-redbrick school building. Steven's head was down and he was dragging his toes, scuffing the leather off his expensive little oxfords and creating a fingernail-on-the-blackboard noise. He hummed the old-lady-and-the-spider song to himself, and I thought I heard him murmur the ending words, "Perhaps she'll die." Maybe it was working.

"You'll go to school next fall. Are you excited about it?"

He shook his head and dragged each toe more loudly.

"Have you met any neighbor children?"

He shook his head again, his head so low his chin was on his chest.

"Are there children in the neighborhood?" He nodded. "But you don't play with them?" He shook his head and kicked at a pebble on the pavement, sending it spinning into the street. Why would his father keep him isolated like that? It was so simple to find some playmates. Simple, and yet it would have made a big difference to Steven. He was one lonely kid.

We pushed open the door of Meredith's shop at ten-thirty and were immediately surrounded by candles and immersed in floral scents. Steven rubbed his nose. I sneezed. Meredith was a fervent believer in aromatherapy. If the shop smelled right, people would not only spend more, they'd feel really good doing it. Or, as I pointed out, they'd have an immediate asthma attack and wheeze for hours.

Behind me, Steven dragged his toes all the way to the back of the shop, where Meredith was arranging flowers. He listened to us for a moment, then began to explore.

She handed over the letter. "You can read it if you want. I made you sound like a model tenant."

"I am a model tenant."

Her right eyebrow raised. ''Well, except for damn near blowing up the building.''

''Not my fault.''

She plunged a rose into a green florist's block. ''What are you going to do if they don't renew?''

''They will. But I've got to get this over to them, like, ASAP.'' I looked around for Steven. ''Steven?'' No answer. My heart skipped a beat, then I spotted him in front of a display of Easter rabbit candles, a picture frame in his hands. His cheeks were waxen.

''What's the matter, Steven?'' I followed his gaze to the picture frame. It was a small, simple walnut frame, with a sample picture of a smiling young woman with short brown hair hugging a boy, who at first glance looked like Steven, all set in a beach scene with sunlight, sand, and sea.

I glanced at Meredith, who shrugged. ''Does this look like someone you know?'' I asked him.

''Mommy.''

''Where—?'' My question died on my lips. I'd promised Holman not to ask Steven questions about Elena. I hadn't specifically promised not to ask about his mother, but I was sure she was included in the forbidden questions.

Meredith solved the problem for me. ''Steven, did you and your mother go to the seashore?'' He nodded. ''You can have the picture if you'd like,'' she said.

He nodded and hustled to the door.

''You sure? You're giving away your profits.''

She laughed. ''Call it an investment.''

I couldn't laugh. Holman wasn't simply a pretty face. I briefly considered telling her about his temper last night, then dropped it. I was afraid it would only spike her interest.

We drove next to my apartment building, where I tried to talk to Larry about my lease renewal, but he didn't answer his bell, so I shoved the letter under his door.

Steven still clutched the picture frame. So far I hadn't

succeeded in getting him to talk, and it was almost noon. I swung by the *Denver Daily Orion* next.

I settled Steven at Jason's desk and quickly scanned the day's mail, then stashed it in my purse. My voice mail was largely stuff that could wait, except for one from Cleota Banks at the Little Nothings lingerie shop.

"Stella, please don't forget to stop by today. I've got a problem with the accounts and I need your help. I know you said you'd be here, but I wanted to make sure you wouldn't forget. Thanks." Of course, I had forgotten.

Steven had wandered out to see Zelda, so I telephoned the missing persons bureau. I explained my concern about Elena Ruiz, who had been listed as missing since last Thursday or Friday. I was told no such report had been filed.

Why had Grant Holman lied to me? Was his insistence on no questions to Steven about Elena merely that of an overprotective father, or was there more to it?

Next I called Stokowski. No new homicides. Period. I was running into brick walls. It was even more important to find out what Steven knew.

I grabbed my purse and went out to where Steven and Zelda were eyeing each other uneasily. "Lunch, Zelda?"

"Excuse me?" she said, locking her desk drawer. "You mean actually go to lunch with you?"

"Sure, Steven's hungry, I bet. Right, Steven?"

He nodded, inching toward her. He was gazing straight at her earrings, fascinated.

Her hand went self-consciously to one earlobe. "Something the matter, kiddo?"

He shook his head.

"Don't stare. It isn't polite," Zelda said nervously. She pulled a green snake-shaped eraser from her pocket. "Here, you want this neat eraser?" He looked at it, then at her. "Go on, you can have it, so long as you don't stare anymore."

He reached out and took it, shoving it deep into his trouser pocket. He started for the door.

"He's not talking, is he?"

I shook my head.

Zelda leaned toward me. "Look, Stella, I'd rather stay here. Now don't get mad, but check his trouser pockets."

"How can you say that?"

"His pocket bulges. My little brother stole things at that same age."

"What's he doing now?"

"Time."

OVER HIS PROTESTS, I checked his pockets while we waited in the fast food line. In one he had the little picture Meredith had given him, a pebble, and some paper clips. In the other, the eraser Zelda had given him.

I wasn't all that comfortable with first Meredith and now Zelda giving him things. It was as if they were trying to fill up his loneliness, but loneliness isn't an empty well, and giving him things would only make him think he could have anything he wanted. I vowed to firmly refuse the very next offer of a gift to him.

We dined on fast food, Steven taking tiny, polite nibbles and carefully wiping his mouth after each bite. It would have taken ages to finish if Steven had eaten even half his meal. As it was, we arrived at the Little Nothings shop at twelve-thirty.

Cleota Banks is a very gifted woman who has blossomed since she came to work and sew for Little Nothings. In her eyes, sensuality is life, and every holiday is an opportunity to celebrate it. But I really wasn't prepared for this year's Easter decorations.

Little Nothings was done up in pre-Easter glory with balloons, ribbons, and even a banner that said, "For the Second Coming."

Strategically placed helium balloons displayed and filled

out Cleota's latest lines of dainty pastel undies. In one corner there were explicit white chocolate and pastel Lick'em Offs in a particularly salacious display labeled "Incredible Edible Wear," under a banner that read, "For Easter—to help your beloved rise from the dead."

I wasn't absolutely positive how Grant Holman would view Steven acquiring an encyclopedic knowledge of women's intimate undies, but I thought I could guess. I was glad Steven's head was down and he was scraping his toes; hopefully he wouldn't see it all.

"Cleota, I think I'd better do this another time."

"I've *got* to have help with these accounts, Stella, and I know you can whip through this in no time. Here, these are the printouts. You start, and as soon as I have a break in the customers I'll join you. Everything's listed as you told me to do, but the balance doesn't come out right, or even within two hundred dollars."

"Look, I'm not sure Steven should really be here."

"Nonsense. He's too young to notice anything. He can sit up at the cash register with me and help."

I leaned closer to her. "Maybe not the cash register..." She smiled at Steven. "Don't worry, I'll keep an eye on him. Stella, this has to get straightened out or the IRS is going to be down on me."

Steven was peering at a relatively safe but colorful display of hair clips set up near the counter. How much trouble could a kid get into with hair clips?

I went over Cleota's figures, trying to understand how she'd done it. Then I went over each item, cross-checking with the receipts, and found the error.

And a new sale to Jason. A very expensive item, a Cleota corseletta, shipped overnight mail to...Bipsie Lotts in Los Angeles. The very city where Jason's "sick friend" was. Coincidence? Bet not.

Cleota saw me pause over the notation and receipt. "Now, Stella—"

"He's sent old Bipsie intimate undies before. She's a very real person, isn't she?"

Cleota was silent, the kind of silence that says, "You betcha."

I'd seen the damn corseletta when she finished it. It was a breathtaking, screaming black leather and ostrich feather boob-boosting corset that went better with whips and chains than hidden beneath clothing. Anyone who could wear that corseletta wasn't all that sick. "If you ask me, Bipsie Lotts is right up there with Dee Licious and Sal Lacious, not exactly shrinking violets."

"Don't jump to conclusions."

"Don't *jump?* What more do I need to hit me over the head that Jason's intimately interested in another woman? Or are you trying to tell me Bipsie is a man? That would be better? Please!"

"All I'm saying is, you don't know the whole story."

"Do you?"

She shook her head. "No, I don't. But Jason's a decent man."

"Oh, great. It's nice to know I'm sharing a decent man as opposed to an indecent one. Thanks."

Cleota's sad eyes stopped me. I had met her nearly a year ago when we were both briefly, and unjustifiably, in jail. She knew a whole lot more than I did about indecent men. I closed my mouth and showed her the accounting error, set her straight on how to manage in the future, and then took Steven and left. At least Cleota hadn't given Steven anything.

It was a measure of my upset that I didn't even worry about Steven having liberated anything, nor did I remember to buy a new nightie, one that covered me up. I didn't even think of it until I was a good block away.

USUALLY IN MARCH the sun is strong enough to chase the cold out by midafternoon. The wind was a little brisk and the temperature a bit too chilly, but I needed to be outside where the stiff wind could blow the turmoil out of my heart. Someplace where, if my eyes were a little red and stingy, I'd have a good excuse. I was in no mood to return to the Holman house, where I'd be closed in with my disgust. I wanted to clear my mind of all that by focusing entirely on Steven in a perfectly peaceful place.

We headed for City Park and the children's playground, just right for a little trust-building. If nothing else, maybe I could get Steven to talk to me by dangling him from the top of the jungle gym.

For a while Steven climbed and played on the gym equipment, but then he wanted to walk. The wind felt good against my cheeks, although my fingers were cold. I had started to put my hand into my pocket when Steven slipped his little hand into mine. I was idiotically pleased.

We came to the lily pond where I'd hunted for crawdads as a kid. Then it had been a pretty pond, surrounded by young trees and small evergreens and filled with water lilies. Now weeds crowded up to the edge of the pond, the junipers had overgrown, and where they overhung the water, a thin sheet of dirty winter ice trapped decaying leaves. It wasn't the pretty wilderness pond of my youth.

Steven dropped my hand. "Look, Stella! It's wild here." He spoke! Spontaneously. It was going to work. Now I just had to keep him going.

He found a little path through the low, horizontal junipers and pushed through toward the water's edge. No listless dragging of his toes now. I trotted after him, ready to grip the neck of his jacket and yank him back from the dirty, icy water if he stumbled.

He stopped abruptly. "A rabbit!"

He was truly talking. At least, almost. Seven words, after all this. I bit my lip so he wouldn't know how excited I was. I looked where he pointed. A tiny, scrawny, brown-and-gray rabbit huddled almost at his feet. I was so excited about his talking, I didn't think about why the rabbit didn't move.

He swooped down and grabbed it.

"Don't pick it up!"

"It's a rabbit for me."

"He's wild, he might bite!"

"He's mine."

I don't think I've ever felt so cold so fast as I did realizing that he was talking because of the rabbit—and now I had to tell him to leave the rabbit there. What if he stopped talking again?

I knew if I waited any longer I wouldn't be able to do it. I bent close to him, put a hand on his shoulder. "Honey, it's a wild rabbit, complete with fleas. He lives here and he needs to stay here. You need to put him down."

He jerked away from me. "No! He's mine."

"His mother will miss him."

"His mother's dead."

"No, she's waiting in the bushes for him."

"No, she isn't." He pointed with his finger, clinging tightly to the bunny. "She's dead."

Sure enough. A large brown rabbit was stretched out just under the edge of a juniper, eyes glazed, ears stiff. Dead.

"How'd the mother rabbit die, Stella?"

"I don't know, Steven. Things like that happen. We don't always understand why."

He considered this for a while, then announced, "This rabbit's mine now. I caught him." He started walking to the car.

"Wait, Steven." He turned toward me, eyes trusting and intense. It was so tempting to stall, but the longer I let him go on thinking he could keep it, the harder it would be. "Steven, honey, he has to stay here. He lives here. He loves it here."

"No, he doesn't. He wants to be with me."

"Honey, put him down. Let's let him tell us what he wants."

Steven finally put it down, thank heavens above. We watched while the rabbit got its bearings. It blinked. It wiggled its nose. It didn't move.

"See? He wants me."

"Shhh! It's not moving because it's scared. Be quiet until it tells us."

The rabbit wobbled. It hopped two tiny steps away, teetered on its feet, and tumbled over.

Steven swooped it up again. "He's hungry. There's no grass for him to eat here. He needs me. Please, Stella?"

For the first time since I'd met him, Steven's eyes were shiny and his cheeks had a hint of pink. I was weakening, and so afraid he'd stop talking again.

Truth was, if I'd been by myself, I'd have snatched that bunny up, taken it home, and nursed it back to health. But in the back of my mind I heard Grant Holman's voice. "You did what? You let him bring a wild rabbit home? He'll come down with plague from the fleas, or rabies from a bite. We'll all be infected. You're fired." And I would never learn what Steven had seen. And never find Elena.

I knelt beside him, stroking the little rabbit, feeling its bones under its furry skin and its tiny heart beating at an astronomical rate. It was starving and pitiful. This was awful. He clutched the rabbit to his chest, legions of fleas undoubtedly leaping to his jacket. "Mommy would let me keep him."

"Honey, you need to put him back."

"He'll die here. It'll kill him."

"Honey, put him back, under the bushes."

He frowned, eyes brimming. "I don't want to kill him."

"You won't kill him."

"Yes, I will. Just like before."

The wind on my face suddenly felt icy, chilling me to the bone. Steven's hair was blowing wildly, whipping his face.

He was so forlorn. "Steven, honey, you didn't kill anything before."

His eyes were haunted, almost sunken in his face. "I killed my mommy."

ELEVEN

WHAT DO YOU SAY to a five-year-old who confesses to matricide? His words echoed in my head and sent shivers down my spine. I couldn't even respond for a minute or so.

The wind blew across his hair, ruffling it in a fine ripple of dark brown on his forehead. His eyes were wide and blue and dry and intense, as if his whole soul were poured into them and every fiber of his being was taut as the wind stirred the fur on the hapless rabbit in his arms.

"Steven—" I started to say, then stopped. Was I merely morbidly curious, and would asking him about this send him back into a mute state? Retraumatize him? But he'd have been barely four then. How could a four-year-old possibly kill an adult? If I knew what he was thinking...

"How did you do that?" Then I held my breath.

He frowned, his chin trembling lightly. "I wanted peanut butter and grape jelly and she made honey. When I cried she said I was bad and I hit her and I stomped on her."

I couldn't help myself, I had to ask. "And then what?"

"And she got real quiet, then I went to school. And my daddy came and got me."

"And then what happened?"

"I was hungry and he made dinner. The bunny's hungry, too."

"Was your mommy sick?"

"I don't know. The rabbit wants something to eat."

"Are you hungry, too, Steven?"

"Yeah."

How could a little kid hitting and stomping a full-grown woman kill her? My eyes stung, and not just from the wind in my face. My gut was in a turmoil from heartache for

Steven, anger at Holman for not clearing this up, and pity for the both of them. What a terrible thing to happen to a little kid. No wonder he had a bed full of weapons. And no wonder they weren't enough to make him feel safe. I held out my arms to him. He walked into them, still clutching the rabbit, and rested his head against my stomach.

I didn't know what to think. It sounded for all the world as if this kid had had trauma I'd never imagined. One thing was certain; Grant Holman had a lot to answer for.

Steven twisted in my arms and looked up at me. "The rabbit's really hungry, Stella. We have to get him some food."

The rabbit. What was I going to do about the rabbit? I couldn't tolerate the idea that Steven would think he killed the rabbit, especially when he thought he'd killed his mother. And he was right about the rabbit dying if it stayed there. It would; it was virtually dead already.

On the other hand, Grant Holman's house was tidy to the point of obsession. Of course he was hoping to have a rabbit move in, probably wanted a whole herd of them. I tried to convince myself that it was entirely possible that he would think an emaciated, flea-ridden wild rabbit was the perfect pet for his son.

"Steven, what do you think your dad will say about the rabbit?"

"He'll kill it."

Oh, dear. Of course, the rabbit could die anyway, and Steven would still be traumatized. Either way I'd be responsible for some disaster, but Steven was talking, and for me that was the bottom line. That made it all worthwhile. I would just have to present it to Grant Holman in a positive light.

We stopped at the animal hospital on the way home and got the bunny emergency care, including saline rehydration and defleaing to the tune of sixty dollars I couldn't afford, but the animation on Steven's face convinced me I was right.

I assured myself Holman would agree and slapped down my credit card, adding to the already large balance hanging out there.

When the veterinarian showed Steven how to hold some alfalfa pellets for the bunny to eat from his sweaty little hand, Steven was ecstatic. Words poured from his lips. "Stella, his name is Buckley. He's eating. Stella, he likes me. Can he live in my bed? He won't poop. He has little claws. He says he likes to ride in cars. He says he likes me to feed him." And on and on.

It was nice, very nice. The sound of his voice was sheer pleasure. He chattered away, telling me the rabbit said this and the rabbit said that, and I said "Great!" and "Wow!" and "Swell!" It occurred to me that I might be able to get him to talk about subjects that scared him by using the rabbit. Buckley, the mouthpiece.

"Steven, we need help finding Elena. Will Buckley help us?"

He grew rigid, barely breathing. "Maybe."

"Do you think the rabbit knows where Elena went?"

He picked the rabbit up, looked into his eyes, then turned to me, absolutely solemn. "Buckley says the vampire took her."

"Where's that?"

"Buckley's scared. He says the vampire will get him."

"How does he know about vampires?"

"He just knows."

If I ever found out who told Steven about vampires, I'd wring their neck. Better yet, I'd bite it.

STEVEN AND I were in his large backyard, sheltered from the wind by the brooding pines that bordered the lawn. The rabbit was reviving. He sniffed the ground curiously, then nibbled on some of the tender young grass shoots that signaled the beginning of spring. He looked as if he might live, at least until Grant Holman discovered him.

Steven squatted, stroking Buckley's fur gently, his eyes alight, but I remembered the despair I'd seen there when he said he'd killed his mother. Elena's disappearance would be doubly devastating to Steven. Holman had to do something about it; no child should, could, live with that. Had Elena known this? The few times she had started to talk about him, he had been there, so she would say "later." We never got to "later."

It occurred to me that Holman might accept the idea of a pet rabbit if we had it all set up with a home in the shed. Maybe I could even sell him on a father-son bonding experience, like building it a hutch so it could live safely and comfortably under the bushes.

I walked down the garden path, which widened at the end, forming a small patio by the shed. It would have been charming but for the overhanging vines and the bricks and tools strewn carelessly to the side of the path by the shed. My feet slipped on ice nearly invisible in the gloom. I managed to stay upright by sheer luck; otherwise I'd have been flat on the stones, right where Steven said the vampire got Elena. I knelt, examining the paving stones for a telltale stain. Nothing.

The shed was a typical old wooden garden shed, about six feet wide and eight feet long, built into the corner of the yard. Two small windows on the side, like sleepy eyes, looked onto the back of the house in a blank stare.

"Steven, bring the rabbit over here. We'll make a nest for him in the shed."

Steven swept up the rabbit and stood, knock-kneed and defiant, the rabbit squeezed and gasping in his arms. "No! The vampire lives there."

"Honey, we'll make him a nice warm bed, and inside the shed nothing can get in to hurt him."

If he clutched the rabbit any closer he'd terminate its life. His lip trembled. "The vampire'll eat him."

"Hold him loosely, honey. He can't breathe. Vampires

don't eat rabbits." I moved over closer to him and put an arm around his shoulder, and he leaned trustingly into me. "There aren't any vampires, honey. Someone just told you that to scare you."

He twisted his head from side to side. "I saw it."

My breath caught in my chest. "What did it look like?"

"Dark. Big. He grabbed Elena and took her into the shed."

"Why was Elena out here?"

"She was taking trash out."

There were no bags of trash here, but they could have been picked up, depending on when the trash haulers came. Something to check on.

"Tell you what, Steven. Let's look in the shed and see if there's any sign of a vampire. If there is, we'll take Buckley inside, but let's try it." I marched to the shed and pulled on the door. It gave with a drawn-out creak. "Did you hear that noise when the vampire took Elena?"

He shook his head no.

"And where were you?"

He pointed up at the window of Elena's room. He probably couldn't have heard the sound of the shed door through the closed window. I peered inside.

"Don't go in there!" Steven yelled. "The vampire lives there!"

I flung open the door and stepped inside. "Nope, no vampire here."

The smell of dust, mice, and mold filled my nose, making me sneeze in rapid succession. I loathed mice; I hoped I wouldn't find one. At one time this shed had been an orderly home for an obsessive tool keeper. Peg-Board with outlines of each tool covered the walls, but now few of the tools hung in their places. Rakes, brooms, and a snow shovel stood in the back corner, with a wheelbarrow and an ancient power lawn mower. Overhead the beams were open to the roof.

A workbench stood along the side wall with an assortment of tools and little jars of screws and nails jumbled together with a small, curved, tree-pruning hand saw on top, all waiting to be put in their proper places. It looked as if they'd been waiting a long time. Dust lay thick on the saw.

The flooring was concrete, with dirt, old sawdust, and a few leaves from last fall scattered haphazardly over it, as if they had blown in during a storm. I stared at it, trying to see a pattern, looking for something that would prove Elena had been here. Actually, I was looking for proof that Steven was telling the truth, that he had seen Elena dragged in here, but I couldn't find a thing.

With my toe I scraped away the dirt and sawdust, looking for telltale stains on the concrete, but it was unstained. "All that's here is the smell of old air, dirt, must, rust, and mice. It's perfect for a wild rabbit."

Steven shook his head. "He wants to sleep with me."

"No. Absolutely not. You could roll on him in the night. He'd get squashed. He must have his own place."

Steven stood flat-footed on the stone path, eyes wide and terrified, clutching the rabbit to his chest. "Not in the shed."

"Look, it's a great place. Try it, just for me. Come see. There's no vampire here."

Steven approached cautiously and peeked inside. "He won't like it."

"Of course he will. Put him down."

"No."

I'd already struck out how many times today? My luck surely had turned for the better by now. "Try him. Trust me."

Steven glowered, but he stepped over the threshold. He glanced around, then frowned and pointed at an old wheelbarrow tipped up against the wall. "The vampire brought the wheelbarrow inside."

This vampire was sounding a lot like my brother's imaginary friend, RedWing. "Steven, please? Let Buckley tell us."

Steven's eyes narrowed skeptically. "Aw right," he said. "But he won't like it." He put the rabbit on the floor and stepped back.

The rabbit sniffed the air, then the dirt and sawdust on the floor, then he squeaked and hopped like crazy to the door of the shed, through Steven's legs, and out into the cold and wind. Steven whooped and ran after him. I banged my head on the wooden doorjamb. "Damn, damn, damn."

Steven returned to the door of the shed. "Stella, the rabbit says he could live in the basement where it's warm."

"Maybe he could just live in the doghouse with me."

Steven frowned. "We don't have a doghouse."

I took one long, last gaze around the shed. No chains, no medal lay conveniently on the floor, only a faint track of the wheelbarrow in the dust at the far end of the shed. I ran my hand lightly along the door jamb, looking for any sign of scraping or struggle. About a foot and a half up from the floor my hand caught on a sliver.

I knelt to get closer and found a shred of black plastic caught in the sliver. Then I saw two long strands of dark hair caught in the rough edges of the woodwork. Elena's hair, I was sure. I touched one of them, trying to see if I would have one of my spells and maybe see more of what must have happened here. My fingers were cold, but there was no tingling, no vision, no taste of blood.

I left the hairs there and rose clumsily; my head was clear, but my limbs felt like wood. I closed the door to the shed and went after Steven, wishing I could break down and cry and cleanse myself. But none of that would come until I found Elena and knew at last what had happened to her and why.

IT WAS NEARLY six o'clock, and I expected Grant Holman any time. Steven and I were in the basement making a place for Buckley. I was more convinced than ever that Steven was my key to Elena, and the rabbit was the key to helping Steven tell about it. Now I had to find a way to tell Grant he had a new pet and convince him Steven needed to keep it.

We located a fine big box and put in some clean rags, a water dish, and some alfalfa pellets. While we bedded down Buckley, Steven sang the old-lady-and-the-fly song. I decided to pry a little more about his mother and the vampire.

"Steven, remember this afternoon? Why did you say you killed your mommy?"

He straightened up, his lower lip pouting. "Because I did."

"I don't think you could do that."

"Yes, I can. I did. Daddy says I'm not supposed to talk about it."

"Well, if you want to any time, I'll listen."

His eyebrows furled. "It makes my stomach hurt."

"When you think about it?"

He nodded.

"The thoughts come even when you don't want them to?"

"Yeah," he whispered. "In the night."

"Steven, everyone gets bad, sad, lonely thoughts at night."

"Daddy doesn't."

"Well, maybe he does and doesn't talk about them."

"No. He just told them to go away and they did."

"Well, maybe he said that because he didn't want you to worry. He feels bad when you worry."

"No, he doesn't. He gets mad when I worry."

"Well, some people get mad when they feel bad. He really loves you, otherwise he wouldn't get mad."

"He must have loved Elena, too."

"Why?"

"Because he got real mad at her. He yelled at her."

Footsteps sounded overhead. "Steven!" Grant Holman was home.

Steven's lips clamped shut, and he bent over the bunny. "Buckley doesn't remember."

I'd have Steven telling me everything in no time. I was sure of it. For now, though, I had to frame the whole rabbit thing positively for Holman. I wondered if Heather would be an ally. "Steven, do you think Heather will like Buckley?"

"No. And Buckley doesn't like her, either."

Great, just great. "Steven, let's go get you all cleaned up, then you can tell your dad all about your day when we're out for burgers. That will be a better time to tell him. He'll be fed, and chances are he'll be real happy."

Steven looked dubious, as though he'd had previous experience. I hoped it was merely my pessimism, not reality. We raced up the stairs to the kitchen.

Grant Holman was at the kitchen sink, sleeves rolled up, tie loosened, hair tumbled forward. He looked the picture of Mr. Congeniality. Maybe now would be the best time, after all. If we got it over before dinner we wouldn't have to worry. "Grant, we—"

"Steven," he interrupted. "Make sure you get those hands clean tonight. Stella, he needs to be more careful about his appearance. His sports jacket tonight, okay?" Mr. Congeniality dried his hands on the towel and arranged it on the towel rack, lining up the edges so they matched.

I glanced at Steven to find him looking at me. Steven pursed his lips tightly together. I smiled and took his hand. "Race you to the top of the stairs," I said.

"Sports jacket tonight, Steven!" Grant hollered after him.

I stopped at the bottom of the stairs; Steven waited for me. "I thought we were going for burgers," I said.

"Something came up," Grant called back.

"Heather," Steven whispered.

"Steven and I could eat here, you can have a night out," I offered.

"No. We're going as a family."

"Then I'll eat here, you two go."

Steven yanked on my hand.

"No," Holman said, coming to the door of the kitchen, glass in hand. "You come, too. You're a part of us now."

I shuddered involuntarily.

STEVEN FOUND A dozen different ways to slow his cleaning-up process, as though he knew I was trying to hurry so I could talk to Grant about our park outing and Steven's statement that he'd killed his mother. I barely had time to run a brush through my hair and slip into a pair of blue silk slacks and a jazzy multicolored Guatemalan jacket. By the time we were downstairs Holman had his coat on.

"Grant, I need to talk to you about how the day went today, do you have a minute?"

"We're a little late now, Stella. Maybe at the restaurant?"

I had my hand on the handle of the front car door when Grant announced, "We're picking Heather up at her place."

I got in the backseat with Steven. He wrinkled his nose. "See?"

The happy family facade slipped even further at the restaurant. The casual sports atmosphere of the Thunderbird Café was definitely only for those fortunate enough to be in a normal family. For us, it was show time. And to make it all quite dreadful, Millie and Barry Quinley were there, and Louise showed up. It looked like a little Grant Holman worship time.

Millie squeezed in next to Grant, while Steven and I were moved to the foot of the table. I was relieved, but Steven looked disgusted. I don't think Holman realized that Steven had hoped for his father's companionship, now drowned in the expensive perfumes of the women flanking him.

I glanced at Steven, expecting to see pain and disappointment on his face. Instead, he was bent over a little toy he had pulled from his pocket and was jumping it up and down on his leg. At least he had brought something to occupy himself with. Evidently he had endured these dinners before.

For the first time in a long time, my appetite failed me. I ordered only a salad and looked forward to nibbling on a tiny ear of corn.

Barry Quinley, also banished to the foot of the table, sat across from me and buried his head first in his menu, then in his salad plate, consuming a basket of bread with butter. He surfaced only after he'd finished his steak.

I thought I recognized the earmarks of a starving man. "Skip lunch?" I asked, smiling. Great conversation opener.

Barry glanced quickly at Millie, seated next to him, but her attention was strictly on Grant. He cleared his throat. "Dieting. Millie thinks I'm too heavy."

He was, but I nodded sympathetically.

Steven was listening, but I couldn't let this opportunity pass. "You and Millie were at Grant's house the last night Elena was there, weren't you? Did you talk to her?"

He took a sip of wine. His hand seemed to have developed a slight tremor. "She was upstairs with Steven most of the time. Just saw her go into the kitchen to help Louise."

"Do you know what time that was?"

"Must've been close to nine. We'd finished dessert."

"Did you see her go back upstairs?"

"No." He stroked the stem of his wineglass, his gaze following the movement of his fingers. "We were celebrating a breakthrough in this deal, we didn't really see Elena."

"Did you notice if she was upset?"

He sipped his wine again, a rather transparent stalling technique. I couldn't tell whether he was always this way, awkward and reticent, or if it was just my nosy questions.

He was working up to a reply when Louise, sitting next to me, leaned over. "Elena was helping me in the kitchen after dinner. I think she spoke to Grant briefly, nothing special.'' Louise offered wine around and grinned. ''So how was your first day, Stella?''

''We had a great time, ran some errands, went to the park—''

''Stella!'' Steven said. ''Look at this.'' He poked his hamburger. ''Can you cut it for me?''

''It's a hamburger, Steven. We don't cut them.''

''I want it cut.''

''You want attention.'' I excused myself to Louise, who was happy enough to return to Grant's conversation.

Grant hadn't mentioned talking to Elena that night; could it tie in with Steven's account of Grant yelling at her? I cut the hamburger in half.

Millie's giggles were growing louder, as though they had been lubricated with a bit too much alcohol. Barry glanced around at her briefly, frowned, then looked at me, his eyes narrowing. ''She likes a good time.'' He sounded plaintive.

Barry watched Steven play with his toy, a not too subtle way to say he was finished with this conversation. A little smile lurked in the corner of Barry's lips. He caught me looking at him and winked at me as if he thought we shared a joke.

I grinned, vaguely uneasy, and tried a new avenue with Barry. ''Have you and Grant been partners a long time?''

''About a year.''

''You've been pretty successful in that time.''

''Very. Grant's a great money finder. I see to the details and paperwork. He finds the money. I place it.''

'' 'Place it'?''

''According to the enterprise, where it will prove the best investment.''

''So you have connections with companies throughout the country?''

''Throughout the world.''

''Would you need to be here, in Denver?''

He pursed his lips. "I hate travel. I'd need to be here, but Grant can operate from just about anywhere."

"Makes him pretty mobile."

"S'pose so." He glanced again at Steven's toy, then at me, grinned and winked at me again, then reached for yet another piece of bread. This conversation was possibly the worst I'd had since junior prom in high school, when my date had a ten-word vocabulary and pinned a corsage to my skin.

Steven ran the toy up and down his leg like a car at a race track. Whatever joke Barry thought I understood, I didn't get, but it wasn't worth the effort to find out. Steven's head remained resolutely bowed, intent on his toy and singing "perhaps she'll die" to himself. I hoped he thought of Heather, not me.

There was a lull in the general giggle and chatter at the other end of the table. I folded my napkin in a going-home motion, praying it meant the end of the evening.

Millie suddenly leaned forward, her gaze, slightly glazed, fastened on Steven. "Steven, darling. You're so precious tonight. What little toy did you bring to amuse yourself?"

Barry Quinley raised his head, his eyes owlishly blinking at Millie. "Leave him alone, Millie. He's fine."

"I'm just showing an interest in him, Barry. I *love* young people, you know. Just like you do."

Barry's expression hardened, and he shook his head, a reply eloquent although mute. This had the markings of one of those unpleasant husband-wife exchanges that masked hostility and old arguments and had layers of meaning that the rest of us could only sense without understanding. Tension tightened my stomach; even lettuce weighed a ton in it tonight.

Millie laughed, teasingly. "Show me your toy, Stevie, you always bring such cute toys."

"Millie, cut it out."

That only goaded her into more effort. "I want to talk to him. Nobody has said a word to him all night."

What was I? Chopped liver? Talk about annoying. I think that's why I felt an uncontrollable urge to respond. "Steven," I said, "do you want to show Mrs Quinley your toy?" He shook his head. "Maybe later," I replied with my most insincere smile.

"Steven," Grant Holman cut in, "show Millie your toy."

Steven smiled.

Something bad was about to happen.

"Steven, give the toy to Mrs. Quinley," Holman ordered. Steven handed it to Barry, who smirked and handed it to Millie.

She turned it over in her hand, and her face gradually went slack. "Oh, my Lord, look what he has." She handed the toy to Grant Holman, who turned it over in his hand, his eyes bulging.

I tried to see what it was. "Steven, what is that toy?" I asked in a whisper.

"Nothing," he muttered. That's when my breathing grew ragged. I smelled disaster.

"What is it?" I asked.

Grant Holman's face flushed dark red, and his brows made a thick dark line across his face. "Where did you get this?" he thundered. Several of the nearby restaurant patrons looked our way.

Steven's face was pale, but there was a tiny gleam of triumph in his eyes. He had his father's undivided attention, at last. He clamped his lips shut tight and stared at his plate.

Heather leaned over to look at the toy. "Oh...my... Lord!" She snatched it up, and took a good long look, her face a peculiar mask, unreadable because of a tremor in her lips. I couldn't tell whether she was horrified or trying not to laugh.

She handed the toy to Louise, who handed it to me. It was a hair clip. I turned it right side up. It was a hair clip cleverly made from a Chinese figurine of two well-endowed people in an imaginative coupling. Kama Sutra stuff. The tiny gold label stuck to the tiny backside of the tiny woman said "Little Nothings."

I looked around. "Eastern art?"

It was a truly ugly moment, and it didn't pass quickly.

TWELVE

MILLIE GUFFAWED in liquor-soaked hilarity and announced she would buy two of them first thing tomorrow, which immediately endeared her to me. Louise tried to smooth things over, but Holman scowled and called for the bill. Heather glued herself, limpetlike, to his side, nodding and imitating his scowl in a silent yes-speak, treating Steven and me as though we had some vile contagion. My sister and I used to do that same thing when we were eight years old. I guess that established Heather's emotional age level. I was so disgusted I nearly stuck my tongue out at her.

The ride home was deadly quiet. Life is tough without a sense of humor. Holman slid the car into the garage at the back of the yard, opposite the toolshed, and led us in silence to the house. We didn't rate the front door after the offense. At least it gave me a glance at the inside of the garage, which was clean, functional, and held little else besides the garage door opener and a pair of tires resting on the rafters overhead.

It was dark and slippery underfoot in the shaded area beneath the grape arbor. Steven eyed the toolshed nervously and slid his cold little hand into mine.

I considered announcing the presence of the rabbit as we neared the house, but held off. Holman held the door for Heather, who stepped inside and immediately went into a sneezing fit. She must have sneezed seven times in a row. "I think I'm coming down with a cold," she said

"Oh, I'll bet it's—" Steven jerked on my arm. "Just allergies," I finished up.

Holman glared at me. "I'll see the two of you in the library in about ten minutes," he said.

Heather pitched me a raised eyebrow glance that could have been either jealous glee or sympathy, and then melted into the woodwork. Evidently she didn't get involved in these domestic disputes, at least not this one.

Upstairs, I sat on the edge of the bed, in the middle of Elena's beige bedroom, considering approaches. Lectures annoy me, and I didn't know how I'd handle this one, especially since I felt that Holman was equally to blame. After all, he had spent the whole evening ignoring the child. Setting aside the fact that Steven had stolen the hair clip, I figured he'd done what he had to do to get his father's notice.

It was clear to me that Steven's main problem was emotional, and I wasn't going to be able to cure that, not with Holman having the sensitivity of a rock.

Fluffy rattled the bars of the plastic travel cage to tell me he was cold again, so I turned on the lamp. Lips was hiding in the plastic plant, and Fluffy had the baleful look of a lonely male. I reached in and offered him my hand. He jumped into my palm.

"Well, Fluff, what's the matter?"

He blinked slowly.

"Isn't Lips cuddling with you tonight?" When they first got together, Lips had been somewhat shy, hiding beneath the log most of the time, but in the last two months she'd been lying on top of him at night. Lizard courtship. "I thought you'd abandoned me for your sweetheart." He blinked again.

"You've been very handsome with your head bobs and throat swells." He blinked. It was so good to have his attention again. I mean, I wasn't jealous. Lonely, perhaps, but not really jealous. It just warmed my heart to find that he still craved my company once in a while.

I slipped on his little harness and pinned him to my sweater. He might as well come with me, so I'd have someone on my side.

"Stella," came Steven's voice from his bedroom. "Are you scared of my daddy?"

I thought about that for a minute. "No. Why?"

"He's mad."

"Yeah, I think he is, but he'll get over it."

"He got mad at Elena..."

My breath quickened. I went to the door of his room and peered in. He was curled in a ball on the floor in the middle of his armament of toy weapons.

"Steven, don't be worried. Let's go and get it over with."

"He's going to whip me."

My heart bled. "No, he won't. He's upset because you stole something. Now we have to get it straightened out."

"I was bad, wasn't I?"

"It was bad to take the hair clip."

He scrubbed his face. "Stella?"

"What?"

"Don't tell Daddy about Buckley."

STEVEN FOLLOWED ME into the library. A small fire in the fireplace cast a golden glow over the heavy oak woodwork and lit the room with a cheeriness that didn't fit the grim expression on Grant Holman's face. His hands were restless on the desktop, fingering a pen, tapping a ruler. As far as I could tell, he'd been in there all that time doing nothing more than getting ready to chew Steven and me out, maybe even practicing his lecture.

I drew in deep, even breaths to maintain my calm, which I figured was imperative. I'm not at my best when I'm angry. I say things that I regret.

He pointed to chairs for us to sit in. I declined. I'd rather be above eye level in these situations, creating the illusion of control.

"Steven, come here." He picked up the ruler. Steven sidled behind me.

Holman stood up, grasping the ruler in his right hand, and

started around the desk toward us. "You won't believe this, young man, but this is going to hurt me worse than it hurts you."

It's the third oldest cliché in the world, right after "Trust me" and "It's in the mail." I heard it when I was a kid, and it made me just as furious then as it did now. I put a hand out. "Hold it."

Steven cowered farther behind me.

Holman flushed. "Come out here, Steven, take your punishment like a man."

"Wait, we need to discuss this."

"Oh, no, we don't."

Fluffy dove for shelter in the neck of my sweater. I gave Steven a shove toward the door. "Wait outside."

Holman's face was clouded with anger. "Stay where you are, young man. Stella, get out of the way."

"Listen, Grant, Steven's like a lot of children his age who aren't sure what is right and what is wrong."

"He knows what's right from wrong. He's done this before. He's got to learn."

"No." I took another step forward, blocking his advance. "Steven, go. Now. Wait outside the room. And close the door after you." Steven hustled. The door clicked shut. I drew in a breath, hoping to reason with Holman. "He needs to be taught, but there are other ways than beating. You know, he gets something out of it when he can get you to beat him."

He snorted. "He wants a beating?"

"He wants your attention. When you beat him, he gets it, even if it hurts."

"He'll learn the way I learned. I was a bad kid, and my father beat it out of me, and by God if that's what it takes, I'll beat it out of him, too. I won't have him ending up in jail." He sounded like an abused kid grown old.

"Steven's not bad, he's very smart and very lonely. When kids are lonely they take things to fill the empty spot inside.

It's like some adults who buy things or eat things to feel better; so do kids."

"What are you, some social softie, knee-jerk liberal? You think he should just be allowed to continue stealing?"

"I happen to know what I'm talking about. Let me take him back to the shop and have him confess and apologize. A little shame and humiliation can work wonders."

Holman snorted in disgust. "What do you know about kids? You don't even have any."

"I know a lot about kids. I've been one, for a very long time."

I hadn't meant to say quite that, but it broke the tension, so I raced on, unfortunately. "He wants you to spend time with him. Why don't you try talking to him, maybe going to the park with him? He loves the park. We went there today and he found a little rab—" My voice died.

Holman looked up. "He found what?"

"He found a rabbit."

"And...?"

"And that's when he started talking again. He was so taken with the rabbit he talked and that's when—"

"And where's the rabbit now?"

"The important thing here is that Steven is talking, and we can begin to unravel what he knows about Elena's disappearance."

"He doesn't know anything about Elena's disappearance. Where's the rabbit?"

"I think he does. And I think it bothers him. That rabbit is important. Grant, that rabbit made Steven feel loved. Do you hear me?"

Holman's eyes narrowed to furious slits. "Are you telling me my own son doesn't feel loved?"

"All evening Steven tried to get your attention. What was he supposed to do?"

Holman was a scary guy when he was angry. He was practically shaking with anger. "You think I don't love my son? I've been through hell for him." He grabbed my forearm, his fingers pinching dents in my flesh. "Don't you dare say I don't love him."

"Is this how you treated Elena?" I yanked my arm away. "You yelled at her that night. Did you grab her, too? Maybe hurt her?"

I knew from the shift in his gaze that he had threatened her. "You knew from the beginning she wouldn't return. That's why you never reported her missing. And that's why you were looking for a replacement from the moment you knew she was gone."

Holman took a step back; I followed up. "You don't want her found. She'll tell how you treated her. Maybe even press charges. That wouldn't look so good for the flashy on-the-rise entrepreneur. What did you do to her? How badly was she hurt?"

He looked at me defiantly, then his gaze dropped again. Guilty as sin. "She wasn't hurt," he said. He almost choked on his words.

"You merely grabbed her arm and left only a few bruises, right?"

"That's all. I didn't hurt her."

THIRTEEN

NEITHER OF US SPOKE while the tension drained away. In the silence I heard a motorcycle with a lousy muffler roar down the street outside. As the sound died, Holman wiped his face as though wiping the slate of his memory clean, then retreated and sat down heavily behind his desk, sullen.

I was surprised to find that while on one level I was frightened by Holman, on another level I felt almost jubilant, as if, having survived his temper, I'd somehow bested him, a seductive illusion of power.

And I understood now why Steven was so wary and secretive. He never knew what mood his father would be in.

I decided to leave the room while I was ahead, and before either of us resurrected the argument. As I closed the door, I saw Holman sitting stiffly at his desk, fingering the ruler, and felt again that sense of almost elation. I shuddered.

Was my reaction the beginning of adapting to an abusive situation?

Steven was curled in a ball, sitting on the bottom step of the staircase, elbows on his knees, head buried in his arms. He looked up, his face almost skull-like from pallor and the shadows under his eyes. I gave him a half-smile and said, "Hey there. Time for bed."

He looked worriedly at the library door.

"We need to talk, big-time, but let's go upstairs," I said, and led the way.

In his room I sat on the chair. "Come here and sit on my lap, Steven." He came and sat, rigidly upright. "Steven, it was very wrong to take the hair clip from the shop. That's stealing, and stealing is very bad. It isn't right to take things that belong to others." I made my voice very low and sad.

"And it makes people think you're a bad boy. It made your daddy ashamed of what you did." Thank God, I saw a film of tears in his eyes. "What do you think we have to do about this to make it right?"

"You can buy it for me."

"No."

He thought. "Give it back?"

"Yeah."

"Then do I get a whipping?"

"No. Worse. You have to go to Mrs. Banks at the Little Nothings shop and tell her you stole her hair clip and say you're sorry you did it."

He thought for a moment, then spoke up. "I'd rather have the whipping."

"You've had them before?"

"They only hurt at first, then they're over."

Steven shed his clothes with the same precision as before, folding them neatly but tonight placing them on the top of the dirty clothes hamper, since I was sitting in the chair where he'd put them the night before. Every movement he made was careful, planned. He was truly remarkable. If he were six it would be more normal. I lifted his trousers onto my lap and slipped my hand into his pockets, expecting to find the picture Meredith had given him. His pocket was empty. Two to one he had hidden it.

When he was ready for bed I pulled him onto my lap again. "Steven, we have some more talking to do." He looked at me sideways. "I took the heat off you, now you need to do something for me in return." He blinked, thinking.

"You see, I think maybe you've got something Elena gave you, maybe a memento of her, and I'd like you to show me."

He scooted off my lap, his head down, kicking at the carpeting. "They're mine."

"Steven, remember the night Elena went away?" He nodded. "What were you doing?"

"I woke up. She forgot the salt, and she wasn't there." He pointed to her bedroom. "I looked out the window and saw her."

"How does the salt help?"

"Keeps vampires away."

"When you looked out the window, what was Elena doing?"

"Taking out the trash."

"Was anyone with her?"

He shook his head.

"Then what happened?"

"I told her not to go there, 'cause of the vampires. But she went anyway. She waved at me, then she talked to the vampire. She was mad..." His voice rose, and he waved his hands as he spoke.

"Mad? Not scared?" If mad, it seemed sure she knew her attacker—and that it was one of the people there for dinner.

"Mad. And the vampire hit her! BAM. She fell down, and her legs and arms stuck out. Then he sucked her blood until it was all gone and dragged her into the shed and took her into the ground." His voice dropped to a near whisper. "She's underground now, in the vampire's cave. We can't see her."

"Did the vampire come back out of the shed?"

"I dunno." He tucked his chin down on his chest, leaning into me to hide his face. Seldom have I felt such despair from anyone, and never from a child.

I circled his narrow shoulders, hugging him. "Why don't you know?" I asked softly.

"I hid under the covers," he whispered.

Could a heart break from this? "That was a good idea," I said and rubbed his arms. "Steven, why was your daddy mad at Elena that night?"

"He yelled at her."

"Did you hear what he said?"

"She should never, ever, ever talk on the phone."

"Who did she talk to on the telephone?"

He shrugged. "I dunno." He leaned heavily on me again, and we sat for a while in silence, then he pushed away, gazing solemnly into my eyes. "I was really scared."

It was a measure of his trust in me that he'd told me that. "I bet. I would have been scared, too."

"Really?"

"Yeah."

He frowned and put his head back down. I wasn't sure what he was thinking, but whatever it was, he shouldn't have had to face it so young. "Stella? Sing me the spider song?"

I sang it, and he hummed along. When I finished he sat quietly for a minute, humming to himself, then he raised up.

"I know one, Stella!" He had a clear voice and carried the little tune perfectly.

"I know an old lady who swallowed a feather
It was named Heather,
Perhaps she'll die."

He shrieked with laughter. His moods changed quickly, too. "Stella, I got another!
I know an old lady who swallowed some fleas
Just like Louise,
Perhaps she'll die."

There was a certain demonic glee in his eye that left me a bit uneasy. "Steven?" I asked. He raised his head. "Are you going to show me your treasures?"

He thought it over, then trudged over to his bed, pulled out a drawer in the base of his bed, scrabbled around in the back of it, and finally drew forth a shoe box. He tipped the box out, raking the treasures in his hand. I got up and went to his side.

There were special rocks, seashells, a miniature Swiss pocket knife, the picture Meredith had given him, a tiny perfume bottle, an eyebrow pencil sharpener, the eraser

Zelda had given him, a Susan B. Anthony dollar suspiciously like the one on my desk at the office, and a tiny crucifix.

The little cross was exactly like the one Elena wore on a chain around her neck, along with the Saint Don Bosco medal. Where was the medal? She was never without the two.

Figuring that to ask him outright about the crucifix would make him clam up, I hesitated over the dollar, saw him tense, then picked up the crucifix, hoping that in his relief over my not choosing the stolen dollar, he'd talk. "And this?"

He frowned. "I found it." I looked at him, then back to the little cross. It lay in the palm of my hand, cold, then suddenly quite warm. My palm began to tingle, and the sides of my face grew cold and clammy.

I fumbled, turned, and sat heavily on the bed, my legs shaking as I grasped the cross. The edges of my vision narrowed until the room was dark and I saw only a pinprick of light and heard only the sound of my breath, susurrant in my ears.

The light spread from a tiny dot to a figure, unnaturally crumpled on a cold, rocky surface. It was barely a figure, could even have been two, possibly a child alongside, but I knew, positively, it was Elena. I tried to see where it was, to find an identifying landmark, but there was none, only the sound of wind filling my mind and a taste in my mouth, morbidly familiar. The metallic taste of blood.

The room seemed to be closing in; I could barely draw a breath. A blinding pain shot through my head, then echoed inside my head, as though my brain had loosened from its moorings. The pain was so strong I retched, then it diminished, although I still felt ill. The figure hovering before me faded until nothing was left but the dull ache in my head as a reminder.

The room reshaped, warm and lighted. Steven stood at

my knee, his hand resting on my arm, shaking it urgently. "Stella? Stella?"

He was trembling, shaken. "Stella, she was here. I smelled her. She smells like roses."

Did he really smell the scent of roses? Was it there from her room, or had he sensed her presence? I opened my hand and stared at the little cross, trying to elicit another vision. Without success. All I saw was four crescent fingernail dents in my palm from clenching my fist.

I held out the little cross to Steven. "Steven, I'm not going to be mad; neither will Elena. Now tell me the honest-to-God truth. Where did this cross come from?"

"The trash. Down there. By the gate. By the shed. On the ground. Buckley found it for me."

I couldn't shake the sense that this little cross carried danger for Steven. I hadn't paid attention to the others, but Barry had been acutely interested in Steven, all through dinner. I had assumed he was trying to avoid me, but perhaps not. And he had lied at least once about Elena.

"Steven, did you show this to anyone else?"

"No."

"Did you play with it at dinner?"

He hung his head. "Yes."

IT TOOK PRECISION arrangement of his toy weaponry and nearly an hour of waiting until I finally heard the soft snore of Steven's breathing that signaled he was asleep. I heard Grant leave with Heather, presumably returning her to her web.

During that time I pulled my cell phone from my bag, debated whether to call Meredith or the rat, Jason, then compromised and called my answering machine instead. Jason's voice came over the line, warm, gentle, and incredibly sincere. He'd be tied up for a few days; he'd try again. In the second message he said he missed me; however, he didn't miss me enough to leave a number where he could be reached.

I dialed Meredith, who answered on the second ring, rather fast for Meredith. Made me think she was expecting a male caller.

"Meredith, I'm calling because I've irritated Grant Holman and will probably be fired tomorrow, if I'm not killed in my sleep."

"Is he as gorgeous when he's mad?"

"Cut it out. I'm serious."

"Oh, for God's sake, Stella. You don't think he'd really kill you, do you?"

"He's got a bad temper. I guess I believe anyone could kill if they're pushed far enough." I told her about the hair clip incident.

Her laughter made me feel instantly better. "Come on, Stella, if you're that worried, leave tonight. You don't owe him anything."

"I can't. Steven's begun to talk—and, I think, to remember. He may have witnessed what happened. I think if I hang on a little longer—"

"Oh, Lord. You're out there again. What he needs is a professional. What you need is something solid to count on. Have you read your horoscope lately? The one in the *Post* gives you only one star. Now, that's bad."

"Meredith, listen, what do you know about using salt to keep evil away?"

"I knew a priest once who was doing an exorcism and put salt on the windowsills and doorways, to keep the devil out. He did other things, too, with a crucifix and prayer, but I remember the salt mostly. What are you getting into?"

"I don't know for sure."

"Stella, um, does Grant seem real attached to any one woman?"

"Actually, I think at least two women, Heather and Louise, are attached to Grant, and maybe a third. The guy is a woman magnet."

"Well, Steven is a woman repellent."

"Remember that, Meredith. And call me here, at Holman's tomorrow morning. If he says I've left, call the police, okay? It'll mean I'm dead."

Next I broke my promise to myself and scrounged out the telephone number for Bipsie Lotts that I'd found on the invoice at Little Nothings.

The phone rang three times, then an all-too-familiar voice answered. Jason.

I sat there, phone in hand, his voice buzzing in my ears. I wondered what kind of reaction I was having—cold skin, dry mouth, bitter disappointment, but no tears. I hung up.

Damned if I was going to weep over this! From the outset I'd suspected he was up to something, so I wasn't going to get dehydrated crying over the rat. Not me! I'd just kill him.

"Trust me," he'd said before he left. Trust, the word that's so easy to say and so easy to betray. The semimelted chocolate bar from the bottom of my bag didn't begin to fill my emptiness.

Holman tromped upstairs half an hour later, but there had been ear-ringing silence ever after, relieved only by the sound of my jaws crunching corn curls.

Some people starve in depression, I eat. No amount of food—corn curls, cheese puffs, diet cola, chocolate—was filling the void. So far, I estimated, Jason had been an eight-pound problem. I wasn't ready yet for drastic dieting, but my jeans were definitely tight and irritating. Things were going from bad to worse.

I HAD TO ASSUME I'd be fired at breakfast. Had I been a little more circumspect, even bitten my tongue once, I could have been sure of being able to search the house at leisure. Now, it was imperative I try to look through the place in the dark of night, risking discovery, possibly missing vital things because of the dark and heaven knew what else.

I quickly built a tower of Legos topped by a bell in front of Steven's closed but unlocked bedroom door to the hallway. Anyone coming through the door would wake the dead.

The steam heat in the house was down for the night, and my feet were frozen, so I kicked off my sneakers and slipped under the covers to keep warm. In the next room, Steven snorted and rustled around in his sleep.

It occurred to me as my eyelids closed that it wasn't until Jason was seemingly out of reach that I realized how much I missed him, and it wasn't until I was most likely going to be fired that I realized how much I wanted to stay with Steven. Why was it I couldn't realize these things more conveniently and avoid the heartache?

I planned to take a short nap, then wake and search the house. If by some miracle I wasn't fired, I could check out Holman's room under the guise of a little light housekeeping. Maybe locate that missing kitchen knife.

I don't know for sure how long I slept. The next thing I heard was a piercing wail. Steven was having another nightmare.

The green numeral of the clock said it was three-thirty. I bolted from the bed, still in a fog, and flew across the floor.

My feet hit the floor at a run, and I was across the room, still half-asleep, when hideous pain shot through my instep. A moan burst from my mouth before I could stop it. The killer Legos. At that point the bell and Legos in front of Steven's door crashed to the floor.

By the time I'd recovered from the crippling pain in my feet, I could heard Holman's voice softly comforting Steven. I peeked in the door. Holman sat on the edge of Steven's bed, in the only spot not covered with toys, his hair crisply in place, wearing a T-shirt and jeans and loafers on his feet. Shoes. No wonder he wasn't crippled. He was patting Steven's shoulder, talking softly to him in a voice warm and gentle. As I watched, Steven threw himself across Holman's lap, sobbing.

It was a genuinely tender moment, a real tear-jerker. My eyes stung, hot, threatening to spill onto my cheeks. How could this man who had been such a brute a few hours before now be so tender?

Holman must have sensed me watching; he turned toward me. The night-light fell across his rugged features, his cheekbones stood out in sharp relief, but his eyes were shadowed, impossible to read under his heavy scowl.

FOURTEEN

HOLMAN PATTED Steven's back and turned away from me. He didn't need or want my help. Back in bed I pulled the covers up to my neck and stared at the shadowed ceiling. For all that he hated what I said, it seemed he was trying to be more loving. I wished for Steven's sake that I could feel better about him. I heard the murmur of Holman's voice comforting Steven, then his footsteps as he made his way back to his room and the click of his bedroom door, solid and final.

It didn't take a blooming genius to know that if I wanted to search that house I'd better do it quickly; whatever success I was having with Steven didn't begin to extend to his father.

Steven had evidently fallen back asleep; I could hear his light snore. Carefully, so I wouldn't wake him, I slipped on shoes, tiptoed through the Lego minefield, eased open the lock on my bedroom door and stepped into the hallway, and slipped on downstairs.

I reminded myself that lots of people who can't sleep get up and drink a cup of hot milk. I certainly would if I could drink it without gagging.

Great-great Aunt Lucinda always got a swig of tonic from the kitchen when she couldn't sleep. Nearly slept forever the night she took a swig of rat poison instead of tonic. Fortunately, she collapsed on her poodle, who yipped until my great-great uncle Hamilton, the town dogcatcher, woke up and found her. My father, who never liked old Hamilton anyway, thought it was a bit odd that rat poison was stored right next to Lucinda's tonic, but she outlived old Hamilton by another five years, so we all figured it was just Dad's little prejudice against dogcatchers.

The first floor was all done in white on white, magnifying the dim light coming in the windows, so I could see quite clearly. I figured anyone with something to hide would go for someplace dark, the basement or the attic. That morning I'd spotted a flashlight in the cereal cupboard, so I grabbed it and headed for the basement.

On the next to the last step I stopped, my nose full of basement smells, right foot dangling over the step. I hadn't quite heard something. This old house had a hundred different sounds, the grandfather clock in the living room, a car outside passing along the street, creaks in the walls from cooling or heating, and muffled rustlings I hoped weren't mice. I shivered.

I was about to take the last step when something slow and cool touched my neck. I froze. Absolutely still. It moved. The roots of my hair rose in panic. It took another chilly step. I couldn't even budge. All I could think about were those nasty little centipedes whisking across the basement floor when we made a nest for the rabbit. Then I felt a little tug of string. Fluffy!

I'd forgotten all about him. It was miraculous I hadn't crushed him as I slept. I picked him off my neck, raised the flashlight, and frowned at him. He flapped his jaw. His way of laughing. And Meredith thinks he has no sense of humor.

I replaced him on the outside of my sweatshirt and sucked in air to calm myself. The adrenaline pumping through my bloodstream sharpened my hearing to the point where I could hear the rabbit breathe. Truth to tell, sneaking around in a strange dark house at night isn't as much fun as it should be.

The basement consisted of one huge, open room with three doorways leading off it. It was mostly empty except for boxes of Christmas decorations to my immediate right, and two pairs of skis with poles leaning against the wall. Steven and I had half hidden the rabbit's box behind them.

The rabbit flinched when I turned the flashlight beam on him, cringing into the rags in the corner of his box. His eyes were beadier than before. Maybe he'd survive. I shoved his box farther behind a stack of boxes and moved on, shining the flashlight methodically back and forth across the room.

The basement was tidy to a disgusting degree, but more to the point, there was cement flooring throughout, old and undisturbed, even in the furnace room. The house was heated by steam heat, radiators in every room, and the old boiler had been converted to a gas-fired boiler. The coal bin was empty except for lingering coal oil smells and old, torn screen windows leaning against the grimy, coal-blackened wood walls.

I smiled. I realized I was relieved. I had been afraid I'd find an earthen floor and a fresh grave.

The laundry room was last, and the only messy place. A heavy scent of bleach, detergent, and lint filled the air. I sneezed, barely muffling it in the elbow of my sweatshirt. I hate detergent smell.

I pointed the flashlight beam around the room slowly. Soiled clothing lay in piles of lights, darks, and mediums. It spilled out of the laundry chute I hadn't realized was there and filled a basket. It appeared as though no one had done laundry since Elena left. Her "light housekeeping" was a lot like complete household responsibility. I began picking through the laundry on the floor, looking for Elena's clothes. And found them. I recognized the little blue sweater she'd worn the last time she'd come to her lesson.

Elena didn't have many clothes. These, along with the ones upstairs, probably constituted her whole wardrobe. It might not be enough for Stokowski, but as far as I was concerned that and the hairs in the shed and the crucifix were proof she hadn't just walked away. I dropped the sweater back onto the pile and went toward the door.

A sharp creak of stair steps stopped me. I killed the flashlight, my mouth dry. My little list of excuses—hot milk, taking out the trash, looking for a note I'd accidentally thrown away—didn't fit down here.

I glanced around in the near pitch-dark, eyes and ears straining. I swallowed, feeling sick.

I could bury myself in the soiled laundry. Not enough cover. No protection. Possible centipedes. I was too far away to dart behind the laundry room door. The only cover left was the laundry table. It hadn't worked when I was a kid playing hide and seek, and it wouldn't work now.

I stepped to my left, praying I'd find the wall, and bumped into the rough stucco surface. I flattened myself, hard, as if I could melt inside it. A scuff, then a crunch, sounded in the main room. The lights blazed on in the main basement room, beaming into the laundry room. I waited, pressed against the wall, holding my breath.

The faint sound of stealthy steps was closer now, almost at the doorway. I glanced around, saw an ancient fly swatter hanging from a nail. I grabbed it. Raised it high overhead.

I barely recognized Grant Holman's voice. It was steely and rough, almost choked. "I've got a gun. Don't move."

I didn't. Not a hair. I didn't even draw air. I held my arms up, fly swatter poised ridiculously. Holman's shadow lay on the floor. I have not had much experience with guns, but it wasn't the kind of thing I wanted to risk. Being shot is so permanent.

He flicked on the light, blinding me, burning my eyes, making them squeeze shut. "Stella?"

I blinked heavily, eyes burning from the sudden light.

"Stella? What in hell are you doing down here holding a fly swatter?"

"I heard a noise. Put the gun away, okay?"

He snapped on the safety and shoved it into the pocket of his robe, but he didn't let go of it. His cheeks were dusky with whisker stubble; that, combined with his deep-set eyes and the shadows beneath them, made him look like a pirate on a binge. "What the hell are you doing down here?" he repeated.

I sucked in a deep breath. "I couldn't sleep, came downstairs for some milk, and thought I heard something down here."

"In the dirty clothes? What were you going to do, smack him with a fly swatter and tell him to go home?"

"It works on cockroaches."

"Hold still!" he commanded, raising his hand. "There's a bug on your shoulder."

I leapt back out of his reach. "Don't! That's Fluffy."

He gawked, then shook his head from side to side. "You know, you're almost more work than Steven." He thought for a moment, and when he finally spoke he had a sly look in his eyes. "I think you figured maybe I had Elena stashed down here."

I couldn't answer. I didn't trust my voice or my quaking brain.

"And what would I do if I did, burn her in the incinerator?"

"You have an incinerator?" I croaked and breathed a little easier.

"No, dammit! For God's sake, I could have shot you!"

"Would have ruined a fine sweatshirt." Not to mention my favorite teddy.

He was silent, sucking on a tooth. I forgot, he didn't have a sense of humor. Then he spoke in a quieter tone. "Did you find anything?"

"Not a thing."

"Too damn bad." He sounded relieved.

THE SUN WAS UP, and it was 8:25. Steven and I had finished a breakfast of Cocopuffs and peanut butter toast, and Steven was in the basement playing with Buckley. By the time I heard Holman come downstairs, I had read nearly all of the *Denver Post.*

He burst into the kitchen and went straight for the coffee. There were shadows beneath his eyes and a slump to his shoulders that I hadn't seen before, but other than that, he was clean and crisp and ready to whip the day, and probably me, into shape. He glanced at the peanut butter jar, frowned, and stirred sugar into his coffee.

I told myself that if he took the chair next to me, he'd be friendly. If he took the chair opposite, it meant he was going to fire me. I've been studying body language.

He sat down opposite me. "Stella, I need to talk to you."

I braced myself. I've never been fired before. I made a production of dragging my eyes up from the paper, as though I was thoroughly engrossed in the article about the healing properties of Mongolian slime mold. "I'm right here."

"I think I made a big mistake..."

"Oh?"

"I think maybe Steven...or rather I..."

This was turning out to be torture waiting for him to come to the point, but I wasn't about to leave before I could get a stab at sifting through the house. "I'll be packed and gone by noon," I said. I used my most authoritative voice. "At the earliest, eleven-thirty."

"That's not—"

"Look," I interrupted. I couldn't tolerate listening to this drawn-out mess. If this was being fired, I'd take charge; at least I could say what I thought and get on with it. "As long as we're getting things clear here, I need to tell you that Steven is a great kid. He's smart, strong, and very loving, but he's only five years old, and he's an emotional wreck at this point. He needs a lot of support, more than you can give."

I stood up, folding the papers. There was a huge hollow spot in my heart for Steven.

Holman's mouth was a thin, angry line cutting across his face. "Sit down, Stella."

I sat. Some people just can't tolerate losing control.

"Stella, I was trying to say thank you. You're a damn difficult woman, you know. Just the same as you were in grade school, always with a smart remark, full of lip. Except...except now...you've grown...." He paused, looking temporarily confused, then gathered himself together. "Well, I just wanted to express my appreciation for your help with Steven. And I hope you'll stay."

Why hadn't he fired me? Of course, this meant I could still search the house. I answered slowly, as if quite reluctant. "Weeeell, if it's helpful to Steven..."

The doorbell rang, and he left to answer it. He returned, looking desperate, as though trying to find an avenue for escape. He was followed by Millie, wearing a peacock blue silk sweat suit, makeup on, and not a hair out of place.

"I was just out for an early-morning run and thought I'd catch you. Louise said there was a leak in the pipe under the sink. Thought I'd just take a look."

"A leak?" Grant looked at me. "Millie, why are you here about a leaky pipe?" I could see the wheels of his brain turning. "You see, Stella? You're needed. There are problems here for you to solve. I leave this in your capable hands. Gotta go."

"Don't let me chase you off, Grant—" The kitchen door closed after him.

Millie smiled slyly, then peered under the sink. "Well, no leak. I must have misunderstood."

"Millie, answer me. Why are you here about a leak in Grant's pipe?"

It was unfortunate phrasing. Millie had a sly and nasty imagination. "Honey, Grant's pipe has been known to leak in the most unsuitable people. Besides, I own this place. If there's a leak, I see it first, then I call the plumber, if appropriate. And, when Louise comes tomorrow—"

"Louise?"

"She cleans for Grant. Personally." She smirked again. "Or at least she'd like it to be personal. Just like Heather would like her little arrangement to be permanent. They both have a snowball's chance in hell."

I grinned and shook my head. "Not much escapes you, does it? You were pretty clever to notice that toy Steven had last night. Nobody else seemed to pay any attention."

She poured herself a cup of coffee, her hand shaking slightly. Last night's party was exacting its toll. She leaned against the counter, classic gossip-swap body language. "I noticed quite a few things, like, for instance, you don't really believe Elena just walked away."

"What makes you think that?"

"The way you looked when you were pumping Barry last night. Not too subtle. Even Louise noticed. So what do you think is going on with Elena?"

I wondered how much she was really willing to talk about. "I don't think she would leave Steven. I don't believe she walked away."

"You think something bad happened?"

I nodded. "Yeah, I do."

Millie blew on her coffee, sipped, then cautiously put it down on the counter. When she spoke, her voice had lost its brightness. "You think one of us did something?"

I shrugged. "I think someone did. Last Thursday, was Elena upset or worried?"

She frowned, breathing faster. "Ask Louise. Elena helped her in the kitchen. And then, you know, if anyone wanted Elena out of here, Heather did. You should spend some time with her, you know. She's a sly one. She notices stuff, too."

She was waltzing away from something and looking restless. I didn't want her to leave yet. I decided to backpedal. "I didn't mean to upset you. It's just that you and Barry—"

She interrupted. "You didn't upset me. I don't care." She bit her lip for a moment, then spoke in a monotone. "I might as well tell you, someone will. Barry has a crush on Elena. I overheard him one day, propositioning her. Couldn't have been the first time, but it was the last time, by God. At least the last time he did it in our home."

"Elena was at your place?"

"Elena comes Friday mornings. I'm always home then. And Barryboy goes to work before she comes."

"That must've put a terrible strain on your marriage."

Millie laughed harshly, then took a long sip of coffee. She lowered the cup slowly as though reluctant to let go of it, and ran her tongue over her lips. "We've been married for fourteen years, ought to be enough to deaden about anything." But tears were ready to spill out over her too-bright cheeks. She took a deep breath. "Tawdry, isn't it?" Her tough words didn't quite cover her vulnerability.

"Sad."

"Sad, huh?" She traced circles on the countertop with her fingernail. "Pitiful, maybe. Ludicrous for sure. We yell at each other over a chasm filled with bitterness."

I waited for her to continue.

"He always wanted children, and I...I couldn't..."

"Couldn't have them?"

She looked at me, defiantly. "No. I couldn't stand the idea. Two years ago I aborted the one I started. I was drinking too much; it would have been affected. I had a rotten childhood, figure the only sure way to keep from repeating it is to never have a kid." She finished the last of her coffee, replacing her cup on the counter with a clatter. "So what do you think of that? Nasty, huh?"

I was on very thin ice with her. "Painful, for you and for Barry."

When she looked up I noticed a faint sheen of perspiration on her forehead, but the room was cool. "Yeah, well, life's painful. But frankly, I'm goddammed glad Elena's gone, and I'll bet big money that Heather is, too. At least I don't have to wonder if he's sniffing after her anymore."

"Have you talked to Barry about this?"

She shook her head, turning away to stare out the window. A tear tracked mascara down her cheek. I went to her, reached out with my hand, and gripped her shoulder. "Maybe you need to—"

She spun toward me, furious. Her arm was raised, ready to strike. I jumped back.

Her eyes were mere slits in her face. "Don't ever do that! Don't touch me, ever!"

"Easy, Millie," I said and moved back slowly, barely breathing. I wasn't sure what had happened, but Millie seemed to have leaped to some other reality. I'd never seen a flashback, but I thought this might be one. Her eyes were wide now, staring. I lowered my voice, trying to reassure her. "It's okay, Millie. I'm not touching you. I'm sorry."

"Stella!" Steven came tromping upstairs. "Stella, Buckley and I—" He broke off when he saw Millie. His mouth clamped shut. He stared at her for a minute, then turned and clomped back downstairs.

"Steven, it's okay." He kept on going.

The sight of Steven seemed to have recalled her from her planet. She was shivering, but her eyes were focused now. "I'm sorry, Stella. I didn't mean to do that. I guess I lost it a little."

"You do that very often?"

She gazed unevenly at me, distress working her face. "I don't like to be grabbed on the shoulder."

"I didn't grab—"

"Touched, then. It...brings back a bad experience."

"Like a flashback?"

Her expression hardened. "Well, don't worry about it. It's not your problem. None of it is." She slammed out of the house.

FIFTEEN

MILLIE'S EPISODE left me shaken. If she flipped out like that in the morning with only caffeine inside her, what did she do with a skin full of alcohol? And if she'd been drinking enough two years ago to impact a pregnancy, could she be having blackouts now? And what was she sniffing around to find out? Somehow I didn't buy her hint that she was just checking up on Grant and what he was up to. The more I thought about it, the more I realized I'd been completely sidetracked.

I wondered what Heather would say. She didn't strike me as smart enough to catch mice, but killers don't have to be smart, just cunning.

I found her phone number in the white pages and rang, hoping she would be home. She was and reluctantly agreed to see me after I said I needed her help. I figured she thought I meant something about exercise and shaping up. Steven, Buckley, and I set out.

Heather lived in a two-bedroom West Washington Park bungalow in central Denver, almost on the way to Little Nothings.

Sunday night's snow had melted entirely away under fifty-degree sunshine, leaving the lawns bright green, the crabapple trees with a hint of pink in their buds, and the forsythia only a little bedraggled. Fat-leafed tulips were up on the south sides of the houses, and the smell of damp earth, fresh growth, and warm sandstone hung in the air.

Steven had Buckley tucked in his jacket. I managed to persuade him to leave the rabbit in the car by promising a stop in the park later. He dragged his toes on the pavement all the way to Heather's porch.

She opened the door clad in a unitard and thong, looking gorgeous. Hers was a body that never enjoyed peanut butter and jelly. She frowned lightly at Steven but held the door for us, and I thanked her for making time, exclaiming at how convenient it was she was free. Her house was furnished nicely but simply, with an accent on function in the color coral. I glimpsed a *Shape* magazine on the couch, open to an article about ab-flattening exercises and a picture of a muscular, tanned female body in an impossibly tight Spandex ditty.

"I have an early-morning and late-afternoon schedule at the gym. That way I get time to rest up a little. You wouldn't believe how much energy it takes to train people and to do the jazzercise and my own bodybuilding." She sneezed. "Hope I'm not coming down with a cold. Vitamin C is good for colds, you know. Now what were you wanting? A personal workout program? Come on in my gym."

I didn't have to speak much; a nod here or there seemed to do it. Steven trailed beside her, and she sneezed again. "My goodness, you'd think there was a cat or rabbit around here. I'm very allergic. I can't even wear angora."

"A real fashion hardship," I mumbled.

One of the bedrooms at the back of the house was converted to a gym room, containing a Scandinavian torture beast, an ab roller, a Stairmaster, dumbbells and weights.

"You use all this?" Heather was easily as tall as I was, around five foot seven. "You don't look it, but I'll bet you're really strong, aren't you?"

She nodded. "Women don't show muscles the way men do. But, you wouldn't believe how quickly you can build up strength. You're a little old, might take longer, but you can do it."

I was staring at the dumbbell and weights. If she could lift those things, she could lift Elena in her arms.

Heather rubbed her eyes, and they reddened. "Dead weight is tough. You should start on twenty pounds and work up. Maybe even with one-pounders. You can use cans of tomato soup if you don't have weights. I can do about a hundred pounds pretty easily. You're gonna have to work out all the time, though.'' She sneezed again. ''Aerobics and weight lifting is something you can use all your life.''

Not if I can help it, I thought, but I simply smiled and nodded.

''See, I'm a professional bodybuilder and aerobics trainer. I was going to be in *Shape,* the magazine, you know? In a spread—it got canceled, though. Totally the pits, you know? But now I've got an offer to be a professional mud wrestler on television even. Something always leads to something. I just wish it were cleaner somehow.'' She rubbed her nose, which turned a gratifying beet red. ''If I didn't know better I'd say there was a cat in the house. I can feel my eyes swelling. You have a cat at home or something? How're you doing at Grant's with you-know-who?''

Steven knew who, too; he stuck out his tongue at her.

This torrent of words was getting to me, like Buckley's dander was getting to Heather. It made me want to stick to monosyllables. ''Nope. No cats. Steven, why don't you go sit in the living room.''

Heather watched him leave, then leaned over conspiratorilly. ''He's a weird kid, you know. He's got imaginary friends. Pretends he's on the phone with them. There's only one way to handle a kid like that. Beat 'em at their own game.''

''What do you mean?''

''Be as strange as they are, so they don't know what to think. Then, they'll mind. Grant's a pretty attractive fellow, wouldn't you say?''

It sounded like the same question Millie had tried out, but Heather sounded more genuinely interested. ''Not my type. But was Elena attracted to Grant?''

Heather stopped, sneezed, turned slowly, her head cocked to the side. ''At first I thought so. I even thought Grant might be attracted to her, but after I heard them fighting I knew he wasn't. Like with you—"

That stung!

"—but you know who *was* attracted to Elena?"

I shook my head.

"Quiet, nerdy Barry. Practically drooled in her lap. And did Millie pitch a fit! You know, there's something strange about Millie. She's friendly on the outside, but, man, she's a barracuda when she's drinking. And can she drink! She's gonna have cirrhosis of the liver soon."

"That bad? You think she ever has blackouts?"

"You mean where she doesn't remember what she's done? Could be. She doesn't remember the shitty things she's said sometimes, or else she pretends she doesn't. Like last weekend. You should have heard her then. Grant was so embarrassed. We couldn't help but overhear. She and Barry were really going at it, even at dinner. Even if Barry is his partner, it was too much."

"Like what?"

She looked suddenly chagrined. "I wouldn't say this, but you'll see if you stick around there very long. She loses it. Saturday night Barry tried to stop her from drinking, and she accused him of causing Elena to leave and he said she'd blacked out and didn't know what she'd done or said. They probably didn't mean it, but I don't think they're going to stay together at this rate. It was awful. And when Barry put his hand on her shoulder, she slugged him. Hard, too."

"Did she talk to Elena last Thursday night?"

"No. She was mad at Barry, but I didn't see her with Elena, but then she could've, I s'pose."

"Did you notice if Elena was upset?"

"At the dinner, you mean? Well, I was there early, you know, and Grant was pissed about something and she looked unhappy then, kind of red around the eyes, if you know what I mean. I don't know for sure, but I think it had something to do with telephone calls. He says it's an old girlfriend. He got a caller ID box to try to catch her.''

"Did you see Barry talk to Elena?''

She pursed her lips. "I think he might have, but I don't know. How come you're asking all these questions? I mean, you some kind of investigator or something?'' She sneezed again.

"I'm still trying to find Elena—for Steven, you know. How serious are you about Grant?''

She tugged at her thong. "I don't know. He's a little old, you know? He's going to be thirty-five this May.''

"How old are you?''

"Twenty-four.''

"Millie said you might be glad Elena was gone. Why would she say that?''

"Because Millie likes to cause trouble. You watch, wherever she goes it turns sour after she's tired of the attention. Last night? See? You want to find Elena, go after Millie. In fact, go after five. Give her time to have her first monster snort, you'll see what she's like. Look, I gotta go out and get some antihistamines. Keep working those soup cans. It's good for upper arm flab, too.''

Leaving Heather was like stepping away from a word flood. Steven and I went to Little Nothings, where Steven humbled himself, returned the hair clip, apologized, and promised not to do it again. After that we had a great time in the park. The weather was soft, lovely, and indulgent. When we got home I found a message from Grant saying he would be home quite late, so Steven and I had a relaxed time of it. He was almost normal.

By ten that night I'd checked messages at home and at the *Orion,* and found nothing from Elena or Jason. I filled the empty place in my heart with a peanut butter and jelly sandwich, heavy on the jelly.

I had called the shelters and everywhere else I could think of, even checking with the emergency food banks, two soup kitchens, and Our Lady of Guadalupe Church. No one had seen Elena or Maria and her family. They had vanished.

WEDNESDAY MORNING Grant left before we even made it downstairs. It was the first morning when Steven hadn't had a nightmare during the night, and I'd slept like it was my last.

Louise was due at nine; she let herself in the front door with her own key and hung her coat in the hall closet. She was dressed rather nicely for housekeeping chores and looked disappointed when she learned Holman had already left for work.

She said hello, patted Steven on the back, and poured herself a cup of coffee. "I'll start in here if you two have finished breakfast," she said and began unloading the dishwasher.

I nodded and cleared the table. If she was going to be downstairs, I thought, I could search through Holman's upstairs bedrooms without her noticing.

Louise lifted cups into the cupboard, then turned to me. "So have you figured out where Elena is yet?" she asked. "I have to get someone to cover Millie's house Friday morning. Elena always did their place, but I don't have time..."

A cup she was lifting from the dishwasher slipped to the floor, shattering. "Damn! I'm so tired I can hardly—"

I can take a hint, especially when it gives me a legitimate excuse to prowl. "Look, Louise. If you'll watch Steven Friday afternoon when I've got a meeting with my landlord, I'll do the Quinleys'. Where do they live?"

"Lordy, she lives just two houses down. But—"

"Two houses down?"

"Yes." Louise paused and ran a hand over her face. "It's a real relief you're willing to do that. It's hard for me, especially knowing how Millie treated Elena. The cruel things she said to her. I'm sure she didn't mean them. Jealousy talking, of course. She gets...I shouldn't talk about her, she's an old friend, but she drinks a bit, you know."

"If Millie was so hateful, why did Elena keep on going there?"

"I don't know. Maybe because she understood how sad Barry was. Or, God forbid, maybe because I asked her to. Elena was so willing to help out. I may have taken advantage of that. And I've known Millie a long time, and she wasn't always like this. She used to be wonderful, generous, kind. The alcohol changed her. I don't know how Barry puts up with her."

Louise's face was ravaged, as though she hadn't slept in days. It seemed to cost her energy just to talk. She gathered the pieces of the cup and dropped them in the trash, then closed and started the dishwasher.

"Louise, I'd be glad to dust and polish the library and the upstairs here."

She looked up. "I don't know—"

"What, you think I'm going to go through everything?"

She smiled. "Sure. Okay, you're on."

The gods were smiling. For almost no effort and absolutely no lying, I'd managed a chance to plow through the very rooms I most wanted to see. While Louise mopped the kitchen floor, I started Steven playing in his room with his toys and hit the library.

It took me four minutes to discover Holman had a drawer full of electronic toys and telephone bills, one of which I pocketed, and twenty minutes to make sure he didn't have any other hidden files or caches. I polished his desktop and replaced his lamp, pen, and telephone, noting the number identification box. Wiping away my fingerprints, I ran the dustcloth quickly over the top of the bookcases and the game table. Then I sprayed the air with an eighth of a can of Endust so it would smell like I'd polished all the furniture in the room.

Upstairs, Steven was busy arranging his massive miniature army in rows in front of his bedroom door, guns and tanks aimed straight at the entryway with a long broom handle lined up as a giant cannon. If I hadn't been watching for killer Legos I'd have rebruised my sore foot on a plastic soldier. "Steven, I'll be cleaning in your father's room. If you need me, just yell for me."

He nodded and pointed to his army of soldiers and tanks. "See the war?"

"Awesome."

"It's for Louise." His smile was diabolical, but that was part of his charm.

I hustled into the hallway and heard Louise start up the vacuum cleaner in the dining room. I figured I had a safe ten minutes.

The master suite consisted of two rooms with the bathroom in between, the same arrangement as my room and Steven's. Holman's room was done in green and burgundy, in a masculine hunter-gatherer theme with a border of mallard ducks around the top of the walls and plain, functional oak furniture.

A *Money* magazine lay open on the bedside stand along with a half-drunk glass of water, pencil, pad, and telephone. The drawer of Holman's bedstand was stiff and heavy, and it held his gun. Using a tissue, I lifted the gun to my nose and sniffed, not knowing quite what else to do. It smelled like oily metal—no sulphurous smell, no residue of any kind. I checked the clip. Loaded. I remembered him Monday, the night before last, stalking me in the basement, and my hands shook.

According to the director of the Johns Hopkins Center for Gun Policy and Research, slightly less than half of all American households have firearms, so maybe he was merely in the mainstream of middle America. I thought of Steven and his five-year-old curiosity and felt sick. How easy it would be for him to find and play with it!

A stair groaned. It sounded like the fourth step, the one Steven called the telltale stair.

I replaced the gun and caught sight of two navy blue passports at the back of the drawer.

"Stella?"

"Here, Louise," I replied, closing the drawer. I started flinging the bedcovers around just as she entered the room.

"Stella, leave the bed, I'll change the sheets later. I just wanted to see how you're coming." She squinted at the top of Holman's dresser. "You'll need to take everything off before you dust, you know. I don't know how you can use so much polish and still not get the dust."

"I haven't done the dresser yet, Louise."

She smiled feebly. "Well, just leave the bathroom to me."

"Okey-dokey. I'll do a swell job, Louise, you'll see."

As soon as I heard her descending footsteps I returned to Holman's bedside stand, withdrew the gun, and lifted out the passports.

They were fascinating.

Passports obtained in Denver are generally issued from Seattle, but these had been issued from Washington, D.C., a year and a half ago, which probably meant he'd been living on the eastern seaboard then.

Then I noticed the date of birth for Steven. According to the passport he was six years old, not five. No wonder he was so advanced. But at six, why wasn't he in school?

And finally, there was Grant Holman's hairline. In the passport photo it receded markedly, but since I'd known him he had a full head of gorgeous, thick hair, which significantly changed his appearance. Rogaine? Toupee? Mere vanity? Or was Holman changing his appearance for other reasons?

I copied his social security number quickly onto my scrap of paper and slipped it back into my pocket. I had replaced everything meticulously and started to dust when I saw his drinking glass.

There was a solid set of fingerpints on the half-drunk glass of water. Using a tissue, I picked up the glass, took it to my bedroom, and set it carefully in the top dresser drawer. I was pretty sure I could get Stokowski to run the prints.

Two small closets flanked the bed, each tidy and sterile. It took only minutes to zip through his dresser drawers; nothing exceptional there. I gave the room a solid, heavy dose of furniture polish into the air, hoping I hadn't left a glaze on the carpet.

The bathroom was boring. Aside from the usual toilet articles, there was nothing of interest, not even a little fungal salve.

I returned to Holman's room, thinking. Housekeepers have a very intimate view of the people for whom they clean. They know more about the inside, personal life of their clients than almost anyone, maybe even more than a parent or spouse, since they aren't blinded by complications or emotions such as love, hate, or jealousy.

From the doorway I surveyed Holman's room, remembering Elena's sister's home. Maria had a small, crowded house, but she'd had pictures and mementos, things that pointed to a personal history, a past. Here, in the whole house, there were no pictures, no mementos of the past, no pictures of Steven anywhere. Even on Holman's dresser, there were no snapshots, no keys, no coins, not even laundry tags, only an empty dish to hold his pocket change at night.

I could understand a person putting away all the pictures of a dead wife, especially with girlfriends, but why were there no pictures, none, of a beloved child? It seemed odd to me. In fact the whole house was barren, as if he had shed his past and blown into town on the wings of a tornado, settling into a house clean, without personal touches. Perhaps he had chosen an old house to give the illusion of history and depth. It was almost as if his clothes were costumes, creating personalities.

Elena was also a woman and a mother. She knew how Holman treated Steven, and she'd have noticed the missing pictures; she probably had found the passports and the gun. In spite of her cultural and language differences Elena was in a position to know a great deal about Grant Holman and his household—and the Quinleys'. I'd forgotten the Quinleys.

I gave the room one last, good spray and headed for Steven's room.

Steven stood in the hallway, the telephone receiver at his ear. His mouth formed a barely audible "Oh," then he frowned. "Mommy? She's not here."

My heart stopped beating, the blood in my veins barely ran. I stepped forward, reaching for the telephone. He twisted away, said, "Bye," and slammed the receiver down.

"Steven? Who was that?"

Steven stood before me, pale and solemn. "Mommy."

I felt a little weak in the knees. "Isn't your mommy dead?"

He nodded. "Yes."

"But you talked to your mommy on the telephone?"

"Yeah," he said and looked up at the ceiling, puzzled.

"Are you telling me any pretend stuff?"

He shook his head. "No."

"What did she want?"

"She wanted to talk to Elena." He turned away and walked to his room.

"Steven," I said, my mouth suddenly dry, "what did she want to talk to Elena about?"

"I dunno." He squatted beside his tank fleet. "Blam! Blam!" He shot the door of his room. His hand was shaky, his cheeks pale. "Mommy wants me to come with her. She loves me."

SIXTEEN

HIS WORDS LEFT ME NUMB. What did this mean? I could hear the everyday stir of Louise cleaning downstairs, but the few seconds it took to quiet my vaulting emotions seemed to last an hour in some other reality.

There must be a rational explanation, I told myself, perhaps someone maliciously calling. But what if Steven was fabricating it or hallucinating? Could he have lost touch with reality? None of these were good, but at least they were logical, not woo-woo. I wanted to reach out and pull Steven into my arms, into warm reality, fast, before he was lost permanently, but I couldn't seem to move.

I had a sudden scare. Was this child talking suicide?

My voice sqeaked a little when I asked, "Why don't you arrange your micro-machines in battle formation? I need to make a call or two."

I ran downstairs, ignoring Louise's questioning look, to the library to check the caller ID box for the caller's number. The number was there, area code 609, but it was a pay phone. I pulled the February bill from my pocket. Different number. At least it was a real call.

I punched in the numbers for a social worker acquaintance of mine who specializes in children. I knew she wouldn't be willing to second-guess Steven, so I said it was a hypothetical situation and gave her a quick sketch of Steven's situation and the telephone call. "How would you tell if a child is psychotic?"

"Ask. Start by asking if they think what they are telling you is real or imaginary. Ask some obvious questions. If they're in touch with reality they'll usually tell you the truth. Not always, of course." She paused, then in a quiet voice that told me she suspected this wasn't so hypothetical, she asked, "There is the possibility that he is expressing a wish to join his mother. Has he done any self-destructive things?"

"Suppose he talks about violence, plays with weapons, and relates a lot of monster fantasies, especially vampire stories, but he hasn't actually cut himself or hurt himself. Maybe he draws vampires with blood in their mouths."

"Stella, kids can get the idea they caused something from the simplest of things, such as someone disappearing after they've been mad at them. It can be that simple and usually is. But I'd be quite worried because they can hurt themselves from depression at that age. They don't have a concept of death as permanent yet. Has he expressed guilt, responsibility?"

My hands were shaky and my stomach in a knot. "He said he killed his mother."

There was an awful silence on the other end of the line. Finally, she spoke up, her voice carefully modulated. "We generally take whatever the child says as truth at some level. Their understanding is colored by their experience. This is true for all of us, but especially children." Her words were carefully measured, as though she wanted me to know how important each one was. Believe me, at that moment, I knew.

"Like a metaphor?"

"Exactly. A metaphor. So if a favorite toy says—"

"But he doesn't act depressed."

"Kids express depression differently than adults. Adults get immobilized, sad, lethargic. Kids get that way only briefly. Usually in childhood anxiety, fear turns into activity, and sometimes so does sorrow. The energy of life in them is so strong that their sorrow or depression is acute, but in brief periods. That's why people don't realize the kids are depressed. This kid should be evaluated, Stella. He's been through more than many adults with very little support and few coping strategies. You've got to get his father to take him in. Until then, play with him and listen to how he plays.''

When I hung up, I felt ill and shaky. ''Steven, when you talked to your mother on the phone, was she for real?''

He looked at me in disgust. ''Yes.''

''Do you ever think you hear voices, but you are imagining them?''

''When I play pretend.''

I sat down on the edge of his bed.

''Don't sit there!'' he shouted. ''That's the bomb!''

I got up. ''Is that real? Or pretend?''

''Pretend, silly.''

I went through several similar questions, each of which he answered completely logically. I breathed a bit more easily. Whatever else, he seemed able to tell reality from pretend, which according to my telephone consult indicated that he was in touch with reality. But if I believed he was in touch with reality, then his mother, or someone pretending to be her, had been on the phone. I knew the explanation had to be simple, but it all felt pretty spooky. Elena's use of salt to ward off evil was beginning to look reasonable under the circumstances.

I was ready for a change of subject. ''Let's go see your rabbit for a while.''

''He's here.''

Was he slipping into fantasy? ''Where?''

''You don't believe me, so I won't tell you.''

''You didn't tell me the truth about your age, so I don't believe you.''

Steven stuck out his lower lip, pouting. ''Daddy told me never to tell.''

''So how old would your mother say you are?''

''Six.''

''Why are you supposed to keep it a secret?''

He shrugged. ''I dunno.''

I thought I knew why. It all made sense if Steven had

been kidnapped—the passports, keeping him out of school, the phone calls. Each time, it came back to the fact that Steven was telling the truth as best he could, but where on earth did he get the vampire stuff?

There had been nothing on the television about vampires recently, there was nothing in his collection of videos and books about them, so where did he get it? Unless maybe he hid it in his secret place—along with the rabbit.

"Come on, Steven, where's your secret place?" I wheedled.

He sucked on his lip for several long moments, then pointed to the bottom door of his toy cupboard.

"Maybe the rabbit would like to be out for a while."

He opened the door and the bunny hopped out, his nose twitching. The first thing that caught my eye were the jelly beans the bunny had left behind on the cupboard floor. The second thing was a tiny green address book. Elena's.

THE ADDRESS BOOK was pitifully barren. In addition to her sister's address, the Dustbunnies phone number, and my address, I found only Madam Anastasia's address, Elena's mother's address in Mexico with a black line through it, and at the top of the third page, Sister Mary Timothy's address.

Elena was devout and went to confession regularly. Confession would be strictly confidential, but Sister Mary Timothy might be helpful. We left Louise scrubbing bathrooms and hit the road with the rabbit in his box in the backseat and Elena's little green address book in my lap.

Sister Mary Timothy lived in a plain, small brick bungalow on the same block as Our Lady of Guadalupe. I knocked at the front door while Steven kicked at the porch floorboards, pouting because I insisted he leave the rabbit in the car.

The door opened on my third knock, and a bland face with the soft eyes of the perpetually nearsighted blinked at me before asking what I wanted. I explained.

"Sister Mary Timothy knows you're coming?"

"No. She knows my friend, Elena Ruiz. It's very important that I talk to Sister."

Bland doesn't mean acquiescent. The gentle sister initially said no, but when I begged, she finally sighed, opened the door, and led us to a small, stuffy room where the vow of poverty was evident. It was done all in brown, walls, ceiling, and carpet, and filled with furniture that looked as if it had been donated to the poor and refused.

I settled on a couch upholstered in something stiff and prickly that once had been rose-colored, while Steven tried out one of the two harsh, blocky side chairs, then returned to stand next to me. His gaze stopped on a picture on the far wall of Christ with a crown of thorns, a beard, and blood trickling down his forehead toward his very sad, upraised brown eyes. It was a grisly item. My great-grandmother had one like it.

Sister Mary Timothy entered the room in a whirl of energy. She was a tall, self-assured woman in her late forties, dressed in a navy suit, with a simple white collar to relieve the severity and a rather large gold cross on a chain about her neck. Her hair was graying naturally, cut short, and brushed back from her face. She seated herself on the side chair, folded her hands, and gave me a piercing stare. I figured it was her nun-sign to start, so I explained why we were there.

Sister frowned. "I haven't seen Elena for almost a month. The last time I saw her she was very troubled, still burdened with grief for her little boy, I believe. I think that's why she was so taken with this young man." Sister Mary Timothy gestured to Steven. He shrank from her.

I mentioned the church bulletin I'd found and asked about the sermon, "A Mother's Love."

"Elena commented on it. I think it disturbed her, because she referred to it several times in our conversation. The gist of the sermon was the Holy Mother's love for us and how we must seek to emulate her in our love for our children. Elena asked how mothers prove their love. She seemed to think she had to prove her love for Eduardo. I thought at the time she meant prove it to God.'' Sister Mary Timothy pursed her lips. ''She was seeking redemption through atonement. I helped her pray for it.''

''Redemption? I don't understand.''

''She left that poor child with her mother in Mexico while she came here. She had been here perhaps six months when she learned that he had died. I don't know the cause, but she believed it was because she sinned in the eyes of God by leaving him. To earn *money.*''

''I thought that many traditional Mexican and Spanish families believe in gift children, giving the firstborn to the grandmother.''

''They do, but they stay close, visiting, frequently living next door, and such. They don't *abandon* them with the grandmother, and Elena believed she had. She was here *illegally,* mind you. Sometimes God's punishment is very stern.''

I was aghast. Her attitude would devastate Elena. ''But any mother would feel tremendous guilt over her child's death, especially if she had to leave him, even if it was with the best of intentions.''

''Of course.''

''That's a very harsh view.''

''Elena had a harsh view. Life isn't easy. The road is narrow, with many forks in it. I'm sorry I'm not more helpful.'' Sister Mary Timothy frowned. ''There was one other thing. The last time she came, she said she had talked to the dead.''

''Who?''

Sister nodded at Steven. ''His mother. Elena said she called and said she wanted him with her.''

The skin under my left eye began to twitch. ''What did you say to that?''

"I told her the dead don't talk," Sister Mary Timothy said firmly. "Elena had turned away from God. She went to a fortune-teller. A gypsy." Sister Mary Timothy gripped her knees and leaned forward, cheeks flushed. "And that woman told Elena she could help her reach her child. That's why I'm concerned for her."

There weren't many names in Elena's address book, but at the back I'd seen the name Madam Anastasia with a star beside it. "Would that be a Madam Anastasia?"

Sister shuddered. "She's a scam artist."

"Do you know anything about sprinkling salt to ward off evil?"

Sister Mary Timothy's eyes narrowed. "Nothing whatever."

SEVENTEEN

MADAM ANASTASIA lived within a mile of the good sister, in a similar bungalow on the south side of the street, distinctive because of the sun-shaped sign hanging from the porch roof, announcing her ability to read palms, tea leaves, tarot, and horoscopes. No discrimination here.

Steven was flipping his leg up and down, kicking the dashboard, not hard, but irritatingly. "Stella, I don't want to go there. It stinks."

"I need to find out what she knows about Elena. It's about our last stop, okay?" I asked. He nodded, scowling. We climbed from the car into the wintry noontime sunshine. As we mounted the porch steps I noticed little stars and crescent moons drawn on the storm door.

"This house looks weird," I muttered to myself. I was very curious about what she would be like to talk to and how she practiced her craft. I wondered if she had times when she envisioned things happening, like I did, and I hoped she wasn't truly a scam artist. It is so painful when a scammer works the field.

I knocked, then looked at Steven, waiting expectantly at my side. "Have you been here before, Steven?"

"Yeah," he said. He walked to the far end of the porch.

I knocked again, louder, but there was no answer. After two more good knocks we left.

We spent the rest of the day in the park with Buckley. Steven was subdued, tender with Buckley, and ate very little. It was the saddest Happy Meal I'd ever witnessed. We went to bed early that night, long before Grant returned.

I called Meredith, got her answering machine, and left a message to tell her I was still alive. Finally, I called my mother to see how she was doing. She was fine and offered to make tuna casserole if I'd come to dinner the next night, but I begged off.

MADAM ANASTASIA was home the next day. We got there about midmorning, while the air was still cold. Steven was in a little better mood until I said Buckley definitely had to wait in the car.

I knocked.

The door rattled and opened a crack. A small, round face with large, prominent dark eyes under well-defined brows glanced quickly over me in a visual price-check, taking in my turquoise-and-orange jacket, frowning at my lilac tights, resting finally on my boots. She smiled at the boots. They were an expensive Italian leather pair, left over from my affluent accountant days.

She opened the door to me, and sunlight glinted off her in a shower of sparkles. She had mirror sequins, little feathers, and bits of bright cloth tacked to a long silken shawl. My first thought was, A woo-woo queen.

She smiled at me, an irritating, ethereal kind of grin, centered somewhere beyond me. I glanced over my shoulder, but whoever she was grinning at was not a physical presence. I was immediately suspicious, expecting something ridiculous.

She noticed it, I think, because she cocked her head, looking into my eyes. When she finally spoke, she waved her hand in a kind of greeting, and the faint scent of old tobacco wafted out of her cape. "You have no appointment."

"No, but I need to see you."

"So, you are here for a reading. You are nervous." She had a singsong voice that fit right in. "You wish to ask me some questions, child?"

I thought she meant Steven. Then I realized she still couldn't see him. I decided to play it low-profile and stupid, not all that difficult for me. I made round, impressed eyes. "Uh, yeah. I haven't been in the presence of a seer before."

"Come on in," she said and turned away, leaving me to follow her.

Steven stayed carefully behind me. We stepped through a bead curtain into a darkened room that reminded me of some subterranean netherland, permeated with the smell of clove incense and decaying roses, a scent I associate with funerals. Heavy floral curtains hung across the large, north-facing living room window, blocking most of the light. On the far wall glowed two large, lighted aquariums with green gravel and orange ornamental goldfish.

The room was dominated by a large brick fireplace and mantel before which she had set a heavy carved chair, creating a kind of throne effect. The walls were textured and painted a thick marine blue, while the ceiling was white stucco with metallic flecks. It only lacked phosphorescent stars swinging from the chandelier and a few ghostly people vaporizing in the chairs.

Steven and I stood at the entrance to the room, unsure whether we wanted to sit down.

Madam Anastasia swept across the room and seated herself dramatically on the throne. Then she looked up and saw Steven. Her eyes grew wary. "Who are you?" she asked me in a harsh, husky voice, no phoney business now. "Where is Elena?"

So much for her ability to see the present; I hoped she'd at least remember the past. This rougher persona, though, was a definite improvement over the woo-woo queen. I didn't know whether to start in straight and honest or lie my best. I was hampered. Lying in front of a child seems so much worse.

I opted to play it sort of straight. "I'm Stella, Elena's friend; she's missing, and I'm trying to find her. She mentioned you, said you were helpful to her, so here I am."

She looked quickly at her hands, small and gnarled. The

nails were bitten to the quick, the cuticles ragged, the joints swollen painfully. They were the hands of someone who had worked hard for years, and still did. She twisted them, looked at her palms, then steepled them and brought them to her lips as though she were praying. When she spoke she used her rough, husky voice. "Elena was a very passionate woman. She believed deeply in what she was trying to do, but she did not want it to be told."

I came farther into the room. "Madam Anastasia, I'm desperate here. I've looked all over Denver for her. I'm taking care of Steven to hold her job for her until I can find her. She called me the night she disappeared; she was upset and wanted to see me the next day. Anything you tell me will help."

Madam Anastasia sighed. She pointed to a couch, a lumpy affair covered with a fringed cotton throw in gold and navy with stars and moons on it. "Sit down, please."

Steven sat primly on the edge of the couch, sucking unattractively on his lower lip and fiddling with the zipper on his jacket. I didn't know what, if anything, to make of his reaction to Madam Anastasia, or mine, either.

"How long has Elena been missing?"

"Since Thursday night, late."

Her deep-set eyes darkened, and the otherworldly facade slipped entirely. "Holy Mother," she murmured, crossing herself. "You checked with immigration? They take people"—she snapped her fingers—"like that."

I nodded. "They haven't seen her. The police don't have her, she's not in a hospital, not in the morgue. She said she would come to see me last Friday and never arrived. Why did she come to you in the first place?"

Madam Anastasia pulled her shawl closer about her, lowering her voice to a barely audible hum, as if she thought Steven wouldn't hear it if she made it lower. "She wanted a seance."

Ah, the scam-artist pitch. "And did you have one?"

"I refused."

"Why?"

Madam plucked at the fringe on her shawl. "There are people who are seeking comfort; they're lonely and want to contact a loved one. A seance could bring them comfort, some sense of completion or release. For those people I will do a seance. But Elena was seeking something else. She was too intent."

"Why would that make a difference?"

"I thought it would bring evil into my house."

"Evil? How?"

"You cannot always predict what spirits will answer."

Gag me. She was back to the woo-woo. "Are you saying she was appealing to evil spirits? Do you actually believe this stuff?"

Madam Anastasia's eyes narrowed. "Your disbelief will hinder you. Everything in nature has an equal and opposite state. For good, there is evil. If you close yourself to seeing evil you will miss the truth because you will be blind to the complete person."

"You think Elena was evil?"

"She was willing to use any means to achieve her goal. I believe when you try to achieve something, you have to weigh the cost. What she wanted to do had too high a cost."

"What do you mean, cost?"

"Her actions would affect others, maybe hurt them."

"Well, it's pretty obvious they hurt someone. She's—" I caught myself. "She's missing."

Madam Anastasia's gaze seemed to almost burn into my eyes. "You also have the ability to see into people's lives."

"I don't make a living scaring the daylights out of vulnerable, lonely people. Maybe I've got a little intuition, but I don't pretend to more than that."

"You are so quick to judge. You're afraid to trust yourself, and so you cannot trust others. You must follow your beliefs."

"Is that what you do?"

She waved my question away. "You think you know what happened to her, don't you? You must be careful, for it could hurt you, too."

Steven put his hand on my arm; it was cool and trembling lightly. I patted it to reassure him. "Madam Anastasia, what did she ask for?"

"At first she wanted to know if I could reach"—she jerked her head toward Steven—"his mother."

"Why?"

Madam's eyes flickered. "She wanted to know how she died."

I felt cold all over. Steven stiffened and withdrew his hand, shoving it into his jacket pocket. "When was this?"

"About a month, six weeks ago." Madam drew in a breath. She was angry in a quiet, hard way that hinted of inner strength. "I told her to be careful—what she was doing, trying to reach his mother, could hurt her or"—she nodded to Steven—"or him."

"Did you tell her to use salt to ward off evil?"

"No. I believe that what you do or don't do determines what happens. Although I think priests use it sometimes in exorcisms. I told her to be careful. She could get into big trouble, letting things bother her too much. Her nerves were beginning to play tricks on her."

My throat was tight, my voice a mere croak. "How?"

"She came last Thursday morning, very upset. She said she'd heard from his mother. When you begin to hear voices, that's dangerous. I told her so. She swore she'd talked to her."

"Where?"

"Over the telephone." Madam looked intently at me, not so much in anger or in a threat but with a fiery, glowing intensity. It probably frightened her vulnerable clients. It did me. She glanced quickly at Steven, then back at me. "The boy is the key. Trust yourself, and be careful. He could get hurt."

We left Madam Anastasia shivering in her shawl like the queen of doom, and piled into the car. I was skeptical of Madam Anastasia, but her last words left me worried and my hands trembling when I tried to put the car key in the ignition.

Her talk about my ability to see into people's lives was disturbing. And when she said to trust myself, it echoed through my being. I'd lived with that particular character flaw for years, whenever I had one of those spells, and more so when I had to deal with my feelings about Jason. Now self-doubt was nearly a plague as I tried to find Elena and figure out the best way to deal with Steven. The look in her eyes as she had pointed to Steven, pronounced him "the key," and said he could get hurt scared me. I wanted to flee, far and fast.

Logic said, Get out of the situation, tell his father to take him to a psychiatrist, and let events unfold without my interference. But my feelings, my wobbly right-brained reflexes, told me to stay with it, look beyond the surface for the underlying menace. I was torn. Facts are so much more reliable. Of course, if there were any facts of consequence, Stokowski would investigate.

Madam Anastasia herself was a complicated person. I'd gone there skeptical of her, expecting her to try to fleece me through a series of superficial tricks. She was enigmatic, but she appeared to genuinely believe what she was saying, and was it so different from the self-help books lining the grocery store bookshelves? Her belief in the supernatural was in direct conflict with all my training and education. But so were my spells.

I was so frustrated I wanted to beat the steering wheel, but it would have scared Steven to death. I figured I'd better get him to talk about it fast, or he'd stash it into his childhood trauma drawer and have another week of nightmares, this time clearly because of me.

"Well, what do you think of Madam, Steven?"

"You didn't pay her."

"You're right. I forgot." And she hadn't asked. Why? Guilty conscience? "Did Elena?"

"Yup. Twenty dollars every time."

"I thought her house was gloomy. I didn't like it very much."

Steven agreed. "It stinks like dead flowers. But it doesn't have any pictures of Jesus bleeding. They're worse."

"What do you think Buckley thought of her?"

"He thinks she's scary."

"What do you think she was talking about?"

He looked at me, puzzled. "I think she was scared, too. Her hand was shaking."

I hadn't noticed.

"Stella, what are we going to do?"

"Uhmm, I think we'll visit Millie Quinley—but first we have to get lunch."

"Buckley's hungry, too."

We went to the Healthy Rabbits Salad Company and got takeout. Steven got Buckley spinach, and himself spaghetti, which he called worms in blood sauce, after which I settled for sesame chicken salad and toast. We took our lunches to Sloan's Lake for a change of scene.

Around two o'clock clouds gathered over the foothills, absorbing the sunshine until by three o'clock it looked like we were in for a spring snowstorm. I had a giant it's-going-to-get-nasty feeling hanging over me that I couldn't shake, and by three-thirty Steven had grown so pensive he tucked the rabbit inside his jacket and we headed for the car.

"Stella, is Elena with my mommy?"

I shivered in the rising wind. "I don't know, but we'll find her."

EIGHTEEN

IT WAS NEARLY a quarter to four. Tuesday I'd been derailed by Millie's weird flashback, now I wanted to see if with a bit of alcohol on board she'd talk more. I had a feeling she knew a lot more about Thursday night than she was telling. I parked the car in front of Holman's house, and we walked the half block north.

The Quinleys' house stood up from the street like Holman's and had been built in the same era, probably by the same builder, but with an eye toward more function and less cost. It lacked the grace and gingerbread charm, and it was smaller, with a steeper roof, no gables, and no little porches on the second floor. It was still a large, handsome redbrick home, in a style I think of as Victorian dour, with gray stone that embellished the brickwork, formed the foundation of the house, and lined the windows. The wooden gingerbread trim was painted maroon, teal, and dark green, giving it a thick, heavy feeling, as though the occupants were turned in on themselves. Fitting, from the little I knew of them.

Millie answered the door in a cloud of Opium perfume, holding a Waterford highball glass and breathing vodka fumes. Her blond hair floated becomingly about her face, and she was clad from head to toe in an angora lounge outfit the very same color as Buckley's fur. She looked like a slightly smashed, blond-headed mother rabbit.

Steven wrapped a protective arm around his bulging jacket and stared at her outfit balefully. "Elena said that was rabbit fur," he said accusingly.

"Ah, Steven. One of life's little surprises. My favorite child. Any more obscene toys?" She grinned at me and raised her glass. "Drink?" She turned away before I could answer. Steven hugged his wiggling jacket. I hoped Buckley was under control.

We followed her through the living room, pink-and-turquoise southwestern decor with a vengeance, to an astonishing pink adobe kitchen, complete with rough-plastered walls and doorways and wood-framed windows. It was an adobe cottage kitchen, right down to Mexican hand-cast tiles, in the middle of a Victorian dour house. The tiles were lovely, but as a whole it was a nightmare in pink, the inside of a migraine.

Millie went to the counter, dropped ice in her glass, and poured a healthy two inches of Absolut Citron. If I had a kitchen like this I'd have simply glugged down the whole bottle. Before I could close my mouth, words slipped out. "This is a...a...an amazing kitchen."

Millie smiled. "Yeah, wild, isn't it? Southwestern, you know." She sipped her drink while my gaze roved from one painfully discordant item to the next. "Barry says it's loud."

"It's colorful."

Steven tugged at my hand, still eyeing her angora. "Can I go outside and play?"

Millie answered. "Great idea, kiddo."

He made straight for the back door, looking a little too pleased with himself. It made me nervous. I hated to see him escape. It left me alone and defenseless against the pink. "Will he be all right out there?"

Millie rattled the ice cubes in her glass, bruising her vodka. "He always plays out there when he comes over. It's fenced. There's nothing out there he can get into."

I peered out the window and saw Steven lift Buckley out of his jacket to the ground. The yard was basically an empty square of winter-dead grass with ice patches next to an old carriage house that stood in one of the back corners. An ancient vine-encrusted yellow-brick incinerator leaned at an angle near the back gate. "Your garage?"

"No, the garage is on the other side of the house. That's

the old carriage house. The people who owned this place before us used to rent it out as a house." She shuddered. "I can't imagine anyone living there. It's just an old rattrap, empty now except for Barry's old wine bottles and his precious old Studebaker that he thinks is going to turn into a collector's treasure. He thinks he's making wine, but it tastes godawful. Makes good toilet bowl cleaner, though. Basically all that old carriage house does is hold up that stupid rattrap incinerator."

She turned and walked toward a sunlit garden room, actually a winterized porch that had been added on to the house. "Barry promised to take it out. But like a lot of things he promised, it hasn't happened."

I leaned out the kitchen door and yelled. "Steven, don't go in the carriage house, promise?"

"Promise."

I followed Millie to the garden room and took a seat in a chair where I could keep an eye on Steven and still see Millie clearly. Unbelievable how much work it was, watching that kid.

Her blue eyes were lazily observant. "So what brings you 'round here, if it isn't to get a swig?"

"About Tuesday—I didn't mean to upset you, Millie. In fact, I was hoping you'd help me out."

She tensed and glanced nervously toward Steven in the backyard. "I don't baby-sit kids."

"No, no. I know you weren't unhappy to see Elena go, but I'm still trying to track her down for Steven's sake. He's really pretty upset. Is there any chance Barry went back to talk to her after you came home?"

"I don't know. I slept in the den Thursday night." Her gaze flickered unsteadily to her glass. "I was overserved, so to speak. That seems to occur fairly often these days."

"Do you remember when you and Barry went home that night?"

"Right after I saw Barry harassing Elena again. Ten, for

sure. I watched the start of the news in the den. I think I fell asleep after that."

"And Barry?"

Just as I was beginning to wonder if she'd gone to sleep, she perked up and answered. "He probably was asleep upstairs. Washed, brushed, pajama-ed, and dead to the world." She started to get up, then sighed and looked at me. "Actually, I was dead to the world; I have no idea where he was, except he wasn't with me. Hasn't been for quite some time."

At the rate and quantity she was drinking, she'd be pickled before long. She looked at me, her eyes a bit vague, as though she was seeing memories in the air. "We haven't been close for two years now. Not since my uncle visited. That's when it started." A sour expression crossed her face. "Stella, about the other day. That had nothing to do with you. It's a ghost from my childhood. A ghost named Uncle Bill."

I waited for her to continue, but she simply sat there, staring into space with an expression on her face that said it was an ugly place. Two years ago seemed to be a point of pain. Her uncle, a ghost from the past, the start of her drinking, an abortion. All linked, was my guess. I wondered what the actual time sequence was.

Millie closed her eyes. "Have you ever noticed how things repeat? Betrayed by one man, betrayed by another, and another."

"Millie, how does this tie in with Barry?"

"Oh, he's there, right along with the others."

"It sounds like Barry didn't really act on his attraction to Elena."

"Who knows what Barry's done? I'm not sure about a lot of things right now. Look, let's change the subject. I don't mean to talk about this. Think I'll get a little more anesthesia." She rattled the ice in her glass.

"Why do you need anesthesia, Millie?"

"Too many ugly thoughts, Stella. Past and present."

"Are you worried about where Barry was Thursday night? Maybe you saw him leaving or returning to the house?"

"I need another drink." She rose unsteadily and went to the kitchen. She twisted off the cap of the vodka bottle, waving it over the sink. The bottle smashed against the edge of the porcelain sink, shattering and splattering vodka into the sink, over the counter, and onto the floor. "Damn it!" she shouted.

"Millie—"

"Oh, get out of my life!" She whirled, the jagged bottle in her hand, and stumbled in my direction.

"Stella!" Steven's voice howled. The back door banged. "Stella, come quick. Buckley's stuck!"

I was afraid to take my gaze off Millie. I wasn't sure what she was going to do next. Steven's footsteps raced across the floor. "Stella, hurry!" He grabbed my hand, then stopped.

Millie shook herself, blinking, her eyes startled. She looked at the broken bottle neck with surprise, then at me, then back at the mess on the counter. "I had an accident."

I let out my breath. "Accident" didn't quite cover it.

"Stella, come on." Steven dragged me out of the house to the carriage house, a veritable spider heaven. "He's in there."

The door was open about three inches, the smell of mummified insects oozing out. "You promised not to go in there."

"He went in there anyway."

Steven squeezed in through the narrow space; I had to pull and shove until it was wide enough for me. My wonderful lilac tights caught and tore on a splinter.

Inside, it was cold as a tomb and stank of mice, mold, and spiders. Light leaked in through the dirt-encrusted windows and several gaps in the roof. Once my eyes adjusted to the dimness I saw that originally it had held three horse stalls, two of which had been combined to hold a canvas-covered car and several boxes filled with empty wine bottles, stacks of old newspapers, and a pile of rags. When I moved closer to the car, I smelled a mild stench of oil, which I figured came from it leaking onto the wood flooring. No wonder Millie wanted it taken out. The thing was a firetrap.

"He's over here, Stella." Steven pulled me toward the corner, where boxes of empty wine bottles were stacked. He pointed at a narrow crack between the boxes. "He went in there." There are very few poisonous creatures in Colorado, but the few there are seem to live in dark, cool crevices. The three I most fear are brown recluse spiders, black widow spiders, and rattlesnakes. I shook the middle and top boxes and listened for a telltale rattle. Nothing. Of course it was still wintry cold. A snake could be sleeping—or too lazy to rattle a warning.

I found a garden stake and pushed it in gently, hoping to poke the rabbit just enough to drive him out. I heard a rustling sound.

"Here he is! I got him."

Buckley ran straight toward Steven, then dodged past him, streaked toward the other corner, and burrowed beneath a stack of old rakes and tools.

I pulled them away from the wall. The rabbit scrambled out. I lunged. He leaped past me, streaked past a ladder to the loft, raced around the barn, and stopped, panting, atop the wine bottle boxes. I stole toward him.

"Get him, Stella!" Steven yelled.

The rabbit took off, running back around the walls of the barn, making the same hysterical circle to stop again on top of the wine box.

Outside I heard Louise's voice calling out our names. How on earth did she get here? I yelled back, "We're in here. Don't open the door. Just stand there so he won't get out."

"You've got to come out of there. It's not safe in there. This old place could fall down around your ears."

She was right, of course. Steven shouldn't be in there at all. "Steven, you go out. I'll catch him."

"No. He's my rabbit." His voice was verging on hysterical. "I won't goooooo!"

"Steven, wait! I know how we can catch him." I got his attention. "Listen, I'll drive him to the door. You stand just outside the door where he can't see you. Then, when he darts to the door, you snatch him, like you did in the park."

Steven ran to the door. "Okay."

I grabbed one of the old newspapers from the top of the stack. Holding it at my side, I crept toward the rabbit. He twitched his ears. I stopped, then inched forward again. He blinked. I reached slowly for him. He sailed off the box, circling the room, stopping opposite me.

As fast as I could, I emptied the box of the wine bottles, setting them on the ground, blocking the crevices between the boxes. Then I spread two pages of the newspaper over the top of the box, leaving the lid of the box up.

"Ready, Steven? I'm going to try to drive Buckley out." Actually, Steven was Plan B. I moved toward Buckley, driving him on his circle. He hopped, a fraction slower, up onto the first box, the second, then the third and empty one. The paper collapsed. He disappeared into the box. I jumped to the lid, flapped it down.

Holding the lid tight, I picked up the box and carried it to the door. Louise pulled it open. I was out, rabbit, cobwebs, dirt, and all. With a shining face, Steven pulled Buckley out of the box, hugging him to his thin little chest. Now we only had to hope the damn thing didn't have cardiac arrest from being chased around the barn.

Everyone has different reactions to stress. Millie's was drinking. Louise had the anger reaction.

She stood in the middle of the yard, hands waving, face pale and upset. "Come inside. Come away from that terrible place. Steven could have been killed in there, Stella. I don't know what you were thinking of. Does Grant know he has this rabbit? Heather is very allergic, you know. She'll have a fit. Steven, come here, you're filthy.'' She literally dragged us both away from the carriage house and incinerator.

NINETEEN

I TOOK STEVEN and the rabbit home as fast as possible. Louise was right about several things, not the least of which was that Grant Holman would not be pleased about the rabbit, and Heather would raise Cain about it.

We secured the rabbit in a very deep box in the basement, farther away from the steps so that the dander wouldn't float upstairs to Heather. I took off Steven's clothes, piled them in the washing machine along with some of his other dirty laundry, and started a wash. Somehow I had to tell Holman about the rabbit, and fast.

Steven had his foot on the bottom step of the stairs when Grant came in upstairs. Steven ran up to meet him. I heard Grant's voice booming out, "Hey, there, Steven. Where are your clothes?"

"Grant, I have to talk to you. It's crucial," I said.

"So crucial it won't wait until he has on some clothes?"

"Yes." I leaned down to Steven. "Go upstairs and get out some clothes. I'll come up and do your bath."

"I'll do it myself." He marched up the stairs. At the landing he looked back at us. "Dad, you shoulda seen Stella today. She saved Buckley."

Grant grinned. "Who's Buckley?"

"He's my—" Then he clapped his hand over his mouth.

Grant's brow wrinkled. "Your what?"

Steven shook his head, eyes filling with tears, hand gripping his mouth.

I sighed. "That's what I have to talk to you about, Grant."

"Who's Buckley?"

"Buckley is his rabbit."

Holman's face froze. I could feel his blood pressure rising, not a healthy sign. "You mean to tell me that you hid that rabbit from me all this time? You lied!"

I tried to temper things. "Not an outright lie. An omission, actually. I tried to tell you the other night, but you were so busy telling Steven that he had to wear a sports jacket you wouldn't listen."

"You're impossible."

"I'm taking care of Steven's needs, not yours or Heather's. Steven's. That's what you hired me for."

He glared. I glared. The whole thing was ridiculous, frankly a game of control. I hated it. Holman wasn't as angry as he pretended, and he had known about the rabbit, I was sure. At least he had suspected it. "Why don't you spend some time with Steven? Before he goes to sleep, just man-to-man talk to him about his day? Earn some nurturing points. If he had more of your time, he might need the rabbit less."

I left the room. I didn't see any point in provoking him further.

That night, Steven's face lit up when his father came to his bedroom and sat on the edge of the bed, forced a grin, and asked Steven how his day was. He even injected interest into his voice.

"Gee, Dad, it was great. Stella saved Buckley, we visited the fortune-teller, and—what's wrong, Dad?"

I hadn't anticipated Holman's reaction. He went bright red, then pale and sweaty. Finally he grimaced, patted Steven on the head, and said good night. "Stella, I need to see you in the library, as soon as possible."

I was beginning to hate that room.

I was in the hallway at the top of the stairs just ready to descend when the phone rang. When no one answered on the third ring, I picked it up.

A clear, worried voice came through the receiver. "Who is this?"

"Stella—the nanny."

"Where's Elena? I have to speak to Elena."

"Who are you?"

She hung up.

In the library, Holman closed the door firmly behind us. "What were you doing at Madam Anesthesia's?"

"Anastasia. I went there to find out why Elena was seeing her. Did you know Elena thought she had been contacted by Steven's mother?"

"You promised not to bring up Steven's mother."

"I didn't. I'm trying to find Elena. Surely you can understand—"

"I forbade you to talk to Steven about her. And then you went to that fortune-teller, that rank phony, and talked about Steven's mother right in front of him. Against my express orders."

"But Elena—"

"Just like Elena did. You don't know what a nightmare you're opening up. You don't care about Steven, you just want to find Elena at any cost. Even Steven's." Holman's face was flushed and beaded with perspiration, an unhealthy sheen that greased his forehead.

"I'm trying to help—"

"You're causing more trouble—"

"And you're being bullheaded and narrow-minded." Even before my lips stopped moving, I wished I hadn't said that. Holman was raging; even his voice shook with anger. "Out. I want you out of here, now. Before you do any more harm. You have no idea—"

"I need to say good-bye to Steven."

"No." He stood over me. "Not a word. Pack your stuff and leave. Now."

"But Steven will think—"

"I'll take care of what Steven thinks."

GRANT HOLMAN ACCOMPANIED me to the bedroom and waited while I packed. Steven slumbered on, unaware, in the next room. Holman walked me downstairs, handed me an envelope, which I jammed into my bag, then led me to the front door. We walked in silence to my car, and he waited until the engine caught.

At that moment I wanted to annihilate him.

I took myself home via the grocery store, where I stocked up on staples: chocolate chips, marshmallows, corn curls, and diet cola, with a can of anchovies and a loaf of bread for ballast. There's something about the emptiness of depression that begs for the one-two slap of salt and sugar.

And I certainly was feeling alone. While I had Steven to look after, I could dwell on Elena and Steven and Steven's nightmares and almost totally avoid thinking about Jason and his suspicious absence. Now, at home, everything was crashing in, the growing certainty that Elena was dead and the gnawing worry that Jason needed another woman, probably more accomplished, polished, slim, young, vital—Bipsie.

I picked up my mail from the mailbox in the back lobby and climbed the stairs to my apartment. I wondered which of my neighbors, all of whom smiled to my face, had complained to the manager about me, saying I had noisy, strange friends, that I brought gypsies to the building, and that I was to blame for the explosion because the package had been meant for me.

At least Fluffy was happy. He flapped his jaws and winked as soon as I set his cage down in my living room. Lips, however, disappeared under the plastic greenery of the travel cage. It looked to me as though they weren't getting along very well. Perhaps Lips had a headache.

I dropped the groceries on the kitchen counter and slumped into my favorite chair at my round oak kitchen table, spreading the mail on the tabletop, too enervated to take off my jacket. The message light was blinking, but I opened the marshmallow bag and the chocolate chip bag instead. Sustenance first.

Most of my mail was junk—several of those missing children cards with the flat, solemn-eyed faces of waifs looking at me. So many sad children. I shoved them aside and stuffed a marshmallow into my mouth.

If I'd had the cash I'd have jumped on an airplane and headed for a beach, somewhere warm with sunshine and soft air, sea breezes, coconut-scented suntan oil, and nothing to do but snooze or jump the surf. All it would have taken was a passport.

I bit the marshmallow in half and dipped it into the chocolate chips. Easier than making fudge.

A passport I had; cash was the problem.

I pulled Holman's envelope from my bag and smoothed it out. Not exactly plane fare, but it held four crispy one-hundred-dollar bills. He'd paid for last night's dinner with cash, too. That was a significant amount of cash to walk around with, certainly more than my customary ten bucks. I wondered if he paid Louise in cash, too. Why did he pay in cash?

And why so bent out of shape because I went to see Madam Anastasia? Initially, he had been supportive of finding Elena; why the change? I had a vague, uneasy feeling that I knew the answer.

The phone rang, and I turned the volume up on the answering machine so I could screen the message. I was sort of hoping it would be Holman begging my forgiveness. It wasn't. It was Jason.

"Stella, I tried to reach you at Holman's, but Heather said you were fired. You've had plenty of time to pick up chocolate and corn curls and I know you're there sitting at the kitchen table nursing your hurt pride."

There was a pause. "Stella, please pick up the phone. Please don't be out skulking around in the dark getting into trouble. Please pick it up."

The sound of someone begging me to do something was nice. I drew in a breath and picked it up.

"H'llo."

"Thank God you're there." He let out a huge sigh. "I've missed you. What happened at Holman's? How come you...aren't there anymore?"

"I was tracking down names from Elena's address book, and I went to see a nun and a fortune-teller. He went ballistic over the fortune-teller."

"Did he threaten you? If he did, I'll have to kick him in the balls." Guy humor.

"Safe bet, from California."

"Why was he cranked over a fortune-teller?"

"I don't know. He claimed it was because I talked about Steven's mother in front of him, after I'd promised not to. He thinks it gives Steven nightmares."

"Maybe it does."

"Maybe *never* talking about her does."

"Stella, I know you love that little guy, and I know he's a lonely kid who sees things a little differently, but have you considered the possibility that Steven *is* the problem?"

I thought about it. Chills ran over my arm. "I can't. If I accept that, I have to believe he killed his mother."

There was a long silence as he digested this. "Well, maybe he did. Have you thought about the possibility? Kids do things without meaning to, you know. Sometimes they're careless, unthinking, and they just fly off the handle, and the worst happens." Jason's voice grew husky. "They don't mean to. But they get mad, and all of a sudden it's done. And nothing can change that. It happens."

"Who did this happen to, Jason?"

Silence spun out over the telephone line. Finally Jason said, "It's hypothetical."

"And how old were you?"

Silence.

"Jason?"

Silence.

"Jason, think about it. How could he kill a reasonably able, healthy human female? People are tough, they don't just keel over."

"It can happen."

"Nine-point-nine-nine times the kid's being blamed, scapegoated because he can't defend himself."

"I agree. I'm trying to get you to look at the point-ought-one time when the kid has done it—just for your own safety. And think, if you were Holman, and your kid had killed his mother, what would you do?"

"I'd stand by him."

"What about legalities?"

"Whatever it took. And once it was over, I'd take the kid and get the hell out of there, and I'd never look back."

"And what if someone tried to dig it up?"

"I'd—Oh God, Jason."

"Yeah, think about it. Now don't go back there. Don't mess in it. Talk to Stokowski, but don't, repeat *don't,* go back there and get into it. And remember my offer if the lease doesn't go through—"

"I want to change the subject."

Pause. "Okaaaaay, what is it you want to talk about?"

"How's your sick friend?"

Pause. "Not so good."

"Does that mean you won't be coming back soon?"

His voice dropped to a near-whisper level. "I don't know when I'll be back. I really can't leave now."

Visions of Cleota's corseletta danced in my head to the tune of "Jingle Bells."

"Stella, are you still there?"

"Jason, the question isn't where I am, it's where you are."

"I can't talk about that."

"There doesn't seem to be much we can talk about."

"How's Meredith?"

"No change. She's taken an oath of sackcloth and celibacy but is lusting after Holman."

"She finds the most unsuitable men."

"I think we have that in common. I'll talk to you later, Jason."

I hung up, then rang Meredith. She answered after the first ring. I know her very well. It meant she was waiting for a man-call. So much for celibacy.

"Meredith, who were you actually waiting to hear from?"

She missed a beat. Then, indignant, she replied. "I know what you're thinking, and it's not true. I merely called Grant to talk to you, but he said you weren't there anymore. Why'd you leave?"

"What exactly did he tell you?"

"That you left a few minutes before I called. He sounded down. It took quite a while to cheer him up."

"Really, did you volunteer to go over and watch Steven?"

"No. I didn't go that far. I figure you must have a good reason to go."

Meredith's male crap-detector isn't good. Not that my record is so sterling, but I've learned that to warn Meredith is to challenge her, and she can't pass up a good challenge. Sort of like my reaction to Jason telling me not to get into trouble. It immediately becomes a goal. So I hesitated to talk about Holman to her, since I feared that anything at all that I said would only enhance him in her eyes.

"Jason is still in California."

"So, are you soft and seductive on the phone with him?"

"Meredith!"

"You've got to encourage him a little, Stella. He's stuck with you for months now, and all you've done is been honest. That's no way to catch a man."

"I'm not a hunter-gatherer. I want a reciprocal relationship, not a trophy in the den."

"Reciprocal relationship usually means process, endless talking, questions and answers. Men don't like Q and A."

"T and A instead? The big-breast approach to modern maturation?"

"Not quite so crude. They just like to feel nurtured."

"Well, I have a feeling he's getting his nurturing with Bipsie, and—"

"What makes you think he's with Bipsie?"

"I called there, and he answered."

TWENTY

IT WAS A LONG, lonely night, and as loving as my body pillow was, it wasn't enough. Neither was the chocolate, the corn curls, the diet soda, or the last of the anchovies.

I woke with the mournful sound of an equally lonely and evidently unsuccessful cat howling in the alley. A railroad train passed through Denver about that same time. The clock said it was 3:43, my heart said it was lonelytime, and my stomach didn't feel all that great for some reason. I couldn't sleep anymore.

I got up and went to the kitchen, where Fluffy and Lips were slumbering the night away, still in their travel cage because I'd been so self-absorbed I'd forgotten to transfer them to their terrarium. Lips clung to the plastic greenery; Fluffy perched on top of her, his little hands holding her shoulders. Lucky lizard.

Fluffy's eyes popped open when I turned on the light. Unusual, because lizards are sound sleepers, needing every one of their ten hours of beauty rest a night so they can lounge and emote effectively through the day. Fluffy crawled up onto the screen top of the cage and blinked sympathetically at me. I was wearing his favorite sleep shirt, a blue-green leaf-pattern silk with tiny buttons down the front.

"You want to come out?"

He turned his head and blinked twice. I lifted him out, carefully because he's more flighty since Lips entered his life. Lizard testosterone. Barely a month ago he leaped from my hand onto the floor. Unfortunately, I was at my mother's house on her mottled-brown, sculpted carpeting. The two of us had to lie on the floor scanning for an unusual protuberance, and it took two hours to find him. He thought it was funny; I know because he flapped his lips at me afterward.

I put on his little everyday string harness and wound the string around one of the buttons on the front of my sleep shirt. He moved over to a green leaf and turned a lovely, glowing chartreuse. It was like old times. My eyes got leaky. It's pretty sad when your lover is less comfort than a lizard.

I made toast and sat down to munch and sort the mail I'd left on the oak table in a heap. I stacked all the envelopes with windows to the far left, pushed all the coupon mail to the far right, and settled into the few remaining pieces, the missing children postcards and a single envelope with my building management company's logo in the upper left corner. Inside I found a brief note from the building owner, confirming an appointment for my appeal tomorrow at two in the afternoon.

Maybe I'd be better off moving, even if I had to bunk in with Meredith or Jason until I could find a place. How did people who didn't have friends and family manage? Living out of their cars, I suppose. Or under the bridges along the Platte. It frankly infuriated me that I had to defend myself, to convince a judgmental old goat, or whoever, that I was a good person.

I finished the toast and sat back. Overwhelmingly, I wanted my mother to hug me and tell me everything would straighten out. Most of all, I wanted to feel Jason's arms around me. Crummy as Jason had been, I still wanted to feel needed. I don't think anyone gets beyond yearning for love and lovability.

Undoubtedly Elena would want it, too. And after losing a child, a mother, probably the child's father, and her home, it could be very hard to leave Steven, but impossible to lose touch with Maria. Sisters who are that close don't suddenly break off.

I was far too wide awake to go back to sleep, so I pulled out my astrological column correspondence and got down to work. For the first time in days I was ready to read letters. I fanned them out on the table and picked out one that had frogs hopping across the back flap. Looked cheery.

Dear Stella,

I'm a Leo in need of advice. A friend of mine recently was widowed for the fourth time. I'm worried she's going to get a complex because her husbands keep dying on her. She says she's all right and she's financially well off since they all died with large insurance policies, thank goodness, but I think she's hiding her grief. I've heard that ignoring grief can cause a lot of problems for a person. What do you suggest?

Sincerely,
Leo Waiting

P.S. I don't know what her sun sign is.

It occurred to me that her prevalent sign might well be a black widow.

Dear Anxiously Waiting,

I think your friend must be too well acquainted with death at this point and knows better than you what she's doing. I have found a detective on the Denver police force most helpful in situations like this. His name is Lee Stokowski.

Leo tends to be a proud and self-sufficient sun sign, but in this case you would be wise to accept help from Mr. Stokowski (also a Leo). I would also strongly advise you not to press your friend about her grief. She may not have quite the same feelings as you do.

Sincerely,
Stella

Being of reasonably sound mind, I also saved the name and address to forward to Lee Stokowski first thing in the morning.

The next letter I chose was a somber-looking envelope in olive drab with precise block lettering, done by hand. I don't get many like that; in fact, I've never had olive drab. My correspondents tend toward the blues, lilacs, mauve, and pink, frequently sporting little animals and flowers, sometimes even perfumed. Now and again I get just plain white, but not olive drab. I slit it open and shook out the matching letter.

Dear Stella the Stargazer,

My husband is an Aquarian who tells me to go with the flow. He is dying to get a dog, but I just got new, cream-colored carpeting. He says the dog will learn to wipe its feet. Do you think the dog will, when my husband never has?

A Very Tidy Virgo

Some letters take less time to reply to than others.

Dear Very Tidy,

Get a poodle that matches the carpet and buy it some booties.

Sincerely,
Stella

Before the sun rose I managed to get through a good fourth of my correspondence and my horoscope. I take horoscopes seriously on one of those leaps of faith that we humans live by. When I explained it to Jason, I said reading a horoscope also unleashed my subconscious observation. In truth, I believe them because for me they work.

This morning's horoscope was particularly unsettling. I'm a Virgo, and this was not one of the more positive times for me to be involved in anything precarious, but today I saw great turbulence in the stars, risks in relationships, and jeopardy to people I loved. My home box was adverse, Mars was particularly noxious, and financial dealings were definitely out. In other words, it was a great day to stay home and read. It occurred to me that prospects were poor for my lease being renewed.

It was 7:20 in the morning when the phone rang. I had the answering machine set so I could screen calls. Grant Holman's voice boomed out, "I'm sorry to bother you so early. I wonder if you could call me at—" and he reeled off his home number. His voice wasn't apologetic or nearly imploring enough. I ignored it.

I headed out into the cold sunshine for a walk, figuring the wind would blow some clarity into my brain. Because of the horoscope, I left Fluffy, someone I loved, safe in his cage and power-walked by myself to the bakery, planning to pick up a *Denver Post* for the rental ads, just in case.

The sun was bright, but the windchill was around freezing, and my eyes watered from the cold. Feathers of frost clung to the bare tree branches, dropping sporadically to melt cold and wet on my face, like tears.

I could still hope, or wish, that Elena was alive, but I believed she was dead, murdered. And increasingly there seemed to be possible motives for all four of the people at dinner that Thursday night. Grant Holman seemed the most likely, since he had a terrible temper, he had displayed plenty of impulse control problems, and Elena was pursuing the question of his wife against his explicit orders. Holman certainly seemed to be hiding something, although I had discarded Jason's theory that he was covering up for Steven's crime as too far-fetched.

I had only Heather's word for the fact that she wasn't

jealous of Elena; she could be lying through her teeth. Millie was.

Millie was clearly jealous of Elena's appeal to Barry, and heaven knows Barry's motive could easily be rejection leading to anger.

I got back to my apartment at 8:34 a.m. and opened the door to the sound of a ringing telephone. The message machine kicked in before I reached it and I heard Holman's voice.

This time he left a slightly longer but similar message, including the word "please" once. It was better, but not good enough to warrant an answer.

At 8:55 the phone rang again, and I listened to the message again; this time Holman's voice was strained, and I could hear Steven howling in the background. "Stella, if you get this message, please call me immediately. Steven is convinced you're dead. You were right, I should have had you say good-bye. It was a mistake not to, but please call, for Steven's sake."

A much better message, although I noted that he said, "It was a mistake," as though it had occurred independently of him. Ownership of the error is important. Recognizing consequences of behaviors is an early lesson, apparently one Holman had never learned, but I felt so terrible for Steven that I broke down, picked up the receiver, and agreed to talk to Steven. It didn't help, of course. He was convinced I was dead and continued to howl. I agreed that Holman could bring Steven to see me.

They showed up at nine-thirty. Deep circles lay beneath Steven's eyes, made more apparent by the pallor of his cheeks. He stared at me, uncertain. "Hey, Steven, come in, give me a hug and say hi to Fluffy." He came to my arms.

Grant Holman, haggard but groomed, stood in the doorway, one hand on the doorknob as though he was ready to bolt.

Steven raced to Fluffy's cage. "He's not here!"

"He's in the travel cage in the kitchen, with Lips."

Grant cleared his throat. "Uh, Stella?"

"You can come in, too, and close the door."

He moved in cautiously, closed the door gently, and took a seat on the couch, just where he'd sat last Sunday, a mere five days ago, when he'd first come to my place. In that short time the lines in his cheeks had grown more prominent, and his hair looked different. Then I remembered the picture on the passports. His toupee was different, crooked maybe.

"Stella, I want to apologize for my temper. I've got a problem with it, I know, but I've been under a lot of pressure. I've got this deal almost to closing, it's very touchy right now with negotiations every hour. I just can't be tied up with Steven, but if he's upset, I'm upset. Steven and I are that close."

I interpreted his request to mean I had some leverage. Before I agreed to do anything, I was going to get some information. Nicely, of course. "What is this particular deal, Grant? I guess I never understood."

"Stella, I'm not interviewing for a job, I'm just asking you to help out for two more days. From today until tomorrow late afternoon. Heather has classes to teach and some private clients until tomorrow, Saturday, at four-thirty. I should be free by four, but she can handle him from then if I'm not, it won't be for long. I just need to know that he's okay until then. The deal should be solid by tomorrow. Six p.m. is the deadline. Then, regardless, I can be with him. And Louise says she'll have applicants for me to interview on Sunday, and she's sure one of them will do."

"Louise can't get someone before then?"

"She offered herself, but Steven went nuts. You know how he is when he gets started."

"You know, Grant, with all that's happened to him and the issues he has about people and about his mother, he could really benefit from seeing a child therapist."

Grant's face wrinkled in disgust, then smoothed out as he

modulated his response. "I'll take it under consideration. It's a good suggestion."

"The reason I say that, Grant, is that Steven says he talked to his mother—"

"When?"

"Yesterday morning he picked up the phone while—"

"Where were you?"

"Cleaning. Dusting. Louise was downstairs, I didn't hear it ring, but Steven was there and he picked it up. I think it was a real call, not just pretend."

"He shouldn't be on the phone, because"—he shook his head, as if he was clearing it—"because I've had some bad crank calls. He's got enough emotionally to deal with, he doesn't need to have this...woman stirring things up."

"Steven thought it was his mother."

He ran a hand over his face and through his hair, then he glanced toward the kitchen, where we could hear Steven talking to Fluffy. Finally he met my gaze. "It's that woman I was involved with before Heather. She's been calling, making trouble. I think she's doing it for revenge. She's not quite balanced. I don't want him answering the phone. In fact, I don't want you to either. It'll only make it worse, and you don't need to have that to deal with."

"Why not change your number?"

"I will." He glanced at his watch. "But right now I need to settle Steven. I'm absolutely out of time. Will you, please, do this...for him? It's only two more days. Thirty-six hours."

Steven charged into the room and launched himself at me. "Stella, please? I'll give you a prize."

"A prize?"

"Yeah. Special. For you." He dug into his pocket.

"Okay."

Steven handed me a crumpled, sweat-damped wad. I smoothed it out and saw soft, loopy handwriting, much like

Milly's or perhaps Maria's. "Steven, where did you get this?"

"On Elena's pillow."

A chill ran over my spine. "Is this Elena's note?" Steven nodded. I glanced at Holman; his face was suddenly sweaty. He shook his head, but he couldn't meet my gaze.

I patted Steven on the shoulder. "Hey, Steven, would you go to the kitchen and talk to Fluffy and Lips about getting ready?" As soon as he'd skipped into the other room, I turned back to Holman. "Okay, explain."

"Uh, see, I heard Steven crying in his sleep. I thought it was odd that Elena wasn't there, she always was. So I went and comforted him and then looked in her room. At first I thought she was there—the covers were bunched up and it looked like her—but she didn't answer. I started to leave, but when I checked closer I saw she wasn't there. Then I saw the note, but I figured she was just mad and she'd come back. I thought if I left the note there, she could throw it away when she came back and we'd avoid a nasty scene. But she still wasn't back in the morning, and when I checked in her room again I couldn't find the note. Still, I figured it wouldn't matter."

"Didn't you think you might need it if she didn't return?"

"I didn't think it would come to this..." He let his voice trail off as if he hoped I'd let it ride.

"Maybe you were relieved, to some degree. You could start over with someone new, or maybe you plan to leave the area soon anyway."

Before he could answer, Steven came back into the room, carrying Fluffy and Lips in their travel cage. He saw his father silent and piped up. "Daddy? Now I can keep Buckley, right?"

Holman frowned. "Now, Steven, you know rabbits make Heather sick."

"Heather makes *me* sick," Steven whined. "I wanna keep him. He's mine."

"Grant, it seems a small price to pay for peace just now."

Steven put the travel cage in my lap. "I'm gonna stay here with Stella."

"No, you need to be at home."

"I'm gonna stay with Stella. She's nice."

Holman's face reddened. "Steven!"

"You want to kill Buckley, and you don't care about me. I'm staying here. Vampires live in our house. It's not safe."

"There are no vampires!"

"Yes, there are. Vampires killed Elena, and they're gonna kill me. Stella's the only one who's strong." Steven wrapped his arms around my legs. "I like Stella better than you. You're mean. You hit people. You hit Elena, and you hit Mommy."

Grant jumped up, grabbed Steven by the arm, and raised his hand.

"Go ahead, hit me," Steven shouted, his jaw set, eyes fierce. I saw him weighing the possibility that his father would hit him. Slowly he let go of me and faced his father.

Holman's expression went from rage to surprise and then to something else, something like furious respect.

Steven sensed his advantage. His little lips twisted into thin, hard lines. "I'm not going home. It's bad there. I'll get dead there."

The blood drained from Grant's face, bleaching his handsome tan to an unhealthy, mottled gray. The air in the room was thick, as though there wasn't enough oxygen.

Steven's eyes were accusing pools of despair, more disturbing because they looked like the eyes of an ancient. Holman was frozen, gripping Steven's arm in his hand, poised to strike. The tension in the room was so heavy time couldn't move.

Grant Holman struggled to reconstitute himself by rubbing his hand over his chin, the whisker stubble snapping to attention with each calming stroke. I swear I saw him regenerate. His tan reappeared, his face relaxed, and he dropped Steven's arm. "You've made your point, son," he said, then looked at me, a joyless smile playing in the corner of his mouth. "If Stella will agree to stick with us for the next thirty-six hours, I'll agree to work something out about Buckley."

He'd neatly turned the tables. Steven literally jumped to his side; now I was the one who could spoil the party. I smiled. "Nice going, there. Okay, you win. I'll do it. But, Steven, Saturday is tomorrow, and then your dad will be with you. And starting Monday you'll have a new nanny. I'll be here, and you'll be with your new nanny, with no huge fuss from you, okay?"

He nodded.

Grant stopped at the front door. "He's defiant because of you. I'm not saying I like it, but at least he's not a wimp anymore." He slapped the doorjamb and left.

As his footsteps faded in the hallway I looked at Steven, expecting him to feel good, possibly smile and chatter. Instead he planted himself neatly beside me and very solemnly took my hand. "Stella?"

I looked at him.

"We have to pack our stuff, Stella."

"Why?"

"Because anybody who argues with Daddy disappears."

TWENTY-ONE

"WELL, STEVEN, we're not going to disappear. And nothing's going to happen to you, I promise. Now, put your coat on, we're going to the newspaper office."

"Fluffy, too?"

"Fluffy needs to stay here and take care of Lips."

Exactly a week ago Elena disappeared. Last Friday a moaning Chinook had rattled frozen tree branches, windows, and trash cans in the alleys, but today the air was still and smoggy. A thin cloud filter blanketed the sky, holding the stale air in on the city. Oppressive. The sun shone weakly through the dank cloud veil, unable to warm the late March freeze. The city smelled vaguely like an old incinerator. The weather weighed down my spirits, but Steven was unaffected. He pressed his nose against the side window of the car, leaving round smudges on the pane. "Are we gonna see Zelda?"

"Yup, why?"

"I like her. She talks like Mommy."

"If you tell her that, she'll like you even more."

Half a block away from the office I parked, and we crunched over the frozen parking strip to the sidewalk. Steven skipped ahead of me and opened the door.

"Close the door, you think I'm heating the whole outdoors? Place is freezing," Zelda said, but her voice held a light warmth, as though she really didn't mind.

"Zelda, I got a rabbit. His name is Buckley, and Daddy's gonna let me keep him."

Zelda's face lit up. "Yo, Steven-o. You're looking like a real kid today."

"That's 'cause I'm not dressed properly."

Zelda gave me an intense glance, then turned to Mr. Gerster. "See, Mr. Gerster, Stella's got another side to her, one we weren't aware of."

I had the sense that she was trying to tell me something, but I couldn't figure out what it was. "Zelda, could I...?"

Zelda interrupted. "Mr. Gerster was worried that you were getting into trouble again, Stella, and I've been telling him how you are helping out for a few days with little Steven. He's real pleased, aren't you, Mr. Gerster?"

He actually almost smiled. I could tell, because the lines deepened in his cheeks. He cleared his throat. "Stella, I think it's very commendable that you're following a fine female role here. And staying safe, no more of that gallivanting around unsavory sorts."

"Fine female role?"

"Zelda tells me you're baby-sitting. It's good child care practice."

"Good practice? For what?"

Zelda stood up abruptly. "Well, it must be time for lunch. I'll bet you're hungry, aren't you, Steven?"

"No."

"Good, let's go," she said, and grabbed his arm, starting for the coat closet.

I barred the way. "Zelda, wait." I hedged the truth and said, "I've got an appointment downtown to see Barry Quinley, and I need you to take care of Steven while I do that."

Her eyes rounded. "Oh."

"It's a fine female thing to do, so you won't mind, will you, Mr. Gerster? This way Zelda can get as much practice as I do with the nice female thing."

He swallowed. "Well, I suppose..."

"I'll be back in an hour. Steven, show Zelda the things in your pocket that you brought to play with."

Zelda seemed to shrink back into her chair. "Be sure it's only an hour, Stella, I've got a hair appointment."

I fled.

Barry Quinley and Grant Holman shared offices in one of the renovated office buildings on lower Seventeenth Street, fashionably close to LoDo, lower downtown Denver. Not so long ago, this area was the resting place for the down-and-out, and the building where Barry and Grant had their offices had most recently been euphemistically called a "hotel," inhabited by the downtrodden, the wine-soaked, and the defeated. Also known as the easy-to-move. The redevelopers had sandblasted the old red bricks, drywalled over the evidence of despair, polished the ancient brass fixtures, painted it a sophisticated, tasteful cream color, and rented it out for an outrageous sum. LoDo.

It was just after ten-thirty. The sun was still an anemic spot in the sky, generating little to no heat. Steam rose from the manhole covers. I'd parked two blocks north to avoid the cost of a parking lot and to give myself a chance to formulate an enhanced version of the truth about why I wanted to talk to Barry. I shivered in the cold and steered a path around a homeless person squatting on a sidewalk manhole cover for warmth. I wasn't that far from the Samaritan Shelter. They turn the people out in the morning and don't let them back in until sundown.

I set foot inside the building and had to admit it looked a lot better wearing the cream-colored paint than it had wearing simple dirt-brown. It certainly smelled better minus the taint of old ashtray and urine.

It didn't matter to me whether Barry was in yet or not. Plan A was to corner Barry and squeeze as much information as possible from his puffy lips. Plan B was, if Barry was out, to pump his secretary. I had no Plan C. But I had a burning curiosity about Grant Holman and Heather.

My goals were: one, corroborate Millie's story; two, find out what Barry had to do with Elena's plans; three, find out what he saw at the house Thursday night; and four, find out what he knew about Holman, if he would tell me. I figured that if he agreed to see me, then he must have an agenda, too. Maybe guilt. And that might drive him to talk to me.

I decided that if Holman was there and asked what I was doing, I'd try truth. I'd say I needed to see Barry and that Steven was playing with Zelda.

Barry Quinley's offices were on the second floor behind very clean glass walls and muted green carpeting. There were no visible papers, no magazines to read while waiting, and, I assumed from that, no waiting. His secretary was an ice queen of indeterminate age, polished voice, and conservative hemline. She gave me a pleasant but very cool look and refrained from offering help or encouragement. Mr. Quinley, she intoned, was busy all morning.

I smiled and explained that it was very important and that she should at least check with Mr. Quinley, since I was sure he was desperate to see me. She smiled back with an Arctic chill and said she was sorry. I tried a few questions and was met with stony silence. Plan B, pumping the secretary, was a loss, but it occurred to me that this ice queen probably maintained her chill to keep people at a distance from herself as well as from Barry Quinley. So I smiled again, pulled the one chair from its place against the wall to a spot in front of her desk, and began to stare at her. I figured I'd give it a solid forty-five minutes. It took only twenty. By that time she had a dull flush on her neck and a satisfying tic in her left cheek.

Barry Quinley appeared at the door, trying to smile. Social graces were not his strong suit. He was wearing a navy wool suit that would have been outstanding on a tall, rangy man, but merely looked expensive on his rounded shoulders.

His office was decorated in what I call modern ranch maple, lots of maple-colored wood, and leather, with a few collections of barbed wire on the walls. The room had beautifully balanced lighting, with two tall windows looking west to the front range. He indicated a chair and said, "Sit," then slumped into his high-backed leather desk chair, which was at least two inches higher than the chairs in front of his desk.

He frowned at me, puzzled and a little wary. "Why are you here?"

I grinned back at him, hoping I looked just goofy enough to disarm him. "You may not know, but I write a newspaper column as Stella the Stargazer. I've had a lot of women write in about how to safeguard their assets from abusive boyfriends and such, and I've never really known how to answer, so I thought I could do a mini-feature in the paper. Suppose I want to put money in a Swiss account?"

"Then the person simply comes here, talks to me, and I arrange it."

"Well, there's one other thing—"

"There usually is."

I switched topics. "Are you planning to open offices abroad?"

He looked flustered for a moment, then firmed up again. "We're considering it. Nothing is decided."

"Grant's lease on the home you're renting him wouldn't be month to month, would it?"

He didn't answer and I didn't know what to make of the look on his face.

"You know that I'm a friend of Elena's. I've been trying to find out where she went."

The expression on his face was instantly sad. "I hope you do. She's a fine woman. Millie said you were over yesterday asking questions. She said you think something has happened to Elena."

"Don't you think so?"

He blinked owlishly. "I don't know what to think."

"Did you see her when you went back to Holman's later that night?"

"No, no." He realized he'd stepped into a trap. He rubbed his nose again. "Elena is a very attractive woman, soft and gentle. I didn't mean to upset her. She was so pretty and so loving with Steven. I want someone to be loving to me, too. I just thought...I don't know. But she wasn't scared of me. I didn't threaten her, I just...asked. You've seen Millie. She's grown hard and cold, she drinks too much, and she hasn't been a wife to me for months. I know I'm not much to look at, but that doesn't mean I don't have feelings." He ran his hands over his face. "Millie wasn't always that way, just in the last year or two. Something happened. She says she has bad dreams. Looks to me like I'm her bad dream."

"So you went back to try to persuade Elena to—what?"

"I went back thinking that if she was still up, I could talk to her. But her light was off, so I went back home."

"And Millie saw you come back in?"

"Millie was passed out in the den, television blaring. She didn't know a thing."

"Actually, I think she does. What do you know about Grant's argument with Elena?"

"It was nothing. He was pissed off about her using the phone for some long-distance calls and answering the phone. He's got a thing about her answering the telephone."

"Something about a girlfriend calling the house?"

"I've never heard about a girlfriend."

"But he was really upset, shouting?"

"Well, not that upset."

"But you could hear through closed doors."

"Maybe his voice was loud. It carries pretty well."

"Yeah, I'll bet. And you never heard of a girlfriend calling the house pretending to be his dead wife?"

"Oh, that. I think I do remember he mentioned some woman has been calling the house, so he didn't want Elena talking to her. Something like that."

"I never met a man who forgets that his friend got phone calls from a girlfriend pretending to be his dead wife."

"I've got a lot on my mind." He was lying, of course. "Look, this is enough. Elena's gone. I didn't hurt her, didn't scare her, and neither did Grant. That's all there is to it."

"Did you know his wife?"

"Never met her. He doesn't talk about her. Doesn't like to have it brought up. I don't believe in nosing into people's business." He glared at me.

I refused to take the hint. "Do you know when she died?"

"Shortly before he moved to Denver, I think. Again, ask him."

"Millie came home with you after the dinner?"

"Bodily. God knows where her mind was. She'd had a bit to drink."

"She says she stayed in the den on the couch while you went upstairs. You didn't come down to check on her at any time, I suppose."

"No, I didn't. She came home and curled up with a bottle of vodka, and I figured there was no room for me."

"So really, neither of you has an alibi."

"Alibi? What is this? The truth is, I still love Millie, at least I love the old Millie."

"But how do you know Millie didn't wake up and go back to Holman's?"

"She doesn't wake up for hours when she starts on the vodka."

"But you don't *know* for sure. You didn't check on her."

He licked his lips again. "Well, I did check on her. She was there the whole time." A sheen of perspiration stood out on his forehead.

He closed down at this point and ushered me out to the reception area. Holman's office door was shut. I hustled out into the hall and as I turned to the elevator, I saw the doors begin to close. And then I saw Heather, standing in the elevator.

I took the stairs running, two at a time, and lit on the first floor just after the elevator got there. Heather reached the front door ahead of me.

"Heather!" I shouted.

She jerked around automatically. She saw me and her eyes

widened; stricken, she turned and bolted through the door. She had parked midblock, next to the alley. I caught up with her as she was getting into her car.

"Wait, Heather." I grasped the car door so she couldn't slam it. "Hold on."

She turned the key in the ignition. "You tell your friend—"

"My friend?" My stomach got a sick, nasty feeling, like melting gelatin. "Meredith?"

She gunned the engine. "Tell her to stay away from Grant Holman, or something real ugly is going to happen to her pretty face."

TWENTY-TWO

MEREDITH! Interfering with Grant Holman! And why was I so surprised? Didn't she find rotten, unsuitable men with complete, never-fail regularity? On that first Sunday night, hadn't she switched that raggy outfit around, tying it with a scarf and sashaying into the living room, eyes alight as soon as she saw him? Wasn't he a possible killer, and abusive? What more could a Meredith want? He lacked only a pirate's credentials and a sword. Well, actually, he had a sword of sorts. For her, he'd be completely captivating, a real prize. Sarcasm, a respite for the desperate.

I dashed back to my car, jumped in, and pounded the steering wheel for a satisfying half minute, only once accidentally hitting the horn. Then I drove straight to Meredith's candle shop, but she had gone. Jan, her assistant, shook her head at me. "She didn't say where she was going, only that she had to go, she had some terribly important date, and I might need to close up if she wasn't back. I'll tell her you stopped by. Is it important?"

Is life important?

I didn't answer, I just asked her to have Meredith call me on my cell phone as soon as she returned.

I went past Meredith's apartment, circled, checked the alley, and saw her car. I went by the front of her place looking for a parking spot, but as I reached the top of the block I saw her in my rearview mirror. She was heading into her building and holding hands with Grant Holman, who was too damn busy to take care of Steven.

I bet they were having more than egg salad sandwiches. Celibacy, my ass. How many unsuitable men would she have to go through in her quest for love and marriage? It made my head hurt.

I was now half an hour late to pick up Steven. I parked in the loading zone in front of the newspaper office and dashed inside. Zelda's desk was absolutely clear; she was gone. I peeked in the newsroom, but it was empty. I marched back to Mr. Gerster's office, where I found Steven sitting on Mr. Gerster's lap, drawing pictures. Mr. Gerster looked up. "Zelda wanted you to call her, said it was very important."

Yeah, I thought, something on the order of I owe her my fortune and a quart of blood for this one.

"This boy certainly has an imagination, Stella. I hope you haven't been the one telling him about vampires."

"Not me. What're you drawing, Steven?"

Steven looked up. "Cemetery. Mr. Gerster's boy is dead like my mommy." He hopped off Mr. Gerster's lap and brought me the picture, then before he reached me, he turned and laid the picture on Mr. Gerster's lap. "It's for you."

Mr. Gerster patted him on the shoulder, his faded blue eyes misty. He smiled. I knew it was a smile because his lips stretched out. "It's been a long time since I held a little boy. It's kind of nice. You know, it's real easy to let business crowd out your time with a child. And they grow up so fast. Take good care of him, Stella."

Steven skipped out into the hallway. "Stella, I'm hungry."

Mr. Gerster stood up, his long, knobby fingers adjusting his suspenders and smoothing his rumpled vest. For a moment he looked like he wanted to say something more, then he pulled a handkerchief from his back pocket and blew his nose. Whatever it was, he'd decided not to talk about it, but I made a mental note to ask him about it the next time I had some time. I waved good-bye and followed Steven to the front office. "How about Mexican food?"

"I want a hamburger."

We went to Burrito Ito. We got there just before the noon-hour crowd and took the back booth. Jannina, face flushed, bangs standing straight up, swept in from the kitchen carrying plates of steaming chili-and-cheese-laden burritos. She slid them onto the table in the front of the café and laid the bill on the end of the table. She turned, came toward us, saw me, and scowled. Then she saw Steven, and her scowl faded. She snagged water glasses and setups, balanced a basket of chips on top, and swung over to our booth. "What can I get you?" she asked, setting the water, setups, and chips on the table.

Steven looked at Jannina and piped up, "We're looking for Elena, do you know where she is?"

Jannina stared at him for a moment, surprised, then glared at me and said in a fierce whisper, "What do you want from me?"

"Anything at all."

Steven got huge, sad eyes. "I want Elena."

She glanced furiously around the café. "I told her I wouldn't tell—" She looked at Steven again, a huge tear rolling down his cheek.

"Oh, damn." Jannina put her hands flat on the table and leaned forward on them, her face so close to mine I could see the glint of powder on her cheeks. "Look, Elena was upset about this man, Mr. Holman's partner, he kept pestering her. She was gonna leave 'cause of that as soon as she found his"—she jerked her head at Steven and mouthed the word "mother."

"How was she going to do that?"

"She came in here Thursday noon, all excited. She made me promise not to tell anyone. She was real weird about it and said she'd had a phone call and she was going to meet her."

Goosebumps rose on my arms. "Meet who?"

"His mother. I thought she'd gone a little wacko. The woman's dead, isn't she?"

"Where did she say she was going?"

The café was filling up. Jannina thought for a minute, then shook her head. "She didn't say. I asked her where she'd get the money, and she said no problem. But she never had any money. All I can think is she was gonna get it from her sister."

"Do you know where Maria is?"

She shook her head, glancing around, nervous. I thought she was lying now. And probably would again, if I asked straight out. "Jannina, the night I was here, when you talked to Maria, had she heard from Elena yet?"

"No, she was real worried—" She drew in a breath of realization. "Okay, I talked to Maria. She didn't know where Elena was. Alberto was real upset—"

"Because they're illegal aliens, right?"

"Yeah. They've been here years, but…look, I gotta go, he wants a hamburger, what do you want?"

"How do you know what he wants?"

"He always has the same. You gotta watch him, you know. He's bad!" she said, then grinned at him and ruffed his hair.

I ordered a beef burrito, smothered green, and soda pop for both of us, then gave Steven a pen to draw on his paper place mat so I could think.

If she was going to get money from Maria, why didn't Maria tell me when I was there? It seemed to me that the answer was that Elena wasn't going to get money from Maria. Where was Elena going to go? Who was she going to meet? How did this all tie together?

Jannina brought our food and flapped the bill on the table. Of course, the bill, the *phone* bill, that I'd taken from Holman's desk and never followed up on. Where was it? I'd put it in my pocket in my trousers, but I'd taken it out when I changed clothes and put it…in the same drawer with the water glass that I'd never taken to Stokowski. As soon as we finished I paid up and whisked Steven out to the car.

"Where are we going?"

"Home, fast as we can. I gotta find some phone numbers and make a few calls."

I PARKED in front of Holman's house, and we trotted up the steps to the front door as fast as Steven's legs would go. The wind had picked up, blowing cold against our cheeks. Steven's had a hint of pink in them, even though he'd been upset for hours last night. I unlocked the front door, and we stepped inside. "Hello?" I called. No answer.

"I'm going down to see Buckley." Steven ran through into the kitchen. I heard his footsteps pounding down to the basement. I gave one more "Yoo-hoo, hello," then headed straight upstairs to Elena's room. The door to Holman's bedroom stood open. I glanced in; bed made, room tidy, dustless, no one there. In my room there was no sign I'd ever been there. I hurried to the dresser and pulled open the drawers. Empty. Each one was bare, not even liner paper left. The water glass, the phone bill were gone. Even the closet had been stripped. Wastebaskets were empty. Bathroom scrubbed down.

I raced down to the library. Holman's desk was still unlocked. I pulled open the letter drawer, ruffled through the bills. No February telephone bill. I ran to the kitchen, pulled open the dishwasher. It was still hot and damp. There was the water glass, sparkling clean. There was a rumble in the back alley. I looked out. A huge garbage compactor truck was in the alley, just pulling away, heading toward the Quinleys'.

There was still a way to retrieve those numbers. I returned to the library, pulled out the January phone bill, and punched in the numbers for U.S. West.

"My name is Mrs. Grant Holman, and I've lost our February telephone bill. I made several long-distance calls, and my husband has some questions about the amounts for our tax records, can you help?"

Well, of course not.

I was switched to someone else, then yet another, to whom I whined about the emotional stress of doing income taxes. "You can't imagine how stressed my husband is about his income taxes. He has such a bad temper, and he said I absolutely had to find out the amounts and the numbers I called. We got audited, have you ever been audited?" I settled in with my worst whine voice and prepared to continue for hours.

"Hold, please," she said. She gave me the numbers, the amounts, then the length of each call and even the time of day of the calls to Chicago, Virginia, and New Jersey. "My brother gets the same way," she said sympathetically. "Hope this helps."

I felt just a little sick about the lie, but I dialed the number in New Jersey.

It was still ringing when I caught sight of Heather, in her exercise Spandex, body perfect, cheeks flushed as though she'd just come off a fast spin on her Stairmaster. The best I could say was that at least you can't conceal a gun in a Spandex unitard. She leaned against the doorjamb, a peculiar, calculating look on her face. "What's this about?" she asked. I didn't know how long she'd been there before I saw her, or how much she'd heard, but she looked suspicious and angry. I lowered the receiver, rose from the desk, and moved smoothly toward the door, hoping to squeeze past her before things grew uglier. She put a hand on either side of the door frame, effectively blocking it. "I'll just bet I know what your game is. You figure you can snag yourself a money tree, right?"

"I've noticed people accuse others of the things they're doing."

She laughed, a brittle, harsh hiccup that had more to do with anger than humor. "Possibly. That's sure how your little friend sees him. She can't wait to try to rip him off."

"I don't think Meredith considers money."

"I don't think you or she consider much of anything else. Money's power, and you know it. I'm a lot smarter than people think I am. You can't fool me. You're here snooping around because of Grant's big deal that's coming off. You and that Meredith are nothing more than a couple of gold diggers, and I've handled people like you before, so be careful, or you could end up looking worse than a bucket of snot."

"Is that what happened to Elena?"

Her face changed, softening a bit. "I don't know what happened to Elena. But Elena was a good person. She didn't mess around, she loved Steven." Heather shuddered lightly. "And she didn't make trouble." Her face softened further. "I kind of miss her."

It sounded like the truth. "So do I, Heather. All I'm trying to do is find her. Did you ever get a call from a woman asking for Elena?"

"No." There was a worry line on her forehead, but she shrugged. "Tell Meredith what I said." She stepped aside.

IT WAS twenty-five minutes before two o'clock, my hearing time. I called Steven up from the basement, then escorted him rapidly through the house and into the car.

When I buckled the seat belt around his waist, he howled. "You'll squeeze Buckley."

"Is he in there?"

"He was lonely."

"Just keep him in your jacket."

We arrived at my apartment building five minutes late. I led Steven into the manager's office where we joined Larry the manager and the building owner. He was a large, round-faced man with graying hair who was attractive until he launched into an explanation of why he couldn't renew my lease, which list included the fact that since I'd moved into the building there had been gypsies, strange people, a break-in, police lurking about, and a bomb that exploded in the back.

Buckley was squirming in Steven's jacket. "Stella?" Steven whispered.

"Shhh, later," I replied.

I've always thought of myself as a little out of the ordinary, but I've never thought of myself as unsuitable, unacceptable.

Buckley was wiggling more. Steven tugged on my sleeve and whispered, "Stella?"

"We're almost through, honey, just keep him quiet." The landlord continued his litany of my unacceptability. I felt somehow tainted. It was a nasty, soul-searing feeling. I thought I might hate the man. At that point I noticed his nose was an unattractive, turned-up snout, and his eyes were set too close together, like one of Uncle Ralph's hogs.

It was disgusting. Larry, the manager, who at least had been friendly and supportive until the bomb had gone off behind the building, stared uncomfortably at the floor, offering no help. Upshot of the whole thing, I had till the end of the month to vacate. I was an outcast, literally. Homeless.

I left with Steven in tow, clutching his jacket and the wiggling rabbit.

"Now, Steven, what did you want?"

"Buckley had to go to the bathroom."

"Noooo."

"Jelly beans in the chair."

TWENTY-THREE

I GOT MY MAIL, and we went upstairs to visit Fluffy and pick up a few things, like my set of master keys, collected over a lifetime of key fascination. I told Fluffy we would be moving. He looked at me gravely, blinked, then crawled over to Lips and put a little hand on her shoulder. He flapped his lips. It felt very desolate.

I stirred the mail, checking to see if there were any significant letters. Most of them were either windows, bills, which I put off, or the usual solicitations.

I looked around at my apartment and all my accumulated things. I had barely two weeks to find another place, pack, and move. I remembered Maria, who'd packed and moved in a matter of hours. How tough it must have been. She must have been very worried to do it. The kids, the school...but maybe she wouldn't have to change the school.

"Steven, bundle up Buckley, we're going to find Maria's girls. Come on."

SO MANY PIECES of the puzzle were falling into place. Holman's aversion to the police. Steven's nightmares. The caller ID box. The phone calls. The story about the old girlfriend. The passports. How much had Elena put together? That had to be what she was doing when she disappeared.

We parked beside Our Lady of Guadalupe Church, across from the elementary school. Steven sat next to me on the front seat, cradling Buckley gently in his arms like the most doting parent, singing over and over, "I know an old lady who swallowed a feather, I hope it's Heather, perhaps she'll die," and following that with the verse about fleas and Louise. It probably wasn't a good choice of songs to teach him. At least Buckley was thriving. His ears were alert now, his nose twitched energetically, and he ate without cease. There were droppings to prove it. I, for one, would never again view licorice jelly beans in the same light.

The doors of the school burst open, letting forth a stream of brightly wrapped children. "Steven, help me look for her. Do you see her?"

He pressed his nose against the window. "Nuh-uh."

"Do you know what she looks like."

"Yeah. She's got a pink-and-purple jacket."

"Right along with all the rest of them."

We scanned the children until my eyes burned. I'd barely blinked for fear I'd miss her. The children spread out as soon as they hit the pavement like the delta of the Mississippi, each going a different direction in an ever-moving flow, but no familiar little face. My brilliant idea wasn't working. I'd been so sure that Maria would not transfer her from the church school, especially since this one was bilingual. The stream of children had dwindled to a scattered few now.

"There she is!" Steven pointed to a slender little girl with long, dark, wavy hair, wearing a pink-and-purple jacket, blue jeans, and tennis shoes, who was skipping down the sidewalk away from us.

She glanced toward us once, her dark eyes rimmed with velvety eyelashes and her lips parted in a happy half-smile. Steven started to roll down the window. "Wait, Steven. Don't call to her. We'll follow her home so we know where she lives." I started the car. Steven looked at me with disbelief, but he didn't protest. "Roll up the window, please. You watch and tell me where she goes, so I don't lose her."

He held Buckley up to the window and pressed both their noses against the window. "Buckley's watching, too."

"What's her name?"

"Carmen, silly."

Carrying a fistful of drawings, Carmen skipped to the corner. As soon as she crossed the street I pulled out and drove slowly down the street, wondering how on earth I could follow her without looking like a child molester on the prowl. Once across the intersection I pulled to the curb and waited until she was all the way down the block and across the street before pulling ahead again. We did this for two more blocks. Then she turned up the sidewalk to a small house, set back from the street.

I pulled ahead quickly and parked about twenty feet away. Carmen was knocking at the front door. I killed the engine and waited. The house was similar to the one they had left, tiny, worn, and dark inside. The main difference was the lack of evergreens and a plastic geranium in the front yard. For a moment I wondered how they'd managed to find one so like the other, then I scanned the street and realized all the homes were tired, worn, and dispirited.

"Aren't we going?"

"In a minute. I want to make sure Maria's home."

She was. Within moments the door opened and Maria let Carmen in, quickly scanned the neighborhood as if looking for trouble, then shut the door again. "Okay, Steven, now we go."

When we reached the porch I stepped to the side, out of sight of the door. "I'm going to wait here, Steven. You knock real loud, then when she opens the door I'll come up, okay?"

He marched onto the porch and pounded on the door. The sound reverberated around the street, and I half expected the doors on all the houses to fling open and people to shout at me. Not a single one did. I heard the doorknob rattle as Maria opened the door to Steven.

"Steven! What are you doing here? Is Elena—?"

I leaped to the front door, grasping the knob so she couldn't shut it in my face. Hot, stale air rolled out of the house like morning breath, smelling vaguely of garlic and chiles. "Maria, please, don't shut the door, talk to me. I've been everywhere looking for Elena."

"You...where is Elena?" Maria asked.

The expression on her face froze. Her eyes were pink and slightly swollen, her cheeks puffy. The blue sweats she wore looked as defeated as she did.

"Maria, please, let me come in. I've got to talk to you."

A haunted look filled her eyes. "No...I can't..."

I put a hand on Steven's back and gave him a shove forward. He squirmed past Maria into the house. "You've got to, Maria. No one knows I'm here, I won't tell anyone. Not a soul, but I've got to talk to you about Elena. I think something has happened."

Maria's eyes filled with tears and she moved back, holding the door for me. "I've been so worried," she said.

I stepped inside. If anything, this house was even smaller than the last, and more barren, yet Carmen's school pictures were proudly taped to the wall, and the house was tidy.

Maria's shoulders sagged. When she led me to the kitchen she moved heavily, as though grief weighed her down. We left the children in the living room with the television and the rabbit. She slumped into a hard kitchen chair. "Alberto will be angry."

"He is afraid the authorities will find you, right?"

She rubbed her face. "It was so hard to come to America, to leave Mama, my cousins, my friends, my home. We came across the border for the day and never went back. It was that simple. Easy then, but it is so terrible living like this, always afraid the INS will come to the door. Every day worrying that Alberto won't come home. We work hard, pay taxes, but we live like criminals."

"Maria, no one knows I've come here. I'm not going to tell the INS. I'm just trying to find Elena. Tell me about Eduardo."

Maria sighed. "Elena's little boy, Eduardo, died two years ago. Elena believes Eduardo is in limbo, crying for her. A month ago maybe, Elena came to me all excited. A woman had called the house saying she was Steven's mother. Elena figured, if she could get Steven and his mother together again, Eduardo would be redeemed and go to heaven. And it would pay for her sins. So when she died, she could be with him."

Maria's cheeks were tear-streaked when she finished. She wiped them with her hands and dried her hands on her sweat pants. "Elena's dead. I feel it. At night I can't sleep good, I'm so empty. I have dreams, real bad dreams, and every day I wake up and I feel her gone, like a part of me died, too. Even Alberto is worried. I can see the suffering in his eyes." She hesitated, then shook her head. "There's something bad at that house. If Elena was going to leave the house, she'd have called me. I think it happened there."

So did I. "Maria, I found salt on the floor and the windowsills in Elena's room. Do you know why it was there?"

"That's our way of keeping bad things away. We used it in our village."

"And the Saint Don Bosco medal that Elena wore. What was that?"

"That was Eduardo's medal. She would never take it off."

It was falling into a logical pattern for me. "Did Elena say when the woman had called the house?"

"That day." She shrugged. "Elena said Mr. Holman was real uptight about the phone. He got one of those ID boxes so he could tell who called all day. He'd check the box every night."

"Elena told you a whole lot."

Maria nodded. "She was real worried about Steven. She believed he'd die like Eduardo if he didn't get his mother back."

There was a shriek from the living room, and we both jumped up to see. Steven was holding Buckley in his arms, frowning and protesting, "Yes, I am."

Carmen was nose to nose with him. "No, you're not. She's dead."

"What's up, Steven?"

He looked at me, flushed and angry. "I am too gonna see my mommy soon. She told me so, on the telephone."

HOLMAN HAD LEFT a note saying he would be out. I rang Meredith, but there was no answer there, either.

Steven and I ate a frozen pizza in the kitchen, then spent the evening playing in his room. We moved Buckley's box to a corner of my room for the night. As soon as Steven was asleep I dialed Meredith again. She answered on the second ring, sounding pensive. I didn't know what that meant.

"Heather accused you and me of trying to break up her relationship with Holman, Meredith. Any idea where she'd get that notion?"

"Stella, you can't believe what a great guy he is. He's so devoted to Steven. He said he'd do anything to be a good father. Because his own father deserted him. Now isn't that wonderful?"

"Meredith, think carefully, please? If someone threatened Steven, what do you think he'd do? How far would he go?"

"I don't think he'd commit murder, but he'd do about anything else."

I'm not sure why I asked her; she was obviously coming down with a case of hot-pants fever. "Now tell me where you stand in all this."

"I don't know. He's about the most decent man I've met."

"Oh, Meredith, you've met a lot of men who were good and decent, and you didn't give them the time of day. It's the ones with problems of cosmic dimension whom you've been interested in."

"Well, those were my salad days, when I was still green."

"You're stretched out on your couch, now, fluffing your

hair and picturing yourself as the romantic Cleopatra, right?"

"Close. No snakes, though."

"Well, there might be one."

"Oh, yeah?"

"Holman."

"Yummy."

I WAS SO EXHAUSTED I could hardly think straight. I needed a good five to six hours' sleep at a minimum. But even with a chair propped beneath my bedroom doorknob and an elaborate arrangement of toys balanced on the bathroom door, I had trouble falling asleep. It was one thing for Meredith to be so sure Holman wouldn't kill, quite another for me.

I called Stokowski at his office, his home, and even at Zelda's, leaving messages for him on his voice mail, asking him to call me on my cell phone.

What I really wanted to do was to put on a costume, run away, and hide in some safe motel, but if I did that I'd have to leave Steven. If I took Steven with me, Holman would undoubtedly come unglued and accuse me of kidnapping. So I put on my best teddy. That way I could die in good lingerie.

Holman returned around eleven. I heard him tromp upstairs and shut his door firmly.

I kept thinking about motives for getting rid of Elena. Money—she had none. Love—possibly Barry, but it seemed a long shot. Revenge—nothing to avenge. Hate—no one seemed to hate anyone here. Fear—Holman definitely feared something or someone, and it seemed to be the mystery woman. He could have thought Elena was betraying him. Betrayal is a great motivator.

There was the mystery woman calling Holman's house, but she was looking for Elena, and if she'd killed Elena, she wouldn't be calling.

I'd seen Holman lose his temper—he had the capability

to hurt—but he also had plenty of other options. He had passports, and probably had money stashed outside the country. He didn't have to murder an illegal alien with no power to affect his destiny. He could leave the country. In fact, I was almost certain he planned to do exactly that, just as soon as this latest deal was complete.

Millie had flared when I touched her shoulder. She was clearly strong, and fury or panic could give her even more strength, but was she sufficiently jealous over Barry? Possibly; she had no alibi, and Elena would have trusted her, so if she'd called asking to meet her, Elena would have done it. And then there was Barry, the nerd enigma.

Finally I fell asleep, no closer to figuring out anything than before.

I was awakened by a piercing shriek. Steven was having another nightmare. It was only 1:20 in the morning. I scrambled from beneath the bedcovers and carefully took down the toys from the bathroom door. By the time I reached Steven's bedroom Holman was there, rubbing his back and reassuring him. Steven was still hiccuping with his sobs. "What was the dream, Steven?" I asked.

"The vampire killed you, and I was dying, and Mommy was coming to get me."

Holman flinched. "Now, Steven, you're not dying. Don't think about it."

"I can't help it."

"Yes, you can. Just decide to, like a man."

"I can't," he wailed.

"Grant, your secrets are affecting Steven."

Holman composed his face, controlled the anger. "Impossible. You don't know what you're talking about."

I knew he could take Steven and leave the country, and this crime would never be solved. I just knew it in my bones, so I shut up. It was hard, though.

After reassembling the toys, I lay on the bed for a while,

trying to think things through but I must have fallen asleep. It was 5:28 on the digital clock when I woke next.

The room was dark, and at first I didn't know what had wakened me. I opened my eyes, searching for the bathroom door. It was still barely ajar, the toys balanced on top.

I heard a light inhaled breath from the side of the bed, near my head. I glanced to the side. Steven's slight frame, clad in his Superman pajamas, stood stock still, holding the long, terrible, missing kitchen knife.

TWENTY-FOUR

SHOCK IS AN AMAZING THING. It allows a person to do things otherwise impossible, like maintaining a section of the brain that methodically acts and presents a calm, powerful exterior when internally there is a storm of adrenaline-driven impulses.

I was aware on some level that my stomach was lurching dangerously and my ears were filled with the sound of my blood coursing through my veins, but with that trauma overdrive section of the old brain I reached over to him, gripped the knife, and sat up.

The room was shrouded in predawn dusk, Steven's face hidden in the shadow. I leaned toward him, tugging the knife out of his hand, and searched his face. What had precipitated this? I asked him, in the unnaturally calm, quiet voice of a barely controlled woman, "What were you doing, Steven?"

"Guarding against vampires."

Once the immediate danger is over and I have even a second to consider what happens, I lose some of that marvelous calm and control. At this point I had to struggle not to shout at him. "There are no vampires. Where'd you get this knife?"

"In the kitchen."

"Well, you leave it here and get back to bed."

"I'm not sleepy." He trudged across the room to the door, then paused. "Stella, I want to be with my mommy."

He slipped easily through the narrow space of the bathroom door without disturbing my alarm.

The knife blade was a good seven inches long and razor sharp. My hands began to shake now that it was safe to do so. Was Steven really thinking he was protecting me against vampires? Could he have done this to Elena? Or his mother? And perhaps hurt them, accidentally? Was I overreacting?

Jason had said Steven might be the problem. Could Steven have stabbed Elena while she slept? Could Grant have found her and hidden her body? Was that why I'd found her hair in the shed? I shook my head; there would have been blood, lots of it. I peeled back the sheet to the mattress. No knife blade holes. I flicked on the bedside lamp. No bloodstains. I must be overreacting. But perhaps there was another mattress. Not in the basement—I'd already searched there—but perhaps in the attic.

I tiptoed to the door and peered at Steven, who was calmly holding Buckley in his lap, murmuring soft reassurances to him. A rubber knife lay next to him on the floor. An army of plastic soldiers was arranged in front of them, tanks poised, broomstick cannon at Steven's side. Was this quiet, pale child the victim or the perpetrator? What had gone on in this household? I shivered, feeling cold inside my bones.

Was he imitating what he had seen? A wave of nausea swept over me as an even worse scenario occurred to me. Could he have seen his mother killed? "Steven? Did you ever do this before?"

"No."

"Did you see anyone stab someone with a knife before?"

He looked up, eyes so wide and innocent. "No."

"Why did you think of it?"

"You can only kill vampires with a knife in the heart."

"Who told you about vampires?"

He shrugged. I bit my lip. I needed to find out about Steven's mother. Holman refused to talk about her, and he wouldn't be a disinterested source anyway, but there were other ways to find out. If Steven, then a four-year-old, had actually killed his mother, the papers would have carried the story, probably as a headliner, probably nationally. It would be simple enough to do a search, if I could convince anyone on a Saturday.

I knew Holman had been in New Jersey in the past; there had been at least one call to New Jersey and one from there. It was tenuous, but worth a try.

It was barely seven-thirty, too early to catch anyone at the *Denver Daily Orion*, but I called Zelda's office phone, leaving her a detailed message. Then I remembered she and Stokowski were in the mountains for the weekend, so she wouldn't follow it up until Monday.

I thought of Jason, who will do nearly anything for a possible story. I dithered over whether to call him at Bipsie's, but when I finally did, I didn't get an answer there either. Where were Jason and his "sick" friend?

That left only Mr. Gerster. He answered on the second ring. "Mr. Gerster, it's Stella. I think I have an interesting story angle about children handling parental deaths. Would you have any connections in New Jersey at newspapers who might be willing to do a search?"

There was a little pause, then in dry tones he asked, "Were there no children in Colorado whose parents died?"

I knew he'd resist. "It's for Steven, to help him."

He gave me the name of the Trenton paper. "You can try their morgue; usually those people are very helpful. You're not getting into any trouble, are you?"

"How could I?"

IT TOOK MERE minutes to get the number of the paper and connect to the paper's morgue, less to learn they were jammed with a local storm story, but would try to get me information by Monday. Sooner if possible. I gave them my cell phone number and urged them to put it into a priority.

I heard Holman in the hall, walking to the stairs, and raced after him. "Grant, did you know Steven had a kitchen knife?"

He looked at me, his eyes smudged dark from lack of sleep, and shook his head. "He's not allowed to have knives."

"When I woke I found him holding a knife. He said he was guarding against vampires. He could have hurt himself, or me."

He rubbed his chin, looking sick and worried, refusing to make eye contact. "He's never done anything like this before."

"Could you talk to him, Grant? You're important to him."

"I don't have time now. I've got to get this deal tied up. It's only a few more hours, and then I'll have all kinds of free time."

"Grant, something very wrong is going on around here, and it's affecting Steven. If you don't make the time to be a father to him, he could be in real trouble."

"Look, Stella. I pay you to help him. That's why I put up with you, because you do know about kids." He started down the stairs, calling over his shoulder to me, "I'll be home no later than four, and I'll take care of it then. Please don't answer the phone."

His receding footsteps sounded loud and final in the quiet house. I returned to my room and punched in the numbers on my phone for Louise. She answered on the third ring, sounding harried.

"Louise, I know it's early, but has Grant called you about a replacement for me?"

"Not recently, but I have a couple of candidates for him to interview on Monday, and I'm sure one of them will do."

"I'm leaving here this afternoon at four."

"I didn't know. Is something wrong?"

I bit back a very flippant reply. "Yes and no. Grant's deal will wrap up today, but the bad news is, Steven is beginning to deal with some disturbing thoughts, and I think he's closer to being able to talk about them. I've urged Holman to help him."

"Do you think he will?"

"Hope so. The way Steven is now, it will be important

for you to hire a highly qualified person. So there won't be any, uh, problems."

Louise huffed. "I always get the most qualified person."

"You took Elena without checking her out thoroughly. If you had you'd have found she was here illegally and had a significant set of problems."

"Like what?"

"Grief over her own child for one, and illiteracy—"

"She couldn't read or write?"

"No, Louise, she couldn't. Maybe that fit in with what Grant wanted. Maybe he didn't want anyone who would be able to look into his background too closely."

"What?"

I hadn't meant to get into that. I changed the subject. "Did Elena talk about taking a trip soon or ask for her savings?"

"Not a word."

"How much was she saving each month?"

"One hundred fifty a month."

"So she had what, thirteen hundred fifty dollars saved? She didn't ask for it?"

"She could have had it any time."

"How do you have those savings accounts set up, little trust accounts at the bank?"

"Well, no. I keep accounts here on the computer and then when they want it or when they leave I cut a check or give them cash."

"Not very professional." And it didn't pay them interest.

"No, but it's simple and it works. I came up with the savings idea to try to keep them on the job, make an incentive to stay on. Do you have any idea how often these people change jobs? A good third of them find private clients and then simply fail to come to work. The average length of employment is about three months, and most never save a dime. Elena was about my only exception. It doesn't pay to get more complicated. This looks like a thriving business, but it's actually pretty hand-to-mouth, Stella, because of the turnover, the cost of materials, training, advertisement, and failure to pay."

"I don't understand."

"Think about it. I have to advertise to get workers and to get clients. I have to pay the workers during the time I train them, give them certain basic materials and transportation money, and I have to pay to bond them, at least some of them, and then there's insurance—"

"You pay health insurance?"

"No, no. Insurance to protect me from accident claims, theft, damage, that sort of thing. It all adds up. And there's a certain number of clients who fail to pay. If I take them to court, I have bad public relations, and I still have to pay attorneys' fees and sometimes court costs."

"So why do you stay in business?"

"Some days I'm not sure."

"Did Elena complain to you about Barry Quinley?"

"She said he made advances toward her, so in June when Grant called in, I reassigned her. She agreed to work one half-day a week at the Quinleys' if Millie would be there. Now, I know he occasionally approached her whenever she was alone, but she seemed to handle it pretty well after that."

"Did you see him talk to her the Thursday night she disappeared?"

"He was talking to her when I set the trash out on the porch, and she looked kind of bothered then."

"And Millie noticed?"

"Notices everything, and gets upset over everything."

I hung up. So Barry had lied big-time yesterday about approaching Elena, and Millie had seen it and gotten upset.

Louise's assurance that she would have someone for Steven lifted some of the weight from my mental shoulders. I was worrying about it more than Holman.

Holman wasn't as insistent on getting a new nanny as I'd

thought he would be. I remembered his passport. I looked around, calculating. There was nothing irreplaceable here. He and Steven could be gone with the purchase of airline tickets. With no way to stop him. His request for me to care for Steven until only this afternoon was looking suspiciously like a prelude to flight.

BY NINE-FIFTEEN I had fed Steven and packed. The only place I hadn't searched was the attic.

Steven was in his room playing with Buckley. I think I half feared Buckley would be a dead, limp body, but he looked healthy and happy, and Steven was absolutely gentle with him. Around Buckley he had built a tower of wooden blocks, stretching a broomstick handle across it to his bed.

"What are you doing, Steven?"

He pointed to the tower. "I locked up Buckley with Rapunzel. Now they can't ever get away."

"That's nice." Probably wasn't the best thing to say, but he was engrossed in his play and didn't notice.

This was my chance to search the attic and perhaps find traces of Elena or anything else. There had to be some reason the door was always locked.

The attic door was locked, had been since I arrived; however, it wasn't a particularly good lock, and it yielded in short order to one of my old master keys. I left the door barely ajar so it wouldn't be immediately noticeable and slipped up the stairs quickly.

The small room at the top of the stairs was barren except for two file boxes next to the gable window. Beyond it was a huge, unfurnished attic room. There was no bloody mattress, not even a soiled pillow. Nothing except mouse droppings.

I returned to the file boxes, unwound the cord closure, and lifted the lid of the top one. It was crammed with files, dating from five years ago, detailing business ventures. The addresses were mostly New Jersey. I pulled a couple, leafing through them. They seemed to be standard—compilations of correspondence about covering investments, financing, loans—nothing I'd be able to comprehend without much closer study. I'd hoped for more recent files, such as one year ago. I had nearly closed that box when a file marked "Divorce" caught my eye. I yanked it out. It was empty, but worn and creased as if it had held a good inch or two of papers. Where had they gone?

I opened the other box. It was full of the same, but going back ten years. I replaced the lids, wiping them down hastily.

Why wasn't Holman's divorce decree in its folder? And who had taken it? If his wife was dead, why would he need his divorce papers? Perhaps he was fighting her will, contesting her estate. If they were divorced at the time of her death, her estate would go to Steven, bypassing Holman. Maybe money was at the root of all this. That is, if she really was dead. And it was seeming less and less likely.

None of this would have meant a thing to Elena; she couldn't read. Her lack of education was certainly handy for Holman.

What was so important about these papers that the door was locked? I took one last look around and started down the stairs.

I was halfway down when I saw Steven holding his broomstick, looking up at me, his hand on the door. "Steven!"

He slammed the door. I raced down the rest of the steps and heard the broomstick fall against the door. I turned the doorknob—not locked—but the door was blocked and would open only an inch. I pushed again. It was absolutely, solidly stuck. "Steven, move the stick, honey."

"You're the princess, you can't leave."

I reached for my cell phone. It wasn't there. I'd left it on my bed. "Steven?"

"Steven!" Silence.

Through the hairline crack I saw Steven calmly walking away. I ran upstairs, looked out the windows, trying to find some easy solution. The north side of the large attic room had dormers that opened out onto the roof. I tried the windows. They raised with ease.

I leaned out over thirty-five or so feet of dead air. It was zero comfort to see that crocus were blooming below.

If I crawled across about five feet of roof I should be over the tiny, three-foot-wide, under-the-eaves balcony off the master bedroom. There were two hazards. A chimney, which meant I would have to inch along the edge of the roof, and the balcony, which was so small, I'd have to dangle and swing in toward the house to land on it. No problem for the heights-loving and athletically inclined. For me, it meant risking vertigo and a plunge to a bloody end.

I headed back down to the attic door and yelled for Steven. No answer. I pounded on the door. Silence.

Then the telephone rang. Steven answered it, and I could hear his clear, piping voice. "Mommy? I'll be ready." He hung up.

His mother again. What did that mean? "Steven? What was that about?" Silence.

I ran back up to the dormer and leaned out. The roof was steep, the gutters fragile looking, and the height sickening, but I didn't have much choice.

Swinging one leg out first, then the other, I inched out the window. The asphalt shingles were warped and nearly bare in places, like sandpaper with the sand coming off. Slippery.

I sat with my legs stretched out in front and pressed hard against the shingles. I moved first one leg, then the next sideways, then lifted my butt sideways, inch by inch. Once I looked down, and my stomach rolled over; after that I kept my gaze glued to the chimney. If I got there, I'd be halfway.

The sun was bright, but this was the north side, and it was icy cold. My muscles tensed and shivered, making it harder to move. Two feet from the chimney I felt the sand on the shingles slip. I slid down maybe five inches before I stopped, my feet barely above the rain gutter.

I inched up on a diagonal, so I could cross behind the chimney to the other side. When I finally reached the shelter of the chimney I was panting, my palms were sweating, and I was shaking in the chill rising breeze.

I leaned against the chimney, gasping. That had been the easy part. The next section was more worn, more slippery. I had to crawl over it to the balcony, swing my legs over the roof edge, persuade myself to dangle by my hands and swing in, then drop. I gagged thinking about it.

Sweat broke, trickled down my sides and back. I looked out over the neighborhood. I saw rooftops, bare trees, the neighbor's backyard, the Quinleys' backyard, their carriage house with its dilapidated roof, the old incinerator, and the alley, but not a soul was out. From this height, the alley looked almost like a private hallway from the Quinleys' yard to Holman's.

The longer I sat, the worse it became.

I inched out, spread-eagled to have as much body contact as possible and keep sliding to a minimum. Luckily, by the time I was fully stretched out I was almost over the balcony. I eased along, every fiber of me gripping the roof. If I was wrong about the balcony, I was dead.

Centimeter by centimeter I crept to the edge of the roof, and peered over the rain gutter. I was wrong. The balcony was another half foot along.

I groped along the roof's edge until I was over the near side of the balcony. It was the width of the window and maybe actually four feet out from the house. It looked a lot narrower from above. I retched, tasting nervous bile in my throat.

I said a little prayer, grabbed the struts of the rain gutter, and let my legs go out by degrees off the roof, inching down. Almost there. Then I stopped. Caught. My sweater was hung up on the gutter.

I tried to pull up, but I didn't have the muscles. I tried to hang still, but the gutter groaned. Sagged. I slipped. Then stopped. Then slipped again, my sweater ripping slowly. With one gigantic effort I swung my legs toward the window. The sweater gave out.

A burst of pain radiated up from my feet. But I was on the balcony. Alive. Shaking, so I couldn't stand. I slumped, half sitting, half lying on the balcony, gazing in at Holman's green-and-burgundy bedroom.

It took a few minutes before I was able to stand, try the door, find it open, and stagger in. I bumped a little table and caught myself. I made it to the bathroom, took a long drink of water, and threw it up.

"STEVEN, COME HERE!"

He came, carrying Buckley. I wanted to smack him. "What were you doing?"

"I locked you up, like Rapunzel."

"You can't keep people like that. It's bad."

He looked at me, eyes round and suddenly full of tears. "I don't want you to go away. If I'm bad you'll have to stay, no one else will like me. 'Specially Heather."

"Wouldn't it be better to have people like you and still be able to talk to me any time you wanted?"

"Yeah."

"Look, Steven. I'll always have a telephone. You can call me anytime you want me, but you can't lock me up. Come on, I'll show you how to call me at home and at the newspaper office."

It took mere minutes for him to master the telephone, memorize my numbers, including the cell phone, and call each one, leaving messages. I didn't count all the messages, but somewhere around eight I persuaded him to stop.

While he was practicing, I'd been thinking about Barry Quinley. Barry had lied through his protuberant front teeth about the last time he'd talked to Elena. With Millie passed out in the library, he could practically rip out a wall and she wouldn't wake. He could have accosted Elena at the back gate while she was taking out the trash. They struggled. He killed her, maybe even accidentally, then dragged her into the shed. Later that night he could have gone along the alley, gotten her body from the shed, and moved it...where? The carriage house? The Studebaker!

This time I remembered my cell phone. "Get your jacket, Steven, we're going on an adventure."

Steven's eyes lit up. "I gotta get Buckley." He returned, hugging Buckley to his chest. "What're we gonna do?"

"An experiment, okay? Let's see if this key to your house works the back gate."

Steven bounced out of the house, tromping on the paving stones to the back gate. The sun had melted the last of the ice, except for the glacier shaded by the toolshed. I was struck again with the ruggedness of the stone path and the number of loose, broken bricks lying about the shed. "Steven, was it here that you saw the vampire with Elena?"

"Yup. He pushed her down and then he sucked her blood and dragged her in the shed."

I shoved the key into the deadbolt on the gate. It worked.

"Here's our mission. We'll be bloodhounds and inspect the alley from here to the Quinleys'."

"Doesn't sound like fun."

"Well, it is. Look for anything that might be Elena's, like her Saint Don Bosco medal. But don't tell anyone, okay?"

He nodded and set off, head bent, holding the rabbit and staring at the ground. I did the same.

When he was distracted I asked, "Steven, when did your mommy say she was coming?"

"She didn't say."

Steven found a dime, two pennies, several pop cans, and an old red plastic hair barrette, but we found nothing of Elena's. At the Quinleys' gate I tried the key.

"You don't need a key for their gate, Stella. See?" Steven shoved it open.

I stepped into the Quinleys' yard, glancing about. A stocky figure at the kitchen window waved. I waved back. Barry opened the kitchen door and came into the yard, carrying a steaming cup of coffee. "I saw you out here, what're you doing? Isn't it a little early? It's barely ten o'clock."

"Maybe for you, but for me it's been a lifetime already." I watched Barry's face, trying to read his mood. He hadn't been particularly happy with me yesterday when I left his office. "We're taking Buckley for a walk."

He peered at Buckley, nestled in Steven's arms. "So that's the rabbit Millie was talking about. She said he got loose in the carriage house Thursday. It's not too safe in there, you know. It's a damned old firetrap. Should've pulled it down years ago, along with that old incinerator, but I never got to it." He looked at me and blinked. He wasn't smiling and cheerful, but he seemed to have decided not to carry a grudge.

Steven had taken Buckley to the side yard and was showing him the stone chicken in the garden. "Barry, when you talked to Elena last Thursday, did she seem upset?"

"No more than usual, uh—" He closed his eyes briefly. "Screwed up, didn't I?"

"Yeah, the truth this time."

He glanced around, then looked back at me. "I didn't hurt her. I never would. She was so beautiful that night. Just wearing a simple white blouse, so soft and a little too big. I didn't lie when I said I still love Millie, I do. But I was so crazy for Elena. She was so good with children. All I ever wanted was a couple of children and a wife who loved me. A family. I thought Millie wanted them, too, until I learned she aborted her pregnancy." He looked at me, his eyes burning into mine. "Do you understand? She killed the one thing I wanted." He threw the cup hard against the fence.

"She said her uncle visited, her drinking started, and she had an abortion, all the same year. Was she drinking heavily?"

"Do bears...live in the woods?"

"Barry, any idea what her relationship is with her uncle? I've got an idea it all stems from him and something that happened years ago."

"He's boring, only talks about hunting and his precious lodge and how they used to go down there." He stopped, thinking. A frown settled on his brow. "Why would he take a twelve-year-old girl hunting?"

I knew what he was thinking and felt sick. "You'd better ask Millie." His mouth was working painfully, but no sounds came out. I looked for Steven and found him still over by the stone chicken statuette. "Millie said something about betrayal."

"I never thought..." Barry whispered. "Millie was furious last Thursday night. She got drunk at Holman's and said I was insensitive, self-centered, and I betrayed her. I told her I'd do anything to make it up. We came home after that, and she really tied it on. She couldn't possibly have wakened at night." He looked at me, his lips compressed. "I don't want a divorce."

But it sounded to me like he was trying to convince himself as much as me. "Maybe she's worried about more than your attraction to Elena."

"How could she—?"

"She knows you went out and when you came back in."

"Good God! Do you believe that I could—?"

It was a great act. I didn't know quite what to say, so I watched Steven walking slowly over the grass, head down, searching the grass, following Buckley, but I kept Barry in sight out of the corner of my eye.

Barry shook his head slowly, then seemed to notice Steven for the first time. "Hey, Steven, what'cha doing? Looking for pennies? You've got your face practically on the ground.'' Barry said quietly to me, ''Weird kid. Where does he get that vampire stuff?''

''I don't know.''

Steven scowled at him, and Buckley took off straight for the carriage house. Steven was puffing by the time we caught him. ''That's Buckley's hideout,'' he said.

''Barry, yesterday I noticed you have a classic car in there. Could you show it to me?''

He was taken aback. ''Now?''

''As good a time as any.''

''I guess.'' He wedged the door open and pulled the canvas cover off the car. I oooh'd and ahhh'd over it for a few minutes. ''It's great, Barry. Can I see the trunk, too?''

''The trunk?''

''Yeah. I have a thing about them.''

He laughed harshly. ''I'm not very sensitive, but I'm not stupid. You think I have Elena in there, do you?'' He opened the trunk. It was empty.

STEVEN AND I returned home via the alley, and I shut the gate behind us, carefully leaving it unlocked. You never know when you might want to return. ''Steven, where'd you hear about vampires?''

He shrugged without meeting my gaze. ''Can't tell.''

Through the window I could see Heather in the kitchen, hair gleaming, makeup perfect, wearing yet another Spandex wonder garment designed to cover all and hide nothing. I stepped aside, holding the door for Steven. He marched inside, Buckley tucked safely inside his jacket.

Heather whirled on him. ''Steven Holman, you get your skinny little self in here and give me back my bracelet. I've had it with you stealing my stuff. That bracelet was worth over five hundred dollars. Those vampires in the shed are going to come in the night to suck your blood and drag you down to hell for this.''

Steven's mouth fell open, and his feet were rooted to the spot, the color draining from his cheeks. His arms holding Buckley inside his jacket were shaking.

"Heather! Why are you threatening him with vampires? You're terrifying him."

She sneezed. I signaled to Steven to go down the basement with the rabbit, fast. He didn't get it.

She rubbed her eyes, which only seemed to spur her on to greater fury. "Didn't you ever hear of the bogeyman? Well, it's the same thing. Scare 'em into behaving. Worked fine on me when I was a kid."

I tried to signal Steven again, making shooing motions with my hand. He didn't move. "Great, Heather. You're a sterling example. He only steals because he's scared and lonely, but you made it worse. You could have helped him, then he wouldn't need to steal."

"Yeah?" She sneezed. "Well, let me tell you, Miz Shrink. If you want to know what happened to Elena, ask him." She rubbed her eyes again, peering at him and his jacket. "I'm allergic to him, that's what. Have you got something in there, kid?"

I tried to distract her, shooing Steven again. He finally got the message and moved toward the basement. "Were you out there with Elena that night, Heather?"

"Don't look at me! I wouldn't go out there on a bet. I was in the powder room and the kitchen—you can ask Louise, she saw me. Elena was out dumping the trash at the time. Then later I heard her on the stairs."

"Did you see her on the stairs?"

"Well, uh, sure. And she saw me, too." But the telltale pause made me think she was lying. She looked around the kitchen for Steven. We heard his footsteps on the basement stairs.

"Where were Millie and Barry?"

She sneezed again. "There's someone who'd gladly take out Elena. Millie was chewing Barry out in the living room.

I heard them when I was in the powder room. Millie caught Barry trying to sneak a moment with Elena, and she was hot! Now, leave me alone, I'm late for my Saturday Super Step aerobics class."

My cell phone shrilled, startling both of us. Heather spun on her heel and left, and I answered the phone.

It was the woman from the *Trenton Herald* morgue. "Mrs. Holman's full name is Cathleen Maureen O'Hare Holman, and there's no record of her death."

As I thought.

TWENTY-FIVE

SO, THERE WAS NO RECORD of Cathleen Maureen O'Hare Holman's death. If she were dead, it was a secret. That's a pretty hard secret to keep. But if she were still alive and Holman knew it, why wouldn't he tell Steven?

Holman was paranoid about a woman, who could likely be Steven's mother calling. He had passports. He hadn't put Steven in school. He had hired a nanny who would be good with Steven but was uneducated, unsophisticated, and unlikely to go to the police or be believed by them if he took Steven and left one day.

Suppose his divorce papers spelled out custody to the wife. Suppose further that Holman had taken Steven and didn't want to return him. That would entirely explain the mystery woman calling, the orders not to answer the phone, and Elena's obsession with finding Steven's mother and how that affected Holman. But would he kill Elena?

It didn't entirely make sense. Holman didn't need to kill. He had the means to leave the country any time. He was a troubled man, a defensive and hot-tempered one, but he had the money, the power, and the mobility to solve his problem by leaving. He could carry on his business in Europe almost as easily as here. Elena couldn't truly harm him. He was in control.

The front door opened and closed with a bang. It was Grant Holman. Home very early. Eleven-fourteen, to be exact.

He came into the kitchen, unzipping his leather bomber jacket. "Stella, I thought about what you said, and I know you're worried about finding a new place to live. I was able to finish up early, so I'll take over Steven's care. I appreciate all you've done for us, but we will be just fine."

"Grant, may I talk to you for a minute, alone?" I sent Steven to check on Buckley.

I had little to lose at this point. "Grant, the woman who is calling here. She's Steven's mother, isn't she? She's really still alive."

He flinched, then tried to cover it by laughing, but it wasn't convincing. "You've got it all wrong."

"Oh, I don't think so. You took him, didn't you? Perhaps even for good reason, but this kind of trauma doesn't just constitute a little misunderstanding in a person, it lives on, like a monster."

Holman's breath was coming hard and fast, and a dull flush spread up his neck. "You don't understand. I simply couldn't bear to leave him; she was involved with another man, and she and Steven were having a terrible time. He'd complain and cry every time I picked him up."

"But why does he think he killed her?"

Holman ran his hand over his face. "I don't know why. I didn't know that he did, until you told me. The neighbors said they heard them have a big fight, Steven screaming and stomping that morning. The school called me, saying he was upset, crying. When I couldn't reach Cathleen I picked Steven up and went by her place. She was still gone. Steven was crying and saying he didn't want to go home. I was due to leave for Colorado, so I did. I left that day."

"Didn't you ever talk to him about it?"

"He never brought it up." He shook his head. "Look, Stella. I know I'm no saint, but I love the kid, and it was breaking my heart."

"Grant, this is bigger than you realize. Steven thinks he's talked to his mother on the phone and that she's dead and calling him to join her. Kids his age don't understand death, but they can still hurt themselves. Do you understand? I'm worried he will hurt himself to be with her. And to never even tell his mother! How cruel!"

"I left her a note. She knew he was safe with me."

"Elena believed Steven would die without his mother. She was determined to find her."

"I told Elena all about it that night. I made her promise not to contact Cathleen. She was angry and upset, and so was I, but I didn't harm her. She walked out of this house and abandoned Steven. You want to blame someone, blame her."

"I believe Elena is dead. Murdered. And I believe you know something about it."

His voice was flat and intense when he finally answered. "This is all speculation and imagination on your part. Elena left a note. In fact, she's still alive, and she even sent a postcard today. Look!" He threw down a postcard, postmarked Denver, and dated three days before. Written in soft, loopy writing.

Dear Steven,

I'm fine. Sorry to have to leave. Got homsick.

Love, Elena

I looked at the postcard, then back at Holman. "It's not from Elena, Grant. Trust me. That's a forgery."

"You don't know that."

"Oh, yes I do." But the killer obviously didn't know she couldn't read or write English. "I know her handwriting. This is a fake. It means the killer is nervous and trying to prove Elena is still alive."

"Well, if that's true, then it's your fault."

AT ELEVEN-THIRTY or so I left the Holman residence with my overnight case, my cell phone, my lizards, and a pounding headache. The last thing I saw was Steven clutching his rabbit, with Grant Holman behind him looking like the grim reaper. I stopped at the *Daily Orion* to check my mail and my messages and was in the midst of sorting them at my desk when Jason strolled in. His shirt was wrinkled, his chin unshaven.

"Stella!"

I was surprised, even shocked, to see him, but I ignored him, piling the envelopes into neat stacks.

"Stella?"

I shoved one of the piles into my purse.

"Stella."

I picked up the loose files on my desk, stuffed them in the file cabinet, and slammed and locked the drawer.

AT HOME, LIPS jumped into the terrarium and flopped onto the hot rock, and Fluffy flapped his jaws, relieved to be back in his own home. He even wagged his tail. I hated to remind him we would be moving again soon.

I went through my telephone messages, listening first to Zelda's, then one from Jason, who sounded depressed. But, dammit, I could live without a man who kept secrets and left town for a supposedly sick friend. Then, lastly, one from Meredith, asking me to call as soon as possible.

"Meredith," I said when she answered on the fourth ring, a sign of depression, or celibacy, one and the same for Meredith.

"Stella, I need to have a horoscope reading. I want to know if Grant Holman is compatible."

"You don't need a horoscope for that one. He's not."

"You're not giving him a chance."

"Meredith, he's had lots of chances, and he's made a significant mess of his life right now. If you want to hook up with him, you'd better be prepared for a very rough ride. There are lots of decent men—"

"Don't talk to me of decent men. Listen, he's not what

you think. He loves Steven dearly, and all he wants is to give him a good life. He told me about his ex-wife, and..."

"You don't have her side of the story. If you're serious about him, try a left-brain approach. Get a few facts. Even talk to her first."

"She's dead."

"I think she's alive and well and looking for her child, who I believe was hijacked by Grant. If what I suspect has happened, you might be looking at a prison romance, Meredith. So cool it for a few days. Let things come to light on their own."

She was quiet for a minute, possibly tearful, but at least she had a better understanding of Grant Holman and his situation. When she finally spoke up, she sounded resigned. "Are you going apartment hunting today?"

"You want to come?"

"It'd be better than sitting here wondering what-if."

While I was waiting for her I called information in Trenton, New Jersey, asked for the number for Cathleen M. Holman, and got three listings. On the second try I thought I heard the same husky, tentative voice I'd heard on Thursday asking for Elena, but I wanted to make sure.

In my best official tone of voice I asked, "Cathleen Holman? This is Jane Austin Smith, Denver, Colorado. I'm trying to locate a missing person by the name of Elena Ruiz."

"She was the nanny for my son, Steven. He's all right, isn't he? My God, something's wrong, isn't it?"

"Your son is fine. His nanny is missing, and I'm trying to find her. Steven is five, correct?"

"Actually, six. He's small for his age, but very bright. Gifted, even. What happened to Elena? She was going to help me get my son back."

"How was she going to do that?"

"I'm not sure, but she said she believed a mother and child should be together. The last time I talked to her, last

Wednesday, she said she was going to arrange to meet me. I never heard from her again."

"Have you been calling the house?"

There was a pause before she spoke. "Yes," she said in a low voice.

"How did you find them?"

"Oh, a bit of luck really. Grant forgot and used his social security number on a bank account. The private detective I hired tracked him to Denver."

"One last question. What kind of custody arrangement do you have?"

"Sole custody; his father has visitation rights."

"In Colorado the court usually grants joint custody, unless there is some problem with one parent."

"When the divorce went through we were using the same attorney, to save money. Grant was out of the country, but we'd agreed to joint custody. When I realized how easy it would be for him to take Steven and that I wouldn't have the money to follow and get him back, I changed the agreement, swore we had agreed to sole custody. I'm sure he's never forgiven me."

"Grant said Steven didn't want to go home to you."

There was a terrible pause. "Grant adores Steven. And I was with an abusive man at the time. Steven and he didn't get along."

"He hit Steven?"

"Yes, and me."

"Did you know Grant had Steven?"

"He left a note."

I TRIED AGAIN to get Lips to jump onto my hand, but she leaped away as though I was trying to snatch her life's breath. I was about to give up on this little lizard. At least Fluffy still liked me. I put him in his green yarn harness and pinned him to my sweater. It was one of his least favorite sweaters, actually one of my least favorite, too. I was trying for a sedate but realistic presentation of self by wearing a crewneck navy sweater with a white-and-red snowflake pattern and a pair of navy trousers left over from my somber accountant days.

Meredith arrived clad in a luscious raspberry-colored outfit, and we spent the rest of the afternoon and the early evening searching central Denver for a new apartment.

Five hours later the sun had set, a gentle southerly breeze was blowing, and Meredith threw herself into the car. "No more! If I see one more place I'll shriek. You've looked at every apartment in Capitol Hill, from the rat-infested to the frankly fantastic and too expensive. Feed me."

We stopped at the Pig N Whistle Pizza Palace and headed straight for our favorite corner booth, beating out a slower threesome who had taken a scant second to scout the place.

I ordered for us, as I always do, having a vested interest in getting food, as opposed to a few rings of green pepper and a mushroom.

Meredith stopped sipping her water. "You haven't said a word about how you feel leaving Steven and all."

So many feelings were tied up in it. "It's profound sorrow and unfinished business and a sense of impending doom. I can't describe it any other way. I don't need Steven for myself, I just need him to be safe, but things aren't right there, Meredith, and I couldn't fix it. But I know something's coming."

"Our pizza. Eat, you'll feel better."

When we got home around seven, my answering machine was blinking. Meredith dropped onto the couch while I listened to the messages and settled Fluffy back in the terrarium with a couple of pinhead crickets for a snack.

The first message was from my mother, at 6:15 that morning. I'd forgotten to call her, and she was wondering if I still loved her. The second call was from Larry the Snake, manager of my building, the man who had not pleaded for me or supported my appeal. He was whining about how badly he felt that I had to move. Sure—he really just wanted to know how soon he could show the apartment.

The next message was from Jason, saying he missed me and would call again.

Meredith sat up. "He sounded discouraged and agitated at the same time."

"He should be, the louse."

The last message was a strange one. A gravelly, hoarse woman's voice came through the receiver. "Oh, damn, it's a recording. I hope it lasts long enough." Then she cleared her throat and started again. "Stella, please listen to this. My name is Bipsie Lotts. I got your number from Jason." She paused, panting, as though she'd run two flights of stairs. "It's hard for me to talk, so please, just listen for a minute." I heard some strange beeps in the background.

"I asked Jason to come to L.A. because he's the closest thing I have to family. I've got cancer, and very little time left."

She coughed, a long, racking cough that sounded as if her lungs were shredding. It took her a minute to recover, then she continued. "When he was in college he got in trouble with drinking and drugs. Then his mother had a stroke and died, and he took it hard, blamed himself. Used to have nightmares that he killed her. Things went real bad. He was expelled from at least two schools, finally disowned." She stopped, panting, then continued. "I found him passed out outside the club where I worked."

She paused, caught her breath, then continued. "He was zoned out, skinny, broke, starving, looked like hell. Nobody'd hire him. I took him in, cleaned him up, got him a job at the club, let him live with me, clean like, till he was back on his feet. 'Course there's more...he can tell you later."

She paused to catch her breath. "He knows I like gorgeous lingerie. I used to use it in my act. Gives me a thrill, so he sends it. In your place I'd be real pissed, so I wanted to explain. See, I'm a retired dancer. Some as call it stripping, but mine's a class act all the way. You probably caught on that he sent me lingerie. He says not, but he's not a very suspicious guy. Although he did say you were snoopy. That's good. It'll keep him in line in his old age."

She coughed again. "Jason's been trying to hide it, but I know he's real down because you're angry with him. I want to straighten things out as much as possible while I still can."

Her voice was fading. "But I figured anybody hearing what he'd been through would be pretty leery of him, so I made him promise then not to tell anyone. He's kept his promise all this time. I thought it was for his own good."

I probably wouldn't have believed it, except that I heard an overhead paging system in the background, paging Dr. Schultz to the ER. I could barely swallow around the lump in my throat.

"Stella, I gotta go. My arm doesn't hold up, and the morphine's wearing off. I've told him he should tell you. Everything. Sorry I never got to meet you, you sound real nice."

By the time I'd snuffled my way through a couple of tissues I was feeling better about Jason, a little guilty about my suspicions, and pretty sad about Bipsie. I think I would have liked her.

I was still a bit wet around the gills when the phone rang. I lifted it, expecting to hear Jason's voice, but it was Steven instead. His voice quivered. "Stella? I'm scared. Daddy's gone on a trip. And I don't like Louise. She took Elena's medal away from me."

"Elena's medal?" My heart rate quickened. "Where did you get that?"

"I found it today. Near Buckley's hideout."

"At the Quinleys'?"

"Yeah. Stella, can you come over?"

"Uh, not right away."

"Then Buckley and I are gonna run away."

"No, Steven, don't—"

"We'll go someplace nobody'll find us. Where Buckley'll be happy."

"Steven, listen—"

But he hung up.

Where would he go? What if he decided to go to his mother? I had to reach Louise before he slipped away from her.

If she would reason with him, give him back the medal for now, he'd calm down. She probably didn't realize how important it was to him. I punched in numbers. It rang four times before Louise answered. I heard her panting lightly, as though she was out of breath.

"Louise, this is Stella. Is everything all right? Steven called a few minutes ago, upset because you took the medal away from him, and I thought you should—"

"Stella, you're interfering here."

"Steven said Grant's gone and—"

"He and Barry had to go to San Diego suddenly, and he asked me to be here, because you're so obsessed with Elena you're upsetting Steven even more."

"Steven is at risk—"

Her voice changed from cool to angry in an instant. "You know, I'm not getting into this with you. I know you're obsessed with Elena, but she left a note and sent a postcard. Why can't you just accept the fact that she's gone?"

Alarm rippled through me. Why was Louise so defensive? And how did she know about the postcard? "How do you know the postcard was from Elena?"

"It's exactly the same handwriting as the note."

The air in the room seemed to turn to frost, and adrenaline hit my bloodstream. Louise couldn't have seen the note unless she wrote it, because Steven took it.

Meredith noticed the change in me and rose from the couch.

I tried to keep my voice as bland as usual. "Well, maybe I am overreacting. Could you put Steven on again?"

"No. I could not." She hung up.

TWENTY-SIX

I FELT SICK through and through, almost weak with dread. Meredith had thrown on her jacket by the time I put down the telephone.

"Come on!" I said. I grabbed the cell phone, and we headed out the door.

I drove, and Meredith used the cell phone to call 911, requesting help. The cell phone batteries gave out before she could get through.

"Never mind. As soon as we're there, you drop me and go to the 7-Eleven and call. I'll try to get to Steven."

"Where is he?"

"I don't know. He might be in his closet, in his cupboard, in the basement in Buckley's box, I don't know where else." I turned onto Speer Boulevard, racing toward the viaduct and the west side.

Bright lights and a clanging bell sounded on my right.

"Watch out for the light rail!" Meredith threw herself to the left, triggering the seat belt.

I floored the gas pedal. We spurted ahead. She bounced back, the breath knocked out of her.

"We'll get stopped and get a ticket," she gasped.

"Good, we'll have the cops."

"I wonder where Grant went?" Meredith mused. "He was so worried about that deal. It meant a lot to him."

"Must have, to risk Steven."

It was Saturday night; traffic was heavy, and the stoplights infuriating. I ran two of them. Not a single cop stopped us.

I threw my purse at Meredith. "I've still got the house keys in the bottom of the purse, dig them out."

"You stole them?"

"No! Forgot to turn them over."

I halted in front of Holman's twelve minutes later. "Two blocks down to the 7-Eleven, hurry, Meredith. And Meredith, call Jason, you can leave a message on his voice mail."

"What do you want me to say?"

"Just say, 'Wish you were here.'"

I ran up the steps, up the walk to the front porch, noticing there were only dim lights on in the living room. I jammed the key in the lock. The door opened with ease.

The house was quiet, no sounds anywhere. My own breathing was the loudest sound I heard. I hadn't tumbled to her because she was always there, in the background, moving, cleaning, comforting, making sure we all believed Elena had gone to another job. I should have known.

I had stupidly called her just this morning and told her Steven was remembering things about the murder. She must have figured then she had to silence him.

"Steven!" I raced from room to room on the main floor, then ran upstairs. Light shone from Steven's room, but it was empty. I yanked open his treasure cupboard, his closet, Elena's room. Nothing.

I ran to the basement. He wouldn't leave Buckley. At the bottom of the stairs I hesitated, then flicked on the lights. Buckley's box was overturned, the stack of boxes thrown to the floor. I darted through all the rooms. No one.

I called Steven's name. No answer. The only sound was the wheeze of the furnace. I checked behind it and finally in the coal room. Nothing.

Upstairs in the kitchen I found the back door closed but unlocked. I ran for the garage. Empty.

The shed! I slipped and slid down the garden path, under the grape arbor to the back gate. It was standing open.

I yanked open the shed door. Empty.

The Quinleys' carriage house. Could Steven have gone there? It was so far in the dark for a little kid, but he called it Buckley's hideout. And he found Elena's medal there. I took off. "Please let him be alive and all right," I prayed.

Stars glittered overhead in a clear, dark sky. The wind had dropped. A frosty moon rose on the horizon, lighting the way. I tried to merge with the shadow of the privacy fences as I bolted toward the Quinleys'.

It was cold out, in the upper thirties, but I was sweating and my mouth was dry, burning from breathing so heavily. My breath made little puffs before me.

Their gate was ajar. I listened, stuck my head in, and listened again.

The Quinleys' house was lit in nearly every room, as though they had a party going on, yet there had been no string of parked cars, and there were no silhouettes of people, no flicker of shadows on the drapes.

I stepped inside the gate, trying to glide without noise or obvious motion, stubbed my toe on the edge of a flagstone, and stumbled into the incinerator.

This was probably where Steven had found the Saint Don Bosco medal. Slowly I raised myself up and peeked inside. I couldn't see anything. I stuck my hand in hesitantly. I felt cold plastic sheeting and the shape of a shoe. Elena. I knew it as sure as I knew my name.

My eyes filled with tears. I had to blink hard and fast to clear them. There was no time for grief now; I had to get to Steven. Before Louise did.

I stole to the carriage house door. It was open a bare four inches, insufficient for me to enter silently. I hesitated. Then I heard a quiet little sob. Steven.

Only a weak glow of moonlight shone through the gaps in the roof, barely outlining the partial hayloft. It wasn't enough to illuminate the floor.

I leaned against the door and shoved myself through the opening, my clothes rustling against the splintery wood.

There was a sense of motion. I felt the rush of air, heard

the whisper of garments, and ducked to the left. Not fast enough. A glancing blow struck the back corner of my head.

Pain burst on my skull, and a blinding flash of light lit behind my eyes.

I fell, unable to catch myself, my face smacking the earthen floor. Stunned, I lay there, the smell of oil and gas-soaked rags in my nostrils, and felt someone grab my hands.

A rope snaked around my wrists. I tried to yank them away. The effort caused a starburst of pain to blossom in my head. The rope pulled tight, pinning my wrists together.

"Get up."

Louise's voice sent ripples of pain through my head like the toll of the doomsday bell. Then another burst of pain in my thigh as she kicked me.

I rolled over, sat up slowly, dizzy, and wiped my face and mouth on the shoulder of my jacket. "Steven?" I called. My intent was loud, the effect was "Stuh." Very soft.

"Steven?" My voice was stronger. "Where's Steven, Louise?"

"Shut up. Get over there."

I heard a soft, little "Up here," then a muffled wail of despair.

It spurred me on. "What next, Louise? Aren't you afraid Barry or Millie will come out here?"

A match flared, lighting Louise's face. Funny, it looked just like a normal face. No slavering mouth, no incendiary eyes. How could she look so ordinary? She was calm, even matter-of-fact. "Nobody is coming out here. Millie is so inside her vodka bottle, she won't even know what she's done. Barry's in San Diego with Grant."

The light from the match died. I heard her moving toward the far end of the carriage house.

"Did you set that up?" I asked.

"It's the only piece of luck I've had in months. Some little hitch in negotiations, but it meant they had to fly out this afternoon."

She lit another match, threw it toward a pile of straw. I glanced around and saw she had found a bale of straw, broken it, and piled it around the edges of the carriage house.

The wood was old, the carriage house dry and riddled with gaps in the walls and roof. It would go up in minutes. Another match flared. I saw her bend and touch the flame to a pile of trash. It caught; flames hesitated, then licked upward.

"You killed Elena that night when she took out the trash, didn't you? All you had to do was follow her out and hit her on the head with a brick, right?"

"No. It was her fault. She did it. She followed me out to the porch. She wanted her damn savings to go find Steven's mother. I told her it was a huge mistake. She wouldn't listen, started grabbing me. I shoved her, that's all. And she stumbled and went over backward, like a...like a tree."

"Then why'd you pull her into the shed? Why didn't you go for help?"

"She was dead."

The flames fattened on the straw, growing until they rose and caught the bundles of canvas stored overhead in the front half of the carriage house. The back half was the old hayloft.

"You were telling the truth when you said you weren't making any money. You couldn't give her the money because you didn't have it. And you were afraid they'd find out that you didn't have her savings."

The flames reached up the wall, stretching, lapping along the wood. The smoke curled up, rising to the gaps in the roof, natural chimneys. Maybe the neighbors would see and call the fire department.

Louise walked toward me. I could see her face easily in the light. I'd always thought someone like this would be marked by madness. I looked for signs of it. There were none.

"It's your fault, too," she said. "If you hadn't stuck your

nose in it, the kid would be fine. It's your fault he's going to go with you. You did it. Now you can feel how it is to know you've taken a life."

A sick feeling grew in my belly, as if my vital organs had liquefied. I thought I'd try to appeal to her better self, if there still was one. "Sick. It feels real sick. You must have felt like hell all this time. You didn't mean to hurt her, did you?" Louise's shoulders sagged briefly; maybe I'd reached her. "You must have been horrified when it happened."

"She was my best one. She was perfect. I knew the moment she walked in I'd never have to send her back to Mexico."

"Send her back?" My mind was sluggish; it took a moment to understand her. "You sent others back—why? Merely to keep their money? You knew all along that she was illegal, didn't you?"

"Makes a big difference. Cheaper labor. It's a mutual service."

"Slave labor. You basically don't pay them. And you still can't make ends meet?" It was the wrong thing to say. She got angry. Or maybe she got angry because it was easier then to do what she'd decided she had to do. Kill Steven and me.

Where was Meredith? Had she gotten through to the police? I needed more time, but the fire was the timekeeper now. "You brought Elena down here in the wheelbarrow. Weren't you worried they'd find her in the shed before then?"

"Nobody goes to a garden shed in the winter. Besides, they were leaving town first thing in the morning. It was simple. I went back Friday night, rolled her into the wheelbarrow, took her down to the Quinleys', and slipped her into the old incinerator. When she was found, they'd blame Millie, the known lush, who'd had a well-recorded fight over Elena with Barry that very night."

I thought I might throw up. I heard Steven whimper. "Steven, run, get out of here."

Louise spoke up. "He can't. He's too terrified. I told him I'm a vampire." She smiled.

I was enraged. "You're a maggot." Ever tactful.

The heat was growing. I saw Steven's head rise up in the loft. He was holding a squirming Buckley tight against his chest.

Flames ran along the flooring of the carriage house, eating their way along the edge of the building, seeking oxygen. Where was Meredith?

"Stella," Steven whined from the loft, the worst possible place. The heat, the gases, the flames would be reaching for him in seconds.

"It's okay, Steven."

Louise picked up an old pitchfork from the stack of rusting tools in the corner. "You want to go to him?" Louise asked. "He's up there." She pointed up the ladder to the loft.

I rose and stumbled toward the ladder. Then I saw the Studebaker. A hose led from the gas tank to the floor. The source of the gas fumes. Once the flames licked their way to the gasoline the whole place would flash.

"You know I can't climb with my hands tied."

I heard a scuffing noise overhead. Bits of straw dropped from between the loft flooring. Steven peeked over the edge. "Buckley's scared, Stella. He's trying to jump out of my arms."

"Buckley will be all right, honey. Lie down on the floor and cover your face."

Louise forked more of the straw around the edges of the carriage house. I cursed myself for not bringing a weapon—a knife, or even a pen—along. There wasn't a way in the world I could think of getting my hands undone. I wrenched and twisted trying to loosen the tie, but it was tight and bit into my wrists.

Dry, dusty wisps of hay clung to the edge of the loft floor. Bit by bit they caught fire. The heat was growing intense. The air was thickening with smoke. I could hear Steven crying, trying to calm the rabbit. "Steven, he'll get down by himself. Let him go and cover your face."

I closed my eyes against the burning air. I heard the creak of the carriage house door and opened them again. Louise was shoving herself out of the fire. She had dropped the pitchfork near the door. "Hold it, Louise!" I shouted. "I've got my hands free! I'm going to escape."

She stopped, turned, and looked toward me. I ran toward the pitchfork, trying to appear as though I was loosening my bonds.

She jerked back inside, lunged at the pitchfork, and snatched it up. I stopped, whirled, and leaped back to the edge of the loft, pushing into the narrow space between the car and the side wall.

She advanced, her hair disheveled, her eyes dark hollows in her face.

I pushed back, squeezing back farther into the narrow space. I followed her gaze as much as I could, trying to judge when she might thrust the pitchfork at me. Hoping I could drop to the ground in a ball before it pierced me.

She moved slowly, stealthily, like a feral cat, stalking me. The tines of the pitchfork wavering only slightly, aiming at my midriff. Closer. I couldn't move farther back. I was wedged in. I heard a scuff overhead.

Steven shrieked in pain. "I can't hold him. He scratched me."

The rabbit, screeching, terrified, leaped from the loft.

Louise looked up. Her eyes must have been blinded by the acrid smoke, her reactions just a bit slow.

She raised the pitchfork. It missed the rabbit.

He landed squarely on her face, then leaped off, his powerful back legs with their sharp claws lashing her cheeks.

She screamed. She dropped the pitchfork, gripped her

face, and howled again. Blood welled from her cheeks, flowed between her fingers, streamed down her wrists.

I streaked forward, aimed, and kicked with my right foot, the only one I was any good with in tae kwon do, and landed a solid hit straight into her unguarded stomach.

She doubled over.

I followed that with a second right-foot kick to the side of her head. She went down.

"Steven, come on down. Quick. She's down."

He appeared over the edge of the ladder. "I'm bleeding." He coughed. The smoke was heavier. "Buckley jumped off, right at her."

"Now you have to come down, too. Buckley did."

"I can't."

I couldn't reach him. My hands were still tied behind me. "You have to. Buckley did. So can you."

He clung to the top rung. A beam at the far end of the carriage house creaked and groaned. It moved.

"Steven, now! Put your leg over the edge and find the top rung."

He hesitated, then swung a leg out over the edge, fished for a rung, found it. Painstakingly, he turned and lowered himself to the next rung. The beam at the end of the barn crashed down.

Sparks and flames billowed up, shooting like fireworks into the air. We would have been smothered with gases but for the terrific draw of the burning roof and the holes that let in the oxygen.

I heard a moan behind me.

Louise was rising, her cheeks gashed, blood welling out over her face. She wheeled, coming toward me, then stopped and stared up. I followed her gaze up and saw the roof engulfed. Flames were filling the loft.

"Steven, hurry!" The air was hot. The flames were advancing on the puddle of gasoline.

Louise turned and stumbled to the door, slipped, fell, rose, then stumbled once more.

Steven was nearly down, face streaked with tears. "I can't see," he whimpered, coughing. I turned away from him, so I could grab him with my hands still bound. I twined my fingers in his shirt and started forward.

"Hurry! Cover your face. The smoke will get us."

We stumbled to the door. It was shut tight. Louise had wedged it shut.

I braced myself, pushed against the bottom and moved it a few inches. I shouted, "Push, Steven! We've got to get out." I heard him cough. Felt him slump against me, then slide to the ground.

I dropped to my knees, rolled to the ground. The air was a little better.

The fire was crackling and roaring, almost growling, reaching for us, consuming everything it touched.

I shoved my feet against the door and pushed. The corner opened a bit wider. I pushed again, finally wedging it open about ten inches. "Crawl there, Steven." He didn't move.

I let go of the door, rolled over him, turned, then shoved the door open again, holding it with one foot.

With my other foot I shoved on his back until he scraped through the crack in the door. It had to hurt, but at least he was out. The wail of a siren rose over the roar of the fire.

I shoved my face to the crack, sucking in the cooler air, feeling the scorch of the flames on my back. It was a bad moment.

I thought of Jason and how I hadn't ever managed to resolve anything with him. I finally knew what he had so carefully kept secret. I knew he was just what he'd said he was all along, just like Steven.

There was a terrible screech of metal on metal, hiss of steam, then cool air and voices. I vaguely felt arms lifting me.

"Get Steven first," I croaked through a dry mouth.

"We got him, hang on."

I saw Jason's face hovering over me. I must have been dead and gone to heaven.

STEVEN AND I were sucking in oxygen at the side of the fire truck, with Jason fussing over us. "Jason, how—?"

He kissed me. "Meredith called. I came as fast as I could. I saw the flames as I drove up."

"Where's Meredith?" I asked.

"The police have her and Grant at his house."

"Grant? But—"

At that moment Grant rounded the back of the fire truck and swept over to Steven, encircling him with his arms.

"I thought you were in San Diego," I said.

He stared at me for a minute, then spoke in a choked voice. "I owe you an apology, Stella."

Damn right he did.

He swallowed, then continued. "Our flight was delayed at Denver International Airport, and I started thinking about what you said." He brushed his eyes with the back of his hand. "I tried to call home, but when I couldn't get an answer I got worried. I sent Barry on without me and came back here. Then when I got home, the doors were all open. I was looking for Steven, then Meredith came—"

Meredith stepped forward, the flames from the fire lighting her face, glinting off her hair. "I got there just ahead of the police. And they were questioning Grant when I saw flames from the carriage house. God, I thought you were dead. You look awful. There's blood on your face."

I swiped at my face with little success. A large gauze pad was taped over the bump on my head.

Grant held Steven tight, smoothing his hair. "Stella, if you hadn't believed in him, he'd—" He choked. When he regained control, he said, "I thought about what you said all the time I was at DIA, and I called Cathleen. She's coming out."

Steven twisted in his arms, his chin raised, looking straight into Grant's eyes. "Mommy's coming?"

"Yes, son. She's really alive. She's coming to see you."

Steven looked at me, his eyes shining, a faint blush of pink in his cheeks. "Stella. My mommy's alive again." He sank back against Grant, then lurched forward again. "Are we all going to live together again, Daddy?"

"No. But we can all live near each other, maybe next door."

"Is Heather gonna be there?"

"No. Heather's going away."

"Good. I don't like Heather."

Lee Stokowski and Zelda came. I pulled the mask from my face. "Lee, Louise Braden got away."

He knelt beside us and pointed to a trio of people, two officers almost dragging Louise between them. "We got Louise. Did you find Elena?"

Reaction was setting in. My legs were trembling, and I couldn't stop the tears that gathered in my eyes and rolled down my face. Jason sat down next to me, wrapping me in his arms. With Steven right there, I couldn't bring myself to say out loud where Elena was. Steven looked up. "Where's Buckley?"

Zelda took Steven by the hand and led him to the far side of the yard. When they were out of earshot, I said, "Elena's over there," and glanced in the direction of the incinerator. Lee figured it out.

Steven let out a yell. "Buckley!" He stooped and grabbed wildly in the evergreen bush, then emerged, holding Buckley.

"Look, Stella, it's Buckley. He's safe. It's going to be all right, isn't it? Will you come and live with me?"

Jason leaned over my shoulder to Steven. "You can visit. She's going to live with me."

I thought about it. "Maybe."